KILLING TIME . . .

What would Phil think? You know, boss, I don't know how to tell you this, but they're killing my sources. No, that's not why I didn't file a story yesterday. And yes, well, it's only one source really. No, I don't know who they are. What? Well, I guess he's not exactly a source. He wanted to be but they killed him. He said he'd meet me for a beer, but he never showed up. Anyway, he's dead. Murdered. Give me the rest of today and tomorrow and maybe I can find out why. I'll write a real 'Hey, Mildred' story for the Sunday edition . . . But Phil, this murder is incredible . . . But Phil . . . But Phil . . . But Phil . . .

What would Phil think? Phil would think I was nuts. So I thought about another angle. Then I thought about the copy desk. Then I thought about a beer and felt a little better.

THE
COLD FRONT

Sean Hanlon

POCKET BOOKS

New York   London   Toronto   Sydney   Tokyo

This book is a work of fiction. Names, characters, places and incidents are either the product of the author's imagination or are used fictitiously. Any resemblance to actual events or locales or persons, living or dead, is entirely coincidental.

An *Original* Publication of POCKET BOOKS

POCKET BOOKS, a division of Simon & Schuster Inc.
1230 Avenue of the Americas, New York, NY 10020

ISBN: 0-671-65739-9

First Pocket Books printing March 1989

10 9 8 7 6 5 4 3 2 1

To James G. and Frances A.

Chapter 1

Moments frozen in memory still bother me, in dreams I have from time to time. In one dream I am impaled on a stiletto made of ice. In the other, I love a woman I cannot have, an equally painful experience. Her name is Rachel Morgan. Some write to remember. Some write to forget. I write because people pay me to do so. My name is Prester John Riordan. What follows is the background of a news story, which I define as a bit of information tucked between an advertisement and a banality and forgotten moments later.

At the time of the murder, I was enjoying a lazy obscurity as a business writer for the *Anchorage Herald,* which proclaimed itself to be "Alaska's Greatest Newspaper." It was the biggest paper in the biggest city in the biggest state in the most powerful country in the goddamn world. Circulation was about 50,000, not counting the gentlemen of leisure who read for free in the public library.

It had been a particularly sloppy Alaska spring, with a lot of dirty snow to melt and a lot of cabin fever festering in my brain. One Tuesday morning in April I woke up to discover that the fever had become a cold. Thick, messy sludge pressed against my temples and made me slow and dull. It was as if my brain were dripping out of my nose. A thin mist sobered me from the excesses of the night before as my dog Chena and I walked up and down the alley connecting our apartment with the loading dock where Ed Hadley dumped the news of the day into yellow vans bearing the words: "The *Anchorage Herald*—the Greatest with the Latest."

Chena, always on the lookout for something disgusting to sniff, pressed her nose into a slick bank of fading, leftover snow. She was an aging but beautiful black Labrador retriever with a gray speckled beard, arthritic black legs, and a taste for the stick and other thrown objects, so long as they were not thrown too far.

I threw a stick, but I threw it too far. She slouched back to me, her tail drooping and her eyes full of remorse. I led her back to our apartment and filled her food and water dishes before scrambling back down the alley to work.

Breakup time in Anchorage, Alaska. Anchorage is a disjointed swell of city tucked between a half-circle of old, low mountains and the rough gray tides of Cook Inlet. Moving to Anchorage is like running away from civilization to the most distant corner of the free world only to find that you've landed in Kenosha, Wisconsin. The local joke goes that the best thing about Anchorage is that it's close to Alaska. And sure enough, strange and wonderful things can be found just beyond the mountains which rim three sides of the city. I tried to avoid such uncomfortable majesty, and made it a rule not to stray too far from the city and the gridlock strangling its central core. This rule was to be broken time and time again in the next twelve months.

I'd come to Alaska from Chicago in 1984, thinking to leave that faltering city behind me in search of fame, Bitch

Success, and the special joy of drinking alone for hours on end. I'd come north because I'd heard that Alaska was brand-new and wide open and that even the most tired adventurer could find profit and glory here. Besides, Alaska's Greatest Newspaper had a job for me, and, having just lost a good one, I needed another.

Breakup time in Anchorage, Alaska. The winters in Alaska are so long and harsh that they have to be broken like wild and powerful stallions. During breakup, five months of ice and snow melt into little gray rivers which flood the streets, uncovering six months' worth of beer cans, cigarette butts, and candy wrappers. And frozen puke. Mustn't forget the frozen puke. Many Alaskans drink too much in the winter and then stumble about outside. There's not much else to do.

On that April morning I danced around wet candy wrappers and thawing puke as well as I could, toward the mobile lunch truck which camped every morning at the corner of Arctic Avenue and Northern Lights Boulevard, kitty-corner from the proud blue sign marking the front door of Ed Hadley's newspaper. I exchanged a dollar's worth of change for a microwaved burrito wrapped in hot, charred cellophane. No matter how much I want another drink on Monday night, I always save a dollar for Tuesday morning.

"Hey, Pres. What's the news?" the burrito man asked.

"Nothing at all, George. Nothing at all. Things are pretty slow. There's that flood in Aniak, but everything's okay. And Swenson's got that union trouble. I've got a little cold and a little too much of last night. How about you?"

"Doin' fine. Doin' fine. Eat your burrito before it gets cold."

A morning burrito is an important part of an aging reporter's diet. The beans absorb any poison left over from the night before and expel it in the form of gas. From then on, your hangover becomes someone else's problem. This more than compensates for the anti-burrito sentiments expressed by people who don't understand its curative powers.

Thus provisioned, I walked through Hadley's front door, where I was greeted by a seventeen-year-old receptionist who'd dropped out of school to marry a sergeant from Fort Richardson. She had a fetching smile, and breasts beyond her years artfully displayed through a loose, clinging, lime-green blouse.

"Good morning, Pres," she said.

I looked at her cleavage while pretending to examine the two telephone messages she had handed me. One was from a creditor who had tracked me all the way from Chicago, the other from a stranger named . . .

"Is that an 'N' or an 'M'?" I asked, hovering over her abundance.

"It's a 'W'. His name is Jeffrey Williams. Some kind of doctor with the college, I think. Said he wants to talk to whoever covers the Chamber of Commerce. Says it's real important."

"But I don't cover the Chamber," I replied.

She smiled a troubling smile. "Yea, well maybe so. But Phil said I should give the message to you. Anyway, you better call him. He sounded real upset."

As I passed through the classified sales department and into the newsroom, I crumpled up the message from my creditor and tucked the one from Dr. Williams into my shirt pocket.

The newsroom of the *Anchorage Herald* is like every newsroom everywhere, only more so. It was on that day filled with paper and plastic and rattling laser-photo machines and fragile egos and clacking computer keyboards and two dozen styrofoam cups in which swam several dozen waterlogged cigarette butts. I poured some coffee, lit a cigarette, and sat down at my desk to compose my thoughts and eat my breakfast burrito.

Three bites, two sips and several puffs later, my city editor emerged from his morning meeting. I wanted to avoid him somehow. To this end, I yanked out the pink telephone message slip and dialed Jeffrey Williams.

"Chemistry department," the operator said as Phil approached my desk.

"Jeffrey Williams, please," I said, trying to sound rushed, as if I had three stories on the line. I tapped my fingers with pretended impatience and nodded severely at Phil, as if to say, "You'll like this."

"One second, please," the operator said.

Phil's tie and cuffs were buttoned tightly. His face was blotted red with a typical rage.

"Mr. Williams?" I asked into the phone—smiling at Phil, looking at my desk. Phil was in the habit of chewing at the tips of his Bic pens. First he would go for the little stopper, then the cap. When there was no more of the soft plastic left, he'd chomp down on the pen itself, gnawing at the hard tube whenever the news of the day didn't go just right. Every now and then, a pen would strike back by leaking ink into a blue bloodstain just below where his heart should be, spoiling the pocket where Phil kept his pens when he wasn't chewing them.

Williams came on the line: "Yes? Speaking." His was a strange voice, tight and troubled, as if someone were stepping on his toes.

"This is Riordan with the *Herald*. You called. What can I do for you?"

A long pause. I nodded into the receiver for Phil's benefit. Williams said, "Hang on a second, will you?"

I hung on and nodded some more. Williams got back on the line and went right to it, whispering: "Mr. Riordan . . . I've got to see you . . . about a story . . . It's very

important, so I really can't talk about it on the telephone."
He took a big breath and let it out in a slow hush. "Tonight. It's got to be tonight. Where can I meet you?"

I paged through my memory, but like a man addicted to race tracks, I ended up at the same old place. "You ever been to the Governor's Hotel?"

"Yes, of course. The one on Northern Lights. Several times. Quickly now. I've got to go."

"Okay. Meet me in the bar upstairs—on the twenty-eighth floor about eight o'clock. I'll be the guy with the bad leg by the olive tray."

Click.

No reply. No goodbye. Just click. It was an awkward moment for me. Phil was still watching. I improvised. "Well, it'll be nice to meet you after all this time, Dr. Williams. Yes, yes. I know it's a big story, but we get a lot of big stories here at Alaska's Greatest. But I'll check into it, okay. I definitely think it's worth looking into. Okay . . . ? Right . . . Goodbye."

Click. Phil crunched his pen.

"What have you got today?" he asked. Phil asked me this every day. He has a vigilant, if limited, curiosity. He looked like he needed a Rolaids.

"Checking my sources, making the rounds. This one's got a thirty percent probability with a hundred percent payoff. Political stuff. Cocaine in Juneau, that sort of thing."

"What else?" As I said, vigilant.

"What else do you want?" He looked like he wanted to strangle me. "Okay . . . let's see. How about that perennial favorite, 'An Ode To Spring—The caribou dance with caribou joy and the moose shed their winter fur as the streets of Anchorage glisten with the afterbirth of a new season . . .' "

Patience twisted his face. "You did it again."

"What's that? Did what again?"

He came back louder and an octave higher, so everyone in the crowded newsroom could benefit from our conversation. "It! It! You did *it* again. Again. *Again!*" Phil has an extensive vocabulary. That's why they made him an editor.

"What again?"

"Again with the names, that's what. Swanson. S-W-A-N-S-O-N. Got it? Swanson."

"Yea, sure. I got it. Just like the frozen dinner. That's a good way to remember names. You associate them with something you'll remember. I just think of that big ugly galoot sitting in a plastic tray with peas and whipped potatoes. I just let him thaw and I got the name: Bart Swanson."

"His name is Brad."

"Whatever."

Jamie Farrell sidled over to the coffee machine so he could be closer to the action. He fussed with the Cremora and stirred for a long time.

"Details will kill you, Riordan. Details are our business. The big picture you're always talking about doesn't mean shit if you don't get the details right."

"Look, Phil . . ."

"You look." I looked. He explained to me that Brad Swanson was going around town telling everyone that Alaska's Greatest Newspaper had called him Bart Swenson. "That's S-W-E-N-S-O-N, as in your Swan song, Riordan, only drop the 'g' and change the 'a' and squish the words together." Brad Swanson was saying, "Who the hell is Bart Swenson?" Further, as Phil explained—still in a very loud voice—the misspellings were helping him to discredit the rest of the story, which was all about violations of the federal labor law at the Swanson Brothers Construction Company, a Fairbanks corporation that had built part of the oil pipeline. I listened to the tirade, paying more attention to my burrito than to Phil until he said something that made me choke on a bean.

"Chamber!"

"Say what?"

"I said 'Chamber.' You know, like in torture chamber, only drop the torture."

"But Phil. Come on. You're kidding."

"Chamber. Noon tomorrow at the Captain Cook. Be there and be on time and get it right or get the hell out of this newsroom."

"But Phil. Buddy. You can't. I'm your best man. I can't cover the Chamber. What are people going to say? It'll kill me. Think about my readers."

"I'm thinking about your readers and I say 'Chamber.' And if you screw that up I'm putting you on the copy desk."

More bad news. The only thing worse than covering a meeting of the Anchorage Chamber of Commerce is working on the copy desk. The Chamber was a room full of people with more money than I. The copy desk meant that I'd have to read stories I didn't write and correct someone else's spelling. I couldn't even correct my own.

"Are you trying to get rid of me? If you want to get rid of me, why don't you just shoot me? Fire me. Leave me out in the cold. But please don't send me to the Chamber."

Phil smiled the smile of an unpleasant child who'd just plucked the wings off a fly, then walked away.

Jamie came over to console me and gather any information which might help him take advantage of my misfortune.

Jamie was tall, young, and eager. He was my nemesis and I was his. He was hip, cool, and just out of school, where he'd majored in football and getting laid. He combined the bouncing vitality of a professional tennis player with light, almost girlish features and a lush mustache. He was able to talk at length about nothing of importance. This endeared him to the more amorous women in the newsroom, who passed him around like a box of birthday chocolates. This bothered me a lot.

I took my revenge with sullen skill, by constantly reminding him that I was the better journalist. Better in this case means older, wiser, and higher paid. Jamie Farrell wasn't stupid, but he so lacked judgment that he might as well have been. Still, he possessed a quick, weasel mind and an inexhaustible supply of misguided enthusiasm. He'd have made a good reporter some day if events had taken a different turn.

Jamie stopped stirring his coffee and finally took a sip. "Chamber, huh?"

"That's right. Some big muckety-muck's in town to teach the locals a thing or two. Mr. Ed wants me there so this guy doesn't think that Anchorage is populated by boneheads or he would have sent you. I think I'll write a banner story just to show that prick Phil what's what."

I leaned back in my chair, pretending an easy confidence. "You know, sometimes the big stories jump right out at you and sometimes you squeeze them out of nothing. How's the school beat anyway? I really liked your piece on the lady who taught kindergarten for forty years. You're starting to get some style."

"Hey, thanks. So, who's going to do the Iditarod next year?"

The Iditarod is a very long sled dog race. Sled dog racing is the Alaska national sport, and the Iditarod is the hardest and most famous sled dog race of them all. Jamie desperately wanted to cover the Iditarod. Phil desperately wanted me to cover it because it would get me out from underfoot. I desperately didn't want to cover the race because the trail is very cold and the accommodations quite primitive. I never told Jamie that. It would only encourage him.

"I don't know. Me, I guess, if I decide I want to. We'll see how things go around here."

Jamie retreated to his terminal and proceeded to bang out something insipid about the grade-point averages of high school basketball players. I called Swanson, but he never called me back. I worked on my own story about the afterbirth of a new season, with a special emphasis on what happens when abandoned automobiles thaw. But my heart wasn't in it, and I soon relaxed into the afternoon. To kill time, I scanned the various personal files in Alaska's Greatest Computer for items of interest. Phil's notes to himself were harsh and vindictive. Jamie's file was silly. The women on the Sunday desk were carrying on a lascivious computer dialogue about the new hunk of manhood in sports, a discovery I was anxious to share with Jamie.

Then I tried Ed Hadley's personal file, which never failed to disappoint. The code was a fairly well known secret: Punch in "FE" (for fetch) and "AGN-1" (for Alaska's Greatest Newspaper, #1). The magic cursor disappeared for a second as it retrieved a listing of topics and flashed them up on the kelly green screen:

```
SWENSON?
APRIL CALENDAR
OIL REVENUE EDITORIAL
NOTE TO AGN-2
TRAVEL SCHEDULE
MAY CALENDAR
```

I fetched the note to AGN-2, which was usually a personal message to Mrs. Ed Hadley. Mrs. Hadley started out writing letters to the editor as Miss Annabelle Carlisle of Sitka, Alaska. Her letter on the need for more U.S. marshals caught the eye of the pugnacious young publisher from Tulsa, Oklahoma, who'd rescued the Anchorage Herald from a well-deserved obscurity. One letter led to another and they were married. Fifty years later, he was a snarling, fire-breathing legend and she was the nitty owner of a southeast mineral empire who'd come into a vast fortune at the age of fifty-three. AGN-1's note to AGN-2 went something like this:

Dearest Belle,

The executive board of the All-Alaska Fellowship is having a special meeting tonight, April 17. Hugh Smalley is in town to discuss the deplorable condition of agriculture in the interior. He says he knows how to fix things up. He wants me to write an editorial and is looking for a vote of confidence from the Fellowship. We'll have to see about that.

I must attend this meeting, although I'd rather be home with you. Don't wait dinner for me. I'll eat at the club. I plan to be home by ten. If I'm not, don't wait up for me.

With love,
Your Publisher.

They chattered on computers just like the girls on the Sunday desk. I admired the Hadleys for their wrinkled affection, although their management of the *Herald* left much to be desired. I hit the "purge" button, wiping their secret message off my screen.

I drank some more coffee.

I smoked a pack of cigarettes.

I banged out another story about Swanson's union troubles. More cigarettes, more coffee, and some futile flirting with the girls on the Sunday desk. The clock wound down and set me free. It had not been a very good day. Maybe the night would fix it.

The sky was still gray. The sun had risen and set while I was indoors, the almost constant darkness of some months being one of the more disabling conditions of life in Alaska. I trundled through the cold slush which leaked through a hole in my shoe. My ankle squeaked at every step.

Most ankles don't squeak. My right one does from time to time thanks to polio and the heavy leg braces I have worn ever since I learned how to walk. The brace is made of metal, plastic, leather, and Velcro engineered to prevent me from falling down when I put weight on my withered leg. It attracts the attention of old ladies, who offer me their seats on a crowded bus, and young boys fascinated by my silly walk.

"What's wrong with your leg, mister?"

"I had polio when I was six months old."

"What's the polio, mister?"

It's a disease that takes little boys and turns their leg muscles into mashed potatoes, you little twerp. Although largely eradicated by a vaccine discovered in the early fifties, tens of thousands of little boys like you got in just under the wire and were crippled by an epidemic which caused widespread panic in the summer of 1952. That's when I was born. Everybody thought it had something to do with going to the beach. I spent the next two years in the hospital. Mother never forgave herself. Father never knew. When I got out of the hospital, the fever had cooled but my leg stuck out like a tollgate. My mother spent every penny she had on subsequent operations to straighten the damn thing out. She took out a loan to buy me my first leg brace and I've been limping ever since, little boy.

While the questions of little boys are annoying, the indifference of beautiful young women is more so. They look right through me, as if I were some street hustler asking for a fifty-cent loan.

I squeaked and limped through slush, up the elevator, and into my seat by the olive tray in the bar atop the Governor's Hotel. I liked this seat because it provided free olives and a commanding view of the city which festered twenty-seven stories below. If I looked hard enough I could almost see my apartment, where Chena waited patiently for my attentions. Down another block was the low-slung pillbox of the *Herald,* where my accomplishments could be purchased for a quarter—and a bargain at that. North beyond the *Herald,* on a clear day, you can see Mount McKinley, also known as Denali, the Great One. A coven of hippies live at the foot of Mount McKinley and feed off its tourists. You can't see the hippies from the bar atop the Governor's Hotel, but you can see in the foreground mud flats oozing from the city's gray and busy port. To the south and east rise tall buildings owned by the companies which have made big money in Alaskan oil—Arco, Standard, and Enserch. Beyond the big buildings are the town houses and the trailer courts and the condominiums filled with aimless dreamers and alkies and squabbling couples.

And trucks and cars and garish buildings.

Especially the garish buildings. The people of Anchorage seem to like loud pastels, perhaps because they help to brighten the drab winters which imprison the city for so many months. There's a shocking yellow shopping center called the Sunshine Mall, and the abandoned hulk of a pink and purple office building which survived the Big Quake of 1964. The Hilton is a conservative brown trimmed with improbable orange, the movie theater orange with red.

All these things can be seen from the bar atop the Governor's Hotel. I half-listened to whispered gossip while waiting for Williams to show up. I reached for a handful of olives. The bartender delivered a Bud. "This one's on Andrew."

As night follows day, so does the poisonous news tip follow the delivery of a free drink. I nodded at my benefactor and poured some beer into a glass. I watched as the golden brew sent numbing bubbles into the atmosphere and took a healthy swig, lest too many escape. Then I packed up my goods and headed over to Andrew's table, which was situated in a shadowy part of the bar. His face was hidden, but he had a good view of the door. His eyes glowed with the purposeful alertness of a gaming falcon.

"Hey, Andrew. Thanks for the beer."

He lit a match that made his face flare up. He smiled and offered me a seat while making a great commotion of putting away the latest edition of the *Anchorage Herald.*

Andrew Finkelstein was a failed actor who'd turned to politics as the next best thing, but never lost the actor's skill of sucking up all the surplus attention in a room. He had the profile of Mr. Potato Head—all lumpy trunk and toothpick limbs and a wild shock of red hair which defiantly resisted all efforts to comb it. He said, "Prester my boy, all that lies between thee and thou destiny is the ability to spell. I read again how the leprechauns taunt yee with t's that should be d's."

"Thanks a lot, Andrew. What's going on with you?"

Whenever Andrew had too much gin, he'd fall in love with a bar girl or launch into an overblown imitation of Franklin Delano Roosevelt. Now he angled his nose up at an FDR-like angle and blew out a puff of smoke he'd sucked through an FDR-like cigarette holder. "So what's this I hear about the Chamber of Commerce? Surely it can't be true." Andrew had good sources. Most sources do.

"I really don't need this," I complained, moving to gather up my drink and cigarettes.

Andrew pouted, as if he were the offended one. "Please. Don't be angry. I can see your sense of humor has failed you in this crisis." He waved his cigarette holder at the waitress as if it were an orchestra director's baton. "Darling, please. Another gin martini here. And what's that? A *Bud?*" He spat out the brand name as if it were sour milk. "And another Bud for my friend here."

"Two drinks? This must be good. So who do you want me to libel?"

"Really, Pres. Your cynicism shocks me. It's such a cheap posture." He hunched his shoulders and leaned over the table. His eyes darted about, watching out for the other eavesdroppers who frequented the place. "Imagine that, my boy. Farming in Alaska. I really like that as a marketing concept. It's bold. It's fantastic. Once he's done the impossible, no one will question his ability to accomplish that which is merely unlikely."

I lit my own cigarette. "Who is he and what the hell are you talking about?"

"Barley, boy. Barley," he hushed, as if barley was a state secret. "Millions and billions of bushels of barley, from his fields to the kitchens of the world. If he can produce barley in Alaska, he can grow asparagus on the dark side of the moon. If he can do that, he can do anything. Ice cubes in Saudi Arabia. Pay off the national debt. Build a perpetual motion money machine."

"You've lost me. Completely."

An awkward silence ensued. You can tell a lot about people from their silences. Andrew almost never had them. When he did, they were awkward, as if he had a meter running somewhere. I counted the bubbles in my beer. He broke the reverie. "Even the Chamber has its days, Pres.

And if you condescend to attend, tomorrow may be one of them. The biggest ever, if you play it right.''

"How's that?''

"Hugh Smalley, that's how. Big thunder. My sources tell me Entco Investments Corporation has a brand-new toy—a technological Tonka of majestic proportions. It's got something to do with barley, petroleum, and truckloads of cash.''

Smalley. Hugh Smalley. The name rattled around for a second before settling into place. A new name. Someone I'd read about today. "Smalley, huh? He's got a big meeting with the boss tonight over at the All-Alaska Fellowship. What's his story?''

Andrew smiled. He knew he had me hooked. "Oh, not much. Greed. Blood lust. The usual sort of thing. Hates Jews for one, and we don't much care for him. Hates the Rockefellers for another. He thinks they are trying to take over the world with a little help from the Chase Manhattan Bank. His father made billions in Mexican oil and bought himself a small airline. He spent a lot of his loot on this television preacher who doesn't like Jews either. Smalley thinks he's got a monopoly on truth and that the bad guys are out to shut him down. So get this: old Hughie cashes in all the airplanes and the contracts for Mexican oil and puts all his money in the Chase Manhattan Bank. He leverages this into enough credit to bankroll a small South American dictatorship, only instead of doing that he starts buying all the molybdenum he can get his hands on. Now most people don't know what molybdenum is, but if you try to fly a jet plane without it, you'll never get off the ground. His idea was that if he owned all the molybdenum in the world, any government that ever wanted to build a fighter jet or a nuclear bomber would have to come to him, and he wouldn't sell unless they had the proper politics and paid him a gazillion bucks. Well, he didn't quite make

16

it because they discovered more molybdenum in South Africa. The banks called in their debts, but he couldn't pay unless they wanted it in molybdenum. But it's like an old line I heard back East one time: 'If I owe you a thousand dollars, I've got a problem. But if I owe you a million dollars you've got a problem.' Well, Smalley owed them billions and billions of dollars and the banks just lent him some more because if he went under he'd take some chairmen of the board down with him. No bank that I know would ever let that happen. Nice deal, huh?''

"Yea, I guess.''

"Well now he's a farmer. He's in real deep with some nice little setup over at Toyukuk City, a couple of hundred miles down the road from Fairbanks. He took over a bunch of ruined farms on the cheap and now he's bringing in some heavy brains to build a petrochemical plant. Tonight he talks to your boss. Tomorrow he hits the Chamber.''

He snuffed out one cigarette and ignited another. "That's it. You now know everything I know. Make some calls. Contact some sources. I'd try Fairbanks.''

"Fairbanks. Right.''

"That's right. Fairbanks. And your own financial pages. There's been a big boom in Entco stock lately and the floor's dropped out of the barley market. As a matter of fact, you might want to invest yourself. My guess is that the biggest boom is yet to come. A well-placed investment could prove profitable, expecially if it's made right before a newspaper story.''

"Right. I'll invest everything I've got. I'll pawn Chena and sublet my bathtub. Can I interest you in an aging black Labrador?''

"Thank you, no. I prefer cats. They have higher standards, you know. A dog will eat anything and love anyone.''

* * *

17

THE COLD FRONT

Andrew left and I switched from beer to beer and brandy. I don't remember the rest too well. I think I tried to pick up a woman with polyester slacks and a light mustache, but I'm not sure. She must have said no, because I went home alone, to a sleep full of Japanese stewardesses who did absolutely everything without blush or complaint. The Japanese are like that, or so I imagine in my dreams. I was so busy drinking and flirting with women real and imagined that I somehow missed my appointment with Williams. There followed a morning not much better than the night it replaced.

Chapter 2

A CUP OF COFFEE.

Some cigarettes.

And a burrito, of course.

The *Anchorage Herald* is an afternoon newspaper. This means reporters who work there have to get up early, drag public officials out of bed, and write in a lucid fashion before ten A.M. This is no way to run a newspaper. I'm certain it is this schedule more than anything else which has caused the decline of the afternoon daily. The consultants say television news is killing the afternoon papers, but the consultants are wrong. Nine A.M. deadlines are at fault. You just can't expect good reporters to get up early and think before noon. It's unnatural and bound to show up on the printed page.

I was excused from this foolishness, thanks to the sort of luck I've never had with women. When I first came up from Chicago, I too was expected to get up early and I grudgingly did so. But fortunately, I scored an early success with an award-winning piece about a leak in the trans-Alaska pipeline near Port Valdez, a scoop of great local interest which quickly established me as a valuable employee. I used this good fortune as leverage to extract certain concessions from management, a ploy amplified by my timely threat to switch over to the *Anchorage Tribune*, a scrappy competitor run by a brilliant but bombastic Skeptic from Baltimore with the bulk of a linebacker and the voice of a castrato. Phil offered me more money, but I turned down the cash in favor of a more reasonable work schedule. I was supposed to work nine to five-thirty, with a half hour off for lunch. I usually came in at nine-thirty and skipped lunch, except for those days when I came in at ten and worked until six.

I punched in at ten-thirty, just as the deadline approached for the final edition. I'd saved myself an hour's sleep by writing a rough draft of my union story the afternoon before. I called up the story, made some minor changes, and moved it into the city editor's file.

I tried to call Williams while waiting for the inevitable conniption fit. He'd sounded so desperate before, and it seemed strange that we should have missed our connection. I should never have abandoned my seat by the olive tray.

"Chemistry department." A woman's voice again.

"Jeffrey Williams, please."

"I'm sorry, but Mr. Williams isn't here. Can I take a message."

I gave her my name and number, and said, "Oh, by the way. This is sort of a silly question, but what number am I calling? I mean, what chemistry department is this?"

Her reply was drowned out by Phil's conniption fit. "Riordan! Get over here."

I tapped out a cigarette and hurried off the line without listening to her answer. I think she said something about the university. I stopped on the way to tease the girls on the Sunday desk about the new hunk of manhood in sports.

"Jamie's heartbroken," I said, although I'm sure it bothered me more than him.

By the time I reached that nexus of anxiety that was the city desk, Phil looked like a slow-motion heart attack. An essential blood vessel seemed about to burst.

"Gotcha," I said.

"What?" he croaked, his face a knot of unspent fury.

"I said, 'Gotcha!' It's Brad, not Bert. I just put the 'Bert' in to see if you've still got it. Some of the kids think you're slowing down. But not me, boy. You got it, Phillip. You got it good."

He mumbled something about the copy desk in an effort to control himself. His jowls relaxed, but the veins in his neck still pulsed with anger, making his second chin quiver like a nylon stocking with a mouse inside.

"Well . . . What have you got today?"

I tightened up. It was my turn. "Chamber, remember?"

"Right . . . Well . . ."

"Well what?"

"Well get to it."

I slowly, slowly got to it, enjoying the chaos of deadline and glad I was not a participant. I tried to distract my co-workers from their frenzy with aimless chatter and cheery "hellos" as I roamed through the sports and photo departments. I knocked loudly on the door of the morgue so that Old Mary would be sure to hear me. She smiled and invited me in.

"Morning, Preston. What can I get you?"

"It's Prester, Mary. Prester John. You remember, don't you?"

Mary remembered everything, as long as it happened more than five years ago. She had the special distinction of being the only person who'd worked at the *Herald* longer than Ed Hadley. She'd already been there for ten years when he blew up from Tulsa like a bit of bad news. Her face was made of wrinkled folds and she wore her crisp, silvery hair tied back in a bun. She had been shrinking in size for the last decade or two. This last year, she had become shorter than I, an event from which I took little comfort. But her eyes were brightly alive and she'd committed the entire history of Alaska to memory. She remembered the gold rush as if she'd panned a creek herself and she knew every verse of the Alaska Flag Song. If she didn't know something, she knew where to look it up.

"Oh, of course. I must be getting old. Prester John . . . Now I remember . . . Let's see if I can get it right."

She got it right. She always did. My mother is the only other person I know who knows anything about the legendary Prester John.

Mama picked the name out of one of her textbooks. She taught medieval history to recalcitrant rich kids before she left the private school to marry my father, who left her before I was born. One night, when I was old enough to understand such things, Mama fed me cookies and milk in bed and told me that I was a special boy with a special name.

Medieval balladeers sang the legend of Prester John, who was the mythical king of a sprawling Oriental empire. Even as a myth, Prester John was much admired by the people of Europe because he was white, Christian, and rich beyond their wildest dreams. This was back in the twelfth century, when people would believe anything so long as a priest or a minstrel said it.

My mother likes people who will believe anything because she is one of them. Mostly she believes in Belief itself, the more unfounded the better. That's why she believed in Prester John, who never existed except in her mind and in the minds of twelfth-century peasants addled by the plague. She found a certain extravagant chicanery in the myth about Prester John which reminded her of my father, and caused her to burden me with such an unwieldy name. She calls me P.J. for short whenever she gives me advice. My friends call me Pres, although as a rule I try to avoid personal entanglements, as they tend to interfere with the gathering of news.

Mary reminded me of my mother. Both women were old and frail, of a bookish nature, and knew the legend of Prester John. They both liked to order me about, and I accorded them both a grudging obedience.

Mary's library was a cavernous room two stories tall, lined from floor to ceiling with row upon row of three-ring binders of the sort grammar school students use for their English compositions.

"I'm working on a story about a guy named Hugh Smalley. He's the C.E.O. and majority stockholder of the Entco Corporation."

Mary creaked toward a sliding ladder that rolled on metal wheels along the book binder walls. She nudged the ladder over to the "S's." I could almost hear her joints squeak as she eased up three difficult rungs. Her back was so bent that she had to climb up to reach down. She fetched one of the binders, crawled down, and handed it to me.

"You can sit right there," she said, pointing at a folding chair. "Take a load off that poor leg of yours." Then, shaking a bent finger in warning: "And you'd better return that file when you're done if you know what's good for you."

The file filled three crowded pages tucked between "Skagway" and "Statehood." The first story was of the "Welcome to Alaska" genre and consisted of an interview done by my friend, Ralph the Obit Man. The story was laid out next to a yellowing picture of a huge, pear-shaped man shaking hands with Hadley. The caption read: *"Herald* Publisher Ed Hadley welcomes businessman Hugh

Smalley to Anchorage.'' In the story, Smalley mouthed the usual placebos about the Last Frontier: ''. . . a land of great opportunity where a man has room to breathe and doesn't always have the government on his back.'' Ralph the Obit Man went on to describe Smalley as a financial wizard with a special interest in molybdenum. Ralph wrote that he had two-third's of the world's supply locked up until the South Africans destroyed his would-be monopoly. He quoted Smalley: ''Our government plans to destroy the dollar to pay off the national debt. When that happens, minerals like moly and gold will be the best currency in the world.'' In the upper left hand, Mary had scratched a date in her clear but weary hand: *5-7-83*.

With one exception, the other stories in the binder were not about Smalley himself, but about local and national affairs on which he was asked to comment. Ralph had gotten into the habit of using Smalley for the ready quote:

''I'm sorry, but oil is God's own blood.'

Or, ''The deficit is one generation's way of stealing from the next.''

And, ''Those environmentalists are nothing but traitors with flowers in their hair.''

There was one more article in which Smalley wasn't quoted at all. The piece carried no byline, but I assume the story was Ralph's:

9-30-85

ENTCO WINS FARM BID
AT STATE AUCTION

Entco Investments made the winning bid at Saturday's auction of 400 acres of Interior farmland near Toyukuk City. The land was put up for sale after the two owners defaulted on loans from the state's Agricultural Revolving Loan Fund.

These are the eighth and ninth defaults near Toyukuk City this year. Farmers there say the state didn't keep its promise to find a market for Alaska barley. State officials blame their marketing troubles on transportation problems and a record-breaking Iowa corn crop.

Entco acquired the land with a high bid of $101.26 per acre, or $40,120 for the two parcels. The company beat out three other bidders for the land.

State officials declined comment when asked if they expect more defaults this year.

Entco officials referred all questions to company President Hugh Smalley. Smalley could not be reached for comment.

I asked Mary to Xerox all three pages for me. She did so while telling me how much poorer and better Alaska was before they struck oil in Prudhoe Bay.

By the time I returned to my desk, the home edition deadline had come and gone and the newsroom had slowed down to a state of noisy exhaustion. I picked up the phone and dialed the Sunday desk. "Hey, Margaret. You're the best."

A tousled speck of frosted blond popped up from behind a pile of camera-ready recipes and newspaper clips. As soon as she realized I wasn't the hunk in sports, her head dropped back down again. "Come on, Riordan. I'm on deadline."

"But Sunday's four days away. I just wanted to tell you your piece on tomato salads moved me to tears."

She was not amused. "What do you want?"

"How about a drink after work tonight?"

"Sure. Why don't you have one? As a matter of fact, you'll probably have ten."

"Why don't you have one of them with me?"

"Forget it. And if you call me again, I'll tell Hadley you're using the office phone to molest his employees."

"Come on, Margaret. I need your help."

"You need help, all right, but I'm no psychiatrist. What do you want?"

"Answer me this: I have a 400-acre barley farm in the middle of Alaska nowhere. What do I do with it?"

"Grow a bunch of barley and then stick it up your ass." Click.

"Thanks, Margaret."

Then I tried Fairbanks. Andrew was right. You can always find someone to say anything in Fairbanks: 985-8100, long-distance. Alaska is large enough to swallow a dozen of its sister states, but small enough to have only one area code. That's just one of the contradictions of life on the Last Frontier.

"Friends of the Tundra, Geri speaking."

"Hello . . . ahh . . . George Brewer, please."

"One moment, please."

"George Brewer speaking."

"Hello, Friend of the Tundra. This is Pres Riordan, enemy of everything."

"Hey, Pres. What's up?"

"The price of a share of Entco Investments. I hear Hugh Smalley wants to turn your precious tundra into a parking lot."

"I'd say dung hole is more like it, but the truth is we're a little soft on Hughie right now."

"How come?"

"We got our hands full with the conglomerates at the moment. Our number one priority is protecting the Porcupine caribou herd. Besides, farming is a renewable resource and, as you know, we're all for that up here at Friends of the Tundra. We're not going to argue with a man who wants to feed people and provide permanent jobs for Alaskans. It's bad for our image with the economy and all.''

''What about the dung hole?''

''Bad news, but it's just not our fight. Not right now. He seems to be producing some sort of stinky stuff and dumping it on the ground. The people over by Toyukuk City don't like it too much, and I don't really blame them. Smalley is quite the asshole, but right now he not our asshole. We're strictly into caribou.''

''What's the setup?''

He cleared his throat and thought about it a bit. ''He's got 1,200 acres of cheap land, armed guards, Doberman pinschers, and a midget refinery. He plugs into the pipeline at Glennallen for about a hundred barrels a day and has a futures contract for a whole lot more starting in the summer.''

''Petrochemicals?''

''I'd say so. Last year he bought a small petro company in Houston with a strong reputation for research and development. He's bringing all the brain power up to Toyukuk City, which isn't exactly the center of the scientific world.''

''So what's the scam?''

''It's got to be farming or something closely related to farming. That's the law. When the state put the land up for auction, they made it a condition of the sale that the land could only be used for agricultural purposes. That's why the land was so cheap—because of the restrictions. Personally, I think Mr. Smalley is crazy. Any fool knows you can't make squat farming in Alaska. It's been tried before and it just doesn't work. The labor's too expensive, the summer's too short, and it's an awful long haul to market.''

''Listen, George. I've got to nail this story down. Who's your source on this one?''

"I don't have a source on this one. Like I said, it's not our issue. I'm just shooting from the hip. And keep my name out of it."

"Come on, George. You owe me. Remember the White Alice site at Aniak?"

"You don't understand. Smalley is heavy thunder. Very heavy. He's got a wad of bills that would choke a horse and he plays rough. Very rough . . ."

He stopped talking so abruptly I thought the line had gone dead. That happens a lot in Fairbanks. "George?" I said.

"Hang on a second. I'm thinking."

Telephones aren't designed for thinking. They abhor silence and can't communicate the furrowed brow or the sweaty palm. I counted the coffee rings on my desk and then looked around the newsroom. Margaret sure looked nice, the little bitch. George stopped thinking and started talking again.

"I don't have a name, but I might have a little something. About three months back we got word that one of his laboratory men had jumped ship. Some scientist from the Lower 48. It had to do with a lady. We tried to find him, but we couldn't. I figure he went back to wherever he came from. Find him and if he talks you might have yourself a story."

The Anchorage Chamber of Commerce meets every Wednesday in the ballroom of the Hotel Captain Cook. The hotel is named for the great English explorer, who visited the area when Anchorage was nothing more than a mudslide waiting to happen.

Several hundred men in pin stripes lined up for a buffet lunch, but I was not among them. Hadley had one policy against accepting free meals and another against paying for them himself. I sat down at the press table and waited for the other news-gatherers to gather around me with their free food. My stomach gurgled. I greeted my fellow reporters with the attitude of superiority which my hunger had earned me.

"What's happening, Pres? Haven't seen you in a long time," said David Garner, a TV newsman with the voice of Zeus and the brain of Hercules.

The podium was flanked on either side by two long tables glittering with crystal water glasses. Seated there were a phalanx of Anchorage elders—Little Eddie Hadley, the boss's namesake and heir-apparent, Brad Swanson and Robert Phillips, who'd made one bundle in the trailer-court business and another bundle clearing away the trailer courts for a half-dozen small shopping centers. At the head of each table was the representative of a major oil company. When they laughed, everybody laughed. When they frowned, everybody frowned. They all stood up and applauded as Hugh Smalley approached the pulpit.

He looked, at first, like a plain man, round and soft. He was about fifty and shaped like a lumpy avocado, with salt-and-pepper hair cut short and slicked back. His skin had the color and consistency of an undercooked pop tart—soft and fluffy, white and pasty. He'd been spending too much time in Fairbanks, away from the medicinal effects of the sun. He wore the pin-striped uniform of his class and walked to the podium with a bouncing, military-school stride, his heels and toes clacking against the linoleum with every step and his arms swinging in wide, pendulous arcs so as not to collide with the ballooning swell of his avocado hips. His collar was tight and cut his jowls into a wrinkled bouquet.

But he didn't seem funny or pathetic when he took the podium. The congregation fell silent before quick, lively eyes full of fire and ice; they danced with some terrible desire, full of anger at some injury long ago forgotten by everyone but him. His face was large and full, but he held it under strict control, as if the muscles were moved by gears. Click, smile. Click, abiding concern. Click, it's time to talk.

His lower lip was large and puffy and bobbed up and down like the bow of an inflatable raft. The crowd became slow and drowsy, as if all the oxygen in the room was being used in the manufacture of his speech. I struggled to stay alert but found myself daydreaming back to my conversation with Andrew, and how Andrew said the bankers feared Smalley because he owed them so much money; about how he was a house of someone else's cards; about how he was hoping for an economic catastrophe that would make all that molybdenum worth enough to buy us all.

He spoke about "What Alaska Means To Me," which was the only topic the Chamber audience ever wished to hear about, no matter who the speaker. "Alaska is the Last Frontier of ideas, too—our last chance to lift the Malthusian curse which dooms us to ever-greater episodes of human tragedy. But first we must deal with those namby-pamby nay-sayers who would use our money to plug a hole in something called the ozone; who would protect the caribou, but allow the Red Horde to advance upon our shores; who would turn Alaska into an amusement park for over-educated backpackers."

After the speech, I hung out on the periphery of the fawning throng which gathered to shake the fat man's clammy hand. When the crowd thinned out, I cornered him by the smoked salmon tray and got my story. I played dumb and he played nice. Click, smile. Click, thought. Click, words—but not too many.

Chapter 3

THE VERY NOTION OF FARMING IN ALASKA IS SO ABSURD that it's hard to avoid satire or parody. Sure Alaska is famous for producing big cabbages. That's because in the summer the sun just won't quit. But seventy-five-pound cabbages are as silly as they are magnificent. How do you start a story about farming in Alaska? "Alaska is famous for gold, oil, and the cole slaw of the gods . . ."

That wouldn't work, but I didn't have a better idea. So instead of writing my story, I talked to Carl, who is the nicest guy in the world. That's how he survived at the *Herald*, with footprints all over his back. Carl was already an eight-year man at the *Herald*, and as each summer flashed into winter, his forehead got higher and it became more certain he would never get out alive.

He was the last person in the newsroom to realize this. One time he'd tried to escape with a manila folder bulging with résumés and stories he'd written in better times. He even purchased three lumberjack shirts so that he could perpetuate the Alaska myth, which is the solemn duty of all would-be émigrés. Thus prepared, he went Outside in search of a living wage.

But the résumés came to nothing and the lumberjack shirts remained wrapped in pins and cellophane. He came back sadder and without much fight and quickly settled into the rut he'd made for himself. I try to be nice to Carl. I might be like him some day, and then I'll want people to be nice to me.

"Hey, Carl. What's up?" I said, snuffing out my cigarette. Carl's desk was in the middle of the "no smoking zone."

"Not much. I'm doing my Sunday column. It's about this new parking garage they want to build downtown. Take a look."

I peered over his shoulder at one of the paragraphs that would keep Carl at the *Herald* for the rest of his life. "Looks good."

Carl nodded and hunched back over his terminal. I was just stepping away when he bobbed back up and called after me. "Hey, Pres. I almost forgot. I got a letter from Ralph the other day."

That would be Ralph the Obit Man. Ralph is a wise-guy New Yorker who'd worked the business desk before he lost his nerve and retreated to the strange, sedentary world of the copy desk. There he gained his nickname by perversely insisting that each death notice in the *Herald* contain some poignant detail about the deceased, i.e.: "George Graves, who once caught a king salmon with his bare hands, died yesterday at the age of 58." This morbid curiosity earned Ralph the enmity of the countless rookie reporters forced to telephone the families of the recently deceased. He once confessed to me that the obit policy was just his way of relieving the boredom of having to edit and headline death notices.

This puckish aspect of Ralph went largely unnoticed and few complained when he parlayed a small inheritance into a ticket out of Anchorage and the *Herald*. The windfall provided collateral for his purchase of the *Nome News*, Alaska's Widest Newspaper. Although is wasn't necessarily a step up, it was, at least, a step out. Journalists have their midlife crises a little earlier than most. Only a fool would want to be a reporter after the age of forty.

Ralph's letter to Carl went something like this:

Dear Carl,

Small town life is driving me crazy. I'm lucky to get two deaths a month, although I must say that up here you really can get into an obit. Every one is front-page news. We blow everything out of proportion, because it takes a lot to fill the *Nome News*, Alaska's Widest Newspaper.

Mary is fine and the kids are growing up fast. The paper is still struggling along. It takes a while to get the confidence of the people of Nome. Not that I blame them. Look what Senator Rhodes did to their Native corporation.

I really pissed a lot of people off with an editorial I wrote about malingering at the police department. The D.A. tried to punch me out over at the Board of Trade bar and somebody called me on the phone and threatened to hang my dog. When I called the cops to file a complaint, they said they were too busy malingering to do anything about it.

Other than that, everything is fine, except that it's very hard to find the super-wide newsprint to fit this old press of mine. Alaska's Widest is custom-made for lumberjacks with the wing span of a Boeing 747.

Tell Phil I need to talk to him about next year's

Iditarod. I want to work out some kind of deal where we can trade stories. I'll write the Nome color piece if you write us a profile of Susan Butcher and take her picture when she leaves Anchorage.

Say "hello" to everybody. Tell Jamie to either grow a beard or shave the mustache and tell Prester John that if he doesn't watch his step, Phil will make him cover the race. Then he'll have to buy me that beer he owes me.

Sincerely stuck in Nome,
Ralph the Obit Man.

"Ralph's a real card," I said, returning the letter to Carl. Carl agreed and leaned back over his computer terminal. This time he meant it, so I wandered back to the smoking zone and lit one up. Jamie was the only reporter around, and I didn't feel like talking to him. So as soon as he turned my way, I grabbed the telephone and dialed a quotable stock analyst from New York. We talked for a half-hour, until Jamie went home.

I didn't start writing until well past six-thirty, long after the reporters and the editors and the classified salesmen and the display advertising salesmen and the pressmen and the graphic artists in the composing room and the truck drivers and the telephone solicitors and the rest of Hadley's chattel had all gone home. Early in the morning it was just me, a single copy editor, a moonlighting photographer, the security guard, and a constant stream of coded catastrophe from the police radio.

I ate French fries and a burger. My fingers started to crawl across the keyboard, pushing the little green cursor across the face of my computer terminal. I wrote my own headline and started out like this:

THE COLD FRONT

ENTCO FARM PLANTS SEEDS OF BOOM

By Prester John Riordan

There's a lucrative cash crop being planted in the most unlikely of places. Streetwise investors are betting big bucks on rumors that a farming revolution is being cooked up in the run-down remains of the Toyukuk Barley Project. Reports persist that Entco Investments of Fairbanks is on the verge of a barley breakthrough in Alaska's Bush.

For the last ten days, Entco stock has been climbing while the rest of the Dow continues its recessionary plunge. Market tipsters say that's because Hugh Smalley's group is about to knock the commodities market on its ear. Smalley says nothing, but even his denials fuel buyer fever.

"My farm is my business," Smalley said following yesterday's meeting of the Anchorage Chamber of Commerce.

But sources in Fairbanks say Smalley has built a modern agri-business complex on the charred remains of a farm in the northwest quadrant of the Toyukuk River district. The farm has been barren ever since the state's barley project collapsed in a swirl of innuendo following the Bergstrom incident.

Today, guard dogs and Entco security officers prowl the perimeter of the 1,200-acre dustbin and firmly turn away all passersby. Meanwhile, sealed tanker trucks full of oil and a handful of laborers with doctorate degrees daily make the 100-mile trek between Entco's Glennallen station and the petrochemical plant set up in the middle of farm country.

Given Smalley's reputation in the market, brokers view this activity with great interest. They see it as a sign there's a huge harvest of greenbacks being planted in the Bush. In recent weeks, Wall Street has enjoyed a furious traffic in the stock of Entco Investments and Petco, Inc., its petrochemical subsidiary. Today's Dow posted another strong gain of three and a quarter points. The closing price of $43.56 a share represents a 60 percent increase in less than three weeks. Meanwhile, the rest of the Dow continues to fall.

"Look, Entco's a strong stock and if you don't like it you can kiss my a—," Smalley quipped during an exclusive interview with The Herald.

Sources in Fairbanks have been watching Smalley's activities in the Toyukuk district. Speaking on the condition they not be identified . . .

All hell broke loose, and it sounded exciting. The night copy editor shot up from his chair and started to gesture wildly. The police radio broadcast scratchy panic and the photographer charged from the darkroom, camera in one hand, film in the other. Someone else's catastrophe, the stuff of which news is made. The police dispatcher said it all in a tone of voice that sounded a little bored: "All alert, code 44. We've got an 11–29, probable 11–1 lying behind the dumpster in back of the Colorado Club 431 East Fourth Avenue map page three. Respond code red, unit five. Units three and seven also respond code red. AFD paramedics also en route."

Here is an abbreviated glossary of the Anchorage police radio code:

    1) 11–44 means emergency.
    2) 11–29 means death.
    3) 11–1 means homicide.

THE COLD FRONT

The copy editor said, "Let's move it, Pres," and I reluctantly moved it. The photographer grabbed my elbow and rushed me out the door. His car groaned as he turned the ignition. It faltered for a moment before roaring to life; the vehicle needed a tune-up. Slush sprayed to either side as we hurtled out of the parking lot. We ran two red lights and nearly turned a pair of love-struck pedestrians into another news story. A couple of television guys beat us to the scene. Those guys are fast.

My companion clicked away and the television photographer danced through and around the crowd, trying to avoid onlookers anxious to get their faces on TV. The sirens wailed and the little plastic bubbles on top of the squad cars splashed red blotches of light across the buildings and the alley and the horrified faces that were glad it wasn't them. The small crowd of derelicts and fun-seekers had stopped their celebrations to speculate on what had happened and exchange the nervous chatter which the presence of death so often provokes.

The victim wore raggedy tennis shoes, corduroy trousers, and a windbreaker. The windbreaker and the gray athletic T-shirt beneath it were hitched up to expose a small ridge of hairy skin just above his belt. He lay there face down behind the Colorado Club, gargling wet death and attempting a weak Australian crawl in a pool of his own blood. A little river of melting snow caught some of the blood, turned it pink and carried it down the alley and into a drainage gutter. Then his body shook with a twitching shudder and he tried one last spastic stroke before stillness and the hurried attentions of the paramedics.

The television lights flashed hot white as they struggled with the body. One of the paramedics had to fetch a towel to cover its face, which was bruised and pale, the mouth frozen open and flattened a bit where it had pressed against the ground. The paramedics rolled the body onto a stretcher, taking care as if the man were still alive. The stretcher wheels rattled over shards of broken glass and chunks of loose concrete. TV lights followed as they slid the stretcher into the back of the ambulance. The driver hit the dome light and siren but pulled away at an easy speed. No need to hurry. The crowd lingered while the TV crew interviewed the officer in charge. Then everybody went home but the cops, and two old codgers from the public works department who washed away the gore with a garden hose.

We followed a caravan of squad cars to Northern Lights Hospital, where the victim was declared dead on arrival. Then we swung by the police station and waited for an hour and a half while the officer in charge filed a single-page report of the incident:

Responding officer: Sgt. Pillbury
Victim's name: (Withheld pending notification of next of kin.)
Time 19:45 of 4/27/88
Complainant: (Confidential)
Incident: 11–29 with a probable 11–1; victim WMA, approx. 30 years declared D.O.A. Nor. Lts. hosp
Witnesses: Cpt. Brewer, Offs. Cleary, Jordan, Donatelli, Johnson, Howard
Disposition: No charges filed the investigation into this case continues at this time

I tried to get the name of the victim from my friend the Colonel, but he just smiled a secretive cop's smile. He did confirm that it was murder and he said the man had been stabbed in the chest with a sharp object, probably a knife, possibly a stiletto. I asked him what a stiletto was and he told me to look it up.

* * *

We got back to the newsroom just before 1 A.M. It took me five minutes to write the murder story. Murder stories are like that—cut and dried—especially when you don't know much. All you have to do is fill in some blanks and leave other blanks alone. The story went like this:

MAN FOUND STABBED IN SKID-ROW ALLEY

A white male about 30 years of age was killed last night behind the Colorado Club, 431 East Fourth Avenue.

Deputy Chief Oscar Roland said the man was stabbed twice in the chest. The victim was pronounced dead on arrival at Northern Lights Hospital.

Although the police have tentatively identified the man, his name is being withheld pending notification of next of kin.

Police were summoned to the scene by an anonymous caller. The investigation into the case continues at this time.

That done, I returned to the more laborious, if more rewarding, task of finishing my Entco story. The pace of my writing picked up as weariness dulled my senses. I stopped thinking and just wrote. The rest of my story went like this:

. . . they say the research and development project points to a revolution in petrochemical fertilizers and pesticides.

George Michaels of the New York brokerage house of Riley, Childers & Gros attributes the Entco boom to fevered speculation among commodity traders. The buying spree has been sparked by Entco's recent take-over of the Lawson Group, a Houston company specializing in petrochemical research and development. The company's name has since been changed to Petco, Inc.

Said Michaels, "If you put it all together—Smalley and a failing farm and a petro lab—you've got innovation in agri-business. When Smalley makes a move, he goes for all the marbles. If he wants to be a farmer, I start selling manure."

Chamber of Commerce members hoping for a clue to Smalley's intentions were disappointed yesterday. The Entco boss didn't talk farming and he didn't talk fertilizer. Instead, he confined his comments to his own personal vision of Alaska, a favorite topic among Chamber guests. But the usual oath of loyalty to the 49th state did wave a red flag at bullish commodity speculators.

"We are the planet's last great hope—a final chance to get it right. Our challenge is to look beyond the oil boom that has blessed this land with such abundance to the growing market for the simple things that the land provides. Alaska's future is in renewable resources—timber, food, and the vivid dreams of its hearty people."

In other action, the Chamber awarded a Business Beautification Award to Northtown Realty. Roscoe Warner of the beautification committee applauded the company's planting of palm trees in a geodesic dome on the outskirts of Muldoon: "The sight of palm trees is a welcome delight to those of us who must trudge daily through our city's long and difficult winters."

Next week's address will be by General Richard Wohl, commanding officer of Elmendorf Air Force

Base. His topic will be "What Alaska Means To Me."

This last line was pure invention. I was very tired by then and a little cranky. Journalism is a fine field for those who take their grudges seriously.

Chapter 4

I CHECKED IN AT THE NEWS DESK SHORTLY AFTER NOON. By then, Jamie Farrell had expanded my modest murder story into a screaming-mimi headliner full of black ink and dark intent:

PROFESSOR FOUND STABBED
IN SKID-ROW ALLEY

My byline was on top because of my seniority, but most of the facts had been gathered by Jamie while I was still asleep. Page one showed a photograph of the paramedics struggling with the body next to a series of testimonials from students and friends of the victim. His name was . . .

(Continued on page 12)

My Entco story was buried on B-11, perhaps in the hope that no one would find it. I was reading it and wondering about its placement when Phil squeezed a smirk into the sort of cackling laugh normally reserved for a padded cell.

"Riordan," he began, trying to suppress his glee. "You're amazing. You're incredible. You're in it up to your ears.'' Then he stopped laughing and wrenched his face into something between palsy and bliss. "You're finished. Done. The boss wants to see you."

I laid my paper down. The newsroom became very still. Telephones were still tucked on shoulders, but nobody was talking. An epidemic of writer's block swept through the room. Reporters leaned over their terminals, but nobody was typing. The phone rang, but nobody answered it.

The boss wants to see you.

It wasn't about a raise. The waiting room outside Ed Hadley's office had the look, smell, and feel of an Episcopal Church, with all of the pomp and none of the poverty of the Catholic in which I had been instructed. There was even a polished wooden pew to sit on, although it lacked a kneeler on which I might beg forgiveness.

Hadley kept me waiting for a good forty minutes, so that I would have plenty of time to contemplate my sins. By brace had rubbed a raw, sore spot on my leg during the exertions of the previous night and my nose still dripped a bit from the head cold which had pestered me earlier in the week. I tried to talk to Hadley's secretary, but a quick glance was her only reply.

Traffic in and out of the old man's office was frequent and heavy with import. An assemblyman entered with a gloomy countenance. Fifteen minutes later, he emerged with the happy glow of the newly annointed. The sales manager went in looking bad and came out looking worse. Finally, a hawk-nosed young man dressed in flawless blue charged past me with the look of the devil in his eye. Moments later, Hadley's secretary picked up the phone, nodded carefully, and said to me: "Mr. Hadley will see you now."

Ed Hadley was tall and stood straight for his years. He had an enormous head full of wild white hair and perched his bifocals on the knobby ridge of a Roman nose. He looked like a retired B-movie star, except for flapping, elephantine ears and thick, bushy eyebrows which danced across his forehead like caterpillars in heat whenever he laughed, which wasn't very often. Hadley was the last of the old-time newspaper lords, a throwback from the era of Pulitzer and Hearst, when a newspaper was just an extension of its publisher's ego. He'd come up from Tulsa in 1943 and purchased the *Herald* for fifteen thousand dollars. As Anchorage grew and became wealthy, so did Hadley and his *Herald*. The man and his paper became famous for righteous crusades and bilesome attacks on those who dared to disagree. His editorials paved the way for statehood and greased the way for the oil pipeline. When the *Anchorage Tribune* tried to move the state capital from Juneau to Willow, Ed Hadley fought them tooth and nail. He won this fight, but at a great cost. Willow residents and the people who owned land nearby called him a traitor and canceled their subscriptions. His numerous and eager critics whispered that Ed Hadley was getting old, out of touch with the times.

Well, Ed Hadley was getting old. When I get old and my memories start to fade like Polaroids without the fixing solution, I will still remember Ed Hadley standing in the Anchorage depot of the Alaska Railroad on a chilly day in January. Some 300 politicians and business leaders had gathered there to celebrate the state's purchase of the railroad from the federal government. The movers and shakers milled around the station, talking shop and waiting for the "all aboard." Hadley and his paper had touched all their lives in one way or another. But no one would talk to him. Not the governor he'd elected, not the scores of businessmen who bought his advertising space, and certainly not the dozen or so ex-reporters who'd worked for him and then grown up into other jobs. Although the crowd was as dense and festive as the Mardi Gras, there was a circumference of no-man's-land cleared around the old gray lion. I caught his eye for a second, and I will never forget what I saw. Ed Hadley, the Thunder of the Tundra, was confused and a little bit scared. Proud still, but also lonely. The Booming Giant, the Scourge of the Last Frontier, didn't have a friend in the room. His eyes asked me to come over and keep him company, but I turned away and interviewed a state senator instead.

The cows had come home for Ed Hadley.

In the beginning, it was just he and the heiress of a mineral fortune, and that's the way it would end, with a sigh of relief from everyone else. But there was something more, something his many adversaries would never understand. Through all the trouble and all the success and all the years, he stuck by the heiress. First she lost her beauty, then her health, then her wits. Now she was tucked away in a cavernous room on the third floor of the *Herald*, where she feverishly wrote Gothic novels with an Alaskan setting. Hadley made sure her books were never distributed by publishing them himself and then destroying all but a handful of copies. He knew that distribution would only subject his sweetheart to ridicule and attacks from his countless enemies. He loved her, after all, even if she was rich.

This sentimental quality was notably absent when I stepped into Hadley's office.

He and the hawk in blue were playing darts. Hadley looked like a newspaper legend should: sleeves rolled up, tie pulled down, deep lines of civic worry carved into his seventy-two-year-old brow. The publicist cut him a flattering contrast with his smooth, unworried head and tailored suit. Hadley split the bull's-eye.

Henry Blaine extended his hand and crushed my own with his public relations school grip. "Have a seat, Mr. Riordan," Hadley said, pointing to a leather-covered chair situated perilously close to the dart board. "We'll be with you in a moment."

I watched in silence as the two men finished their set, Hadley retrieving the darts and calling out the scores. The old man won sixty-eight to thirty-eight. Then he turned to me, clutching one finely balanced dart in his throwing hand and a cluster of its mates in the other.

He marked me with clear eyes, as if measuring the distance to the tip of my nose. "Mr. Blaine has a problem with your story about Entco Investments. He thinks you're laboring under the influence of some bad information. I thought we should get together and talk about it. Mr. Blaine, you have the floor."

Hadley turned away and looked out the window. I stood up and shifted from one foot to the other, trying to relieve the hot soreness of my leg. Hadley examined the tips of his darts. Blaine began:

"You have no facts, Riordan. Just unfounded rumors and crazy speculation. The only thing you can prove is our stock is going up and that doesn't prove shit. It doesn't take a genius to figure that out."

"That's not true. I've got facts."

"Fuck your facts."

Hadley listened to all this with the attitude of a Father Confessor. I said, "Fact one—Entco buys a petroleum products company. Fact two—Entco buys a worthless farm near Toyukuk. Fact three—Entco buys North Slope crude and ships it to said farm. Fact four—the title on the farmland says you've got to use it for agricultural purposes. It's in the title. That's the law."

Hadley turned away from me and the two men exchanged a conspiratorial glance. With all the heavy symbolism his Mount Rushmore-like face could muster, Hadley walked over to Blaine and handed him a dart. The publicist nodded. They both looked at me.

"All of which adds up to nothing, Pres," the publicist said. You know they're going to screw you when they use your first name. "So how did you decide that Entco is in the fertilizer business? I can quote you more exactly than you quoted Mr. Smalley: 'On the verge of a technological breakthrough.' "

"Fact five," I said, with as much certainty as I could pretend.

"Fact five? What's that?"

"I can't tell you. It's confidential."

(Use of the confidential source should be avoided when possible. However, the serious journalist will need to refer to such sources from time to time. Even more to be avoided—and used only in the most desperate of circumstances—is the confidential source that doesn't exist.)

"What do you mean, 'confidential'? Only the employees of Entco Investments know anything about our research and development activities. And our employees are not in the habit of talking—certainly not to reporters."

I waited for a second, then said: "You see my point. So you admit there's a research project. Can I quote you?" I yanked out a reporter's notebook I'd tucked in my back pocket for just such a moment. "Be careful, Blaine. I'm going to write this down."

Blaine hurled a dart past my ear and smack into some polished oak trimming three feet on my side of the dart board. Hadley let out a gasp that withered the publicist like a dry leaf in a bonfire. Oak doesn't grow in Alaska, and it costs a fortune to ship it up from the Outside.

"Sorry about that, Mr. Hadley," Blaine said. "But I must protest. This is the most irresponsible bit of scandal-mongering I've ever seen. If I owned the *Herald*, I'd fire him. He's grasping for straws."

Hadley walked over to the expensive oak trim, plucked out the dart and rubbed the hole as if it were a wound in his forearm. He turned to me. "This conversation is most certainly not on the record."

Then to Blaine: "As for you, I'll make my own decisions about whom to hire and whom to fire. Now, if you'll excuse us, I think this conversation is over. My secretary will show you to the door. Please leave. I'd like a moment alone with Pres."

Blaine slunk out the door.

Hadley pushed his bifocals back up over the bump in his nose and rubbed his hands together, as if slavering over a big plate of turkey. "Phil Norwood told me all about you." He paused, so I could think about it. "No, Mr. Riordan, I'm not going to fire you. But when you leave here, no paper in the country will hire you. You'll be a nervous wreck, a basket case. They'll put you in a rubber room where you can play handball with your ding-dong. I'll have you blacklisted and branded as the scoundrel that you are. I'll make sure your every working day is a little glimpse of hell. Obituaries, press releases, and long features on the women in my wife's garden club. I think I'll start you off with a nice, long tour of duty on the copy desk. Now please leave. I've enjoyed our conversation."

Jamie told me all about Jeffrey Williams. The young reporter wanted to know all about my meeting with Hadley, but was too polite to ask. Instead, he said "What do you think?" as I sifted through the pile of papers on my desk, searching for the résumé I periodically Xeroxed and mailed around the country. It was buried under a mess of notes, cigarette butts, coffee stains, leaky pens, and out-of-state newspapers.

"What do I think about what?"

Jamie smiled, self-satisfied. " 'Professor stabbed in

skid-row alley,' of course. Not bad, huh? We make a pretty good team.''

He threw a newspaper on my desk, knocking to the floor a brown-stained styrofoam cup punctured with a half-dozen pencil holes. ''I think you're the best reporter since Henry Louis Mencken. Now get out of here. I'm busy.''

He walked away. I examined the paper he'd thrown on my desk. The headline on the final edition was even bigger and more lurid than the one I'd seen earlier. Phil had selected another photograph which showed the victim's head sticking out of the back of the ambulance, mouth open and eyes closed. The name jumped off the written page and into some dusty closet of my memory, where it taunted me from behind a pile of old songs, neglected friends, and books I've never written. Jeffrey Williams. Jeffrey Williams. Something I was supposed to do.

Check that. Something he was supposed to do. Recall hit me with all the sickly force of a watermelon dropped from the fifteenth floor. It wasn't an old name, but a new one. He was supposed to meet me over beer after work and tell me what it was that made him so scared that he whispered on the phone—what made him so desperate that he turned to a newsman for help. He said he'd meet me after work, but instead he met me in the alley behind the Colorado Club and now he was all dead in black and gray on the front page of the *Anchorage Herald*.

Jeffrey Williams. A whisper on the telephone and a bloodstain on the ground. Jeffrey Williams. His fear was real, and so was the way his head flopped about when they lifted him onto the stretcher. When I put the picture and the sound together, it was as if the dead were speaking only to me.

What would Phil think? You know, boss, I don't know how to tell you this, but they're killing my sources. No, that's not why I didn't file a story yesterday. And yes, well, it's only one source really. No, I don't know who they are. What? Well, I guess he's not exactly a source. He wanted to be but they killed him. He said he'd meet me for a beer, but he never showed up. Anyway, he's dead. Murdered. Give me the rest of today and tomorrow and maybe I can find out why. I'll write a real 'Hey, Mildred' story for the Sunday edition . . . But Phil, this murder is incredible . . . But Phil . . . But Phil . . . But Phil . . .

What would Phil think? Phil would think I was nuts. My city editor has a very limited imagination, and besides I was on Hadley's shit list. So I thought about another angle. Then I thought about the copy desk. Then I thought about a beer and felt a little better.

Chapter 5

PHIL PUT ME ON THE NIGHT DESK, WHERE I WOULD BE less likely to poison other employees with my discontent. I punched in at four P.M. and scanned the national wires for items of interest. There was nothing of interest to me. I'd become a journalist so people could read my writing, not so I could read theirs.

I couldn't help but notice an air of jubilation at my demise. Jamie was, of course, thrilled at my reduced circumstances and spent five minutes of every hour telling Phil why he should cover the Iditarod. Carl was glad he wasn't me. And the strange spectacle of my being paid to spell correctly brought a warm, fuzzy glow to my new colleagues on the desk. The same people who had endured my tortured renditions of words like "commitment" and "bureaucracy" pelted me with low-grade sniggering every time I reached for the dictionary.

The computer started to spit the Sunday Outdoors section at me as soon as I sat down. I stitched and trimmed and condensed and fluffed for hours on end. I wrote the worst headlines I could think of to see if anyone noticed or cared: "Salmon species: seeing reds while in the pink" and "Kodiak bear, the lonely game in town." Nobody noticed. Nobody cared. The day workers went home, and the police radio scratched out its weary warnings about traffic accidents (11–23s) and belligerent drunks (10–15s).

I stitched and trimmed some more and thought about what I could do to extricate myself from this unpleasant situation. After a while I decided that maybe I should start with Dr. Williams. Maybe if I wrote a story, the dead professor's head would stop flopping around when he talked to me in my mind.

A thin membrane of ice covered the streets and made each puddle into a treacherous trap. I walked slowly and carefully, my lame leg slipping to the side a bit on every other step. Downtown was lively on the east side of B Street, with people talking on the sidewalk or quietly scooting from one bar to another, a party bathed in neon. The harsh background music of two bar bands and a half-dozen jukeboxes collided in the street. Cars full of shadows cruised up and down the boulevard, hunting for other shadows. A foot cop arbitrated a dispute between a native man and a white woman while the drunk truck carried her boyfriend away. An old woman shivered in the hollow doorway of Frontier Real Estate. She'd traded in her winter coat too soon.

As I shuffled over the ice toward the scene of the crime, one man asked me for a cigarette. Another wanted to know what had happened to my leg.

"Mauled by a bear," I said without slowing down.

The Colorado Club anchors the strip with dollar-a-glass beer and a long mural of Alaska legends painted on the wall above the door. The front door was propped open to provide a clear passage for the patrons and the fresh air and the beckoning twang and yawl of Howdy Bob and His Cowboy Commotion.

Inside, white and brown and black circulated freely around a ratty pool table. Dancing couples did the Heel-and-Toe in frothing puddles of spilled drink. There was another, smaller mural decorating the wall behind the bartender with Day-Glo images drawn in a primitive style—the gold panner and the trapper and the fisherman and the railroad builder, a hodgepodge of memory and legend, a phantasm of what Alaska thinks it used to be. The scenes were captioned with exerpts from the poetry of Robert Service written in thick white letters by a childish hand. My personal favorite, "The Men That Don't Fit In," was given a prominent position near the cash register. A moosehead surveyed the scene from a rough wood rafter above Howdy Bob.

A patron collapsed into a heap on the floor while the Cowboy Commotion screamed to be heard above the din. The band didn't miss a beat as two bouncers dragged the man to his feet and rocketed him out the door, twisting his arm a little too hard.

I read "The Men That Don't Fit In" while waiting for the bartender to come my way.

"Buy me a drink," the lady said, a command rather than a question.

She looked like the Face on the Barroom Floor. She was a white woman of about forty-five with dyed red hair and makeup packed like mortar between her wrinkles. Breasts that had lost their battle with gravity spilled out from her black leather coat and were held in place by the tired buttons of her lumberjack shirt. She tapped the toes of her cowboy boots. I nodded meekly. Her blue jeans strained to contain her swelling thighs. I hadn't had a woman in months. Maybe she would help me to forget them altogether.

"Bartender," I said, trying to sound authoritative, but only sounding loud. "Let's have a beer here, and . . ." I turned to the woman. "What will you have?"

"The usual."

The bartender lumbered our way and rested two meaty elbows on the rim of the bar. "You want something?"

"Yea . . . ahh . . . One tap, and one usual."

I offered her my seat. She climbed aboard, her butt spilling over the rounded curve of the seat. She asked me for a cigarette. I put it to her while lighting a smoke. "I hear somebody bought it here last night. In the alley out back."

She sucked on her cigarette, then sucked on her whiskey and exhaled into my face a combination of smoke and alcohol fumes. "No shit. Wanna dance?"

"Sorry. I don't dance."

"What's the matter? Are you a faggot or something?"

"No. I lost my leg in the war. So what do you think happened?"

"I don't know. I guess you lost your leg in the war."

"No, I mean to the guy that got killed. Think it was drugs?"

"Naw. He was probably a faggot, too."

She hit me up for another cigarette. I counted the bubbles in my beer. She started talking to the guy on her right and asked him if he wanted to dance. He led her onto the dance floor like a sailor wrestling with an untied sail.

I reclaimed my seat and started reading poetry again. There was a scuffle somewhere in the thick knot of dancers swarming over the place. Howdy Bob and His Cowboy Commotion played "Family Tradition" by Hank Williams, Jr. as three bouncers used pool cues to separate the combatants. Glasses shattered and the crowd pressed against the rim of the bar as the bouncers rolled two drunks out the door.

I followed soon thereafter.

I had a drink in each of the seven bars on the two-block length of skid row. The bartender in the Not Much Room agreed that it must have been drugs, but he didn't know a thing about it. A regular at the Norwegian Lounge said he knew all about it and would tell me if I bought him a shot of Wild Turkey and a beer. His memory failed after the drinks were poured.

From there the trail led to the Blue Bear Bar and a large group of large soldiers and to the Walk Inn and a scrawny girl with no front teeth who looked too young and too old at the same time. The marquee of the Wild Berry advertised "22 beautiful girls and 3 ugly ones." Four of my last five dollars bought me a watered-down beer and a painful erection, but no information. I tossed down the beer and started for home. It was closing time anyway.

The street clattered with a sloppy, dying frenzy as the night ran out of energy and the bars evicted their most loyal customers. Loud arguments, drunken laughter, and the horrible feeling of being alone at two A.M. I might have cried and blamed it on my leg, but something familiar clicked in my brain, distracting me.

Maybe it was the last encore of Howdy Bob and His Cowboy Commotion slipping through a crack in the night. Or maybe it was the broken concrete, or the fact that the alley was clean where they had washed the blood away. Or maybe death still lingered in the place, enjoying its triumph of the night before.

One of these things—or something else altogether that I still don't understand—stopped me in my tracks. I hesitated for a moment before turning into the alley. Maybe I could find some clue the police had missed—a tuft of hair snagged on the dumpster or a bloodstained weapon buried under a pile of discarded wine bottles.

Maybe they'd spotted each other in one of the bars and

exchanged some obscure signal that only criminals know. After eyeing each other carefully for a minute or two, one man moved closer to the other and started talking about politics or sports or some other subject on which men can safely disagree. After a while, they bought each other drinks and maybe Jeffrey Williams said he was feeling a little slow and needed a pick-me-up. Or maybe the other guy was moving slowly and Williams had the goods. Maybe they agreed to meet out back in a safe spot where the cops never went and maybe they had an argument there. Things got out of hand and Williams took a knife in the gut. The killer ran away, his mind crazed with panic, his pockets bulging with greed and his palms sweating from the excitement and the cocaine fever.

Or so I figured. It all made perfect sense until you got to the telephone call. Why would a junkie call me about something urgent and important? Junkies and creeps don't need reporters. Decent people do. Or so I told myself as I swayed back and forth on my heels in the alley behind the Colorado Club.

Strange laughter caught my ear. I spun around twice before my eyes came into focus on the soft glow of a campfire in a vacant lot halfway down the block. Bulky shadows passed in front of the throbbing coals and settled into a dark ring of heads shifting around the light. I could feel their eyes hot on me as I turned heel once more and headed for the fire. I didn't know where I was going until a new and wonderful aroma started competing with the stale beer smell and the old garbage smell for the attention of my nose. It was then that I noticed the vacant lot was clean of broken glass and as nicely manicured as a vacant lot can be.

Alex's Outdoor Salmon Bake was a certified Anchorage legend. Although it violated dozens of municipal ordinances, the cops and the health department looked the other way because it performed a valuable public service. Street people have to eat, too, and Alex ran a clean and orderly operation. The cops and the health department also ignored Alex's Steampipe Hotel, a fly-by-night flophouse situated in a crevasse of the underground heating system which the city uses to keep its water pipes above freezing temperature. Street people have to sleep, too, and Steampipe Hotel was better than finding frozen bodies in the morning.

"Slummin', brother?" a thick shadow asked as I approached the fire. I assumed it was Alex. It was.

"Sort of."

Five or six shapes were gathered around a small barbeque grill set upon cinder blocks. Three were huddled on one side and passed a bottle back and forth. On the other side was Alex and an inert lump that could have been a man or could have been a pile of rags.

"Well, sit yourself down," Alex said, patting the ground on his left. He smelled like an old moose. There was a tool belt strapped to his shoulder and an extra pair of shoes dangled from a frayed piece of rope looped around his neck. He wore a billed cap and thick glasses with black frames. His face looked like a relief map of Afghanistan, complete with a gray stubble of beard that looked like a snowy timberline. His nose was the size and shape and color of a tomato.

I sat down. He stretched a leg. A sliver of steel tucked into his boot flashed me a warning. "What happened to your leg, boy?"

"I had polio when I was a kid."

"That so. My cousin had the polio, too, but he didn't wear no wooden leg."

"It's steel. And there's a little bit of real leg in there someplace."

"Well, sit down and tell ole Alex what you need. I'd

introduce you, but those folks are too drunk to do much talkin' and my buddy Naknek's all 'sleep. You look a little drunk, too, now that I think. We got good food to eat and a place to stay and real fine company if you ain't too proud. You don't look too proud. You got a quarter? A sit by my fire cost you a quarter.''

I dug into my pocket and handed him three dimes. "Keep the change,'' I joked. He didn't get it.

"Okay, now a swig a dis here wine gonna cost you another quarter, unless you be thinkin' that ole Alex is a dirty dog and you don't wanna put your lips where a dirty dog's lips a' been.''

That's exactly what I was thinking, but I counted out twenty-five cents and traded them for a shot glass full of something that tasted like grape kerosene. "I need some information.''

Alex smiled. "I bet you talkin' 'bout last night's little party. I seed you standin' over there—bein' still and thinkin' real hard. You the brother or somethin'? You lookin' for a little comeback? You got yourself a gun?''

"No. I'm a reporter with the *Anchorage Herald*.''

Alex leaned forward and started poking the fire with what looked like the sawed-off handle of a tennis racket. The business end of the racket had been sharpened into a broad, flat wedge which he used to flip the charred pieces of salmon. He pinched off a morsel and tossed it into his mouth. "Soup's on, children.''

The three men on the other side of the fire fussed with each other over money. They were trying to figure out who would pay for the food and who for the lodging. The man in the middle had already paid for the bottle. He was getting a little impatient with his pals. Finally, they straightened it out and the guy on the left handed over three greasy bills.

Alex folded the money and tucked it into the side pocket of his coat. "Want some? Cost you a dollar."

I nodded. I fumbled for my last dollar bill and handed it over. Alex poked a sliver of salmon and then skillfully shoveled it up with the sawed-off racket and tossed it into my lap. The grease soaked through my pants and made a penny-sized burn on the inside of my thigh. The first bite made a savory, juicy explosion in my mouth. It was the best salmon I'd ever had. "Delicious," I said.

Alex nodded. "You can't beat the open fire and some of Alex's secret sauce. So you work for the *Herald,* hey? That be ole Ed Hadley's rag. I used to work for that ole prick for a bit. That was long ago before I got the freedom urge. Stitcher in the composing room, I was, 'til the union come to town and try to squeeze a little respect outta that ole skinflint. We all signed up and Mr. Ed just laughed. We all lost our jobs to a buncha pansies he got shipped up from the Outside. Now I use the *Herald* papers for my pillow every night and I feel much better for it. Never read it, though. Too much bullshit for my mind. So what's goin' on in the worl' these days? Is Nixon still in charge? You gonna put ole Alex in the paper again?"

"Maybe. If you want me to."

"I don't want shit from you, boy, 'less it be another dollar for another piece of fish meat. I swear, every spring breakup, just about as regular as the spring itself, Hadley send some youngster down here to the Ave to write it all up about the strip. That's so as to make us look bad so maybe come summer the city'll clean us out 'cause your boss don't like us hangin' 'round like we like to do because we're ugly, or at least Naknek is."

He gave an elbow to the bundle of rags, which rolled over but didn't reply. "We're bad for business, I suppose. Bad for all them property values your boss got himself. So Mr. Ed send you down to ask me 'bout the salmon bake and when's the last time I had a bath and what 'bout the Steampipe Hotel. Where's the picture-takin' man? Hadley always sends along a picture-takin' man to take my picture."

I tried to ask him a question, but he started up again.

"Of course, I suppose you get it wrong, just like the others. Not that I read the paper no more or give a flyin' fuck anyway. Ain't got it right in fifty-three times tryin', I bet. No reason you should be different."

"What's the part they don't get right?"

"Every part."

Alex picked up the wine, took a swig, and then offered it to me. I reached for the bottle. He pulled it back. "Got a quarter?"

I checked my pockets, but I only had fifteen cents left. I handed the money over and with a laugh he poured a half portion into the bottle cap. "I see ole Mr. Ed still pay just enough to keep you alive. Shit, boy, I got twenty-five thousand gold in the bank. Price of gold go up again and I be a real rich man. That's 'cause I live on the cheap. That's how a rag man like me be rich. Most people watch what they make, but ole Alex be cagey and watch what he spend."

I downed the shot. "So what's the part they don't get right?"

"Naknek? Hey Naknek!" he said, nudging the pile of rags.

"Yea?" the pile groaned.

"Where you born?"

The pile shifted onto an elbow. A puffy, scarred face came into the light. He had Oriental eyes and isolated patches of mustache and goatee. "Minto, boss. You know that."

"Pretty boy here thinks you smell like yesterday's fart. Tell him 'bout your first job."

"Ain't never had no first job. Ain't never had no job. I never work for nobody."

"How many bear you ate?"

"Couple of five or ten."

"How much gold you found?"

"Enough for me to need."

"How many mountains you seen?"

"Plenty. Nothin' but mountains way up north of Minto."

"How many rivers you run?"

"Shit. I don't know. How many are there?"

"What you doin' here, then?"

"Waitin', Alex. You know that."

"What you waitin' for?"

"Not too much now. Not much left."

"Take a long swallow, boy. It's all gonna be okay."

Naknek grabbed the bottle and took a long pull. Then he tucked his elbow back in and returned to his slumber. I looked across the campfire and saw that Alex's other guests were sleeping, too. I noticed now that the streets were quiet. The merrymakers had all gone home and the fire was getting low. Alex added a chunk of two-by-four to the fire. He poked the ashes with his sawed-off tennis racquet.

"That's the part they miss, boy. That's the part they miss. They see the death, but nobody of them ever see the life. This here be a dyin' place. Naknek dyin', and I dyin', too. But it's a dyin' place for them folks that's done their share of fine livin'. That be more than a man over there. Naknek is the one of a kind that you not gonna see much anymore. When he growed up, there be huntin' and fishin' and plenty of trappin' and space to move 'round like you never gonna ever see. But the white man come to town with the oil like you and me and chase all that away with his TV and his cars and his three-wheelers so as like the young ones don't even learn how to walk no more. That ole man done just about ever'thin', boy, and if you start right now you'll never do a slice of the things that Naknek done 'cause they can't be done anymore. Alaska be a new place, boy. It's your place now, just like ever'thin' else. I come up here to get away from folk like you and like I used to be and damn if they din't strike the oil and now all the Outsiders're runnin' up here like the salmon come to Bristol Bay.''

He'd run out of wind, not anger. I coughed and waited for a few seconds. ''Look, Alex. I'm not doing that story. I'd love to do that story just like you told it to me right here. But right now I'm working on a murder.''

''Course you are, boy. Course you are. The only ones do that story be the ones that don't know shit. I can't help you but a little bit. I seen it happen for sure, but I didn't get too close 'cause I know it be somethin' nasty. So here's how it is. The dead one waits over there for twenty minutes or so, like he waitin' to meet somebody real important 'cause he was pacin' and fidgetin' and always lookin' over his shoulder and seemin' like every stranger might be the one he waitin' for. So then the Slim Slam Man comes along. He be tall and strong and real mean lookin'. I'm pretty sure it be this here Slim Slam—an evil one we seen hangin' 'round the strip lately. He dressed poor and talk like a uneducated fool, but I figure he ain't really that way and he just scammin' us, though Lord know how come anybody want to scam raggedy men like us. Slim here got some big ole ears just like a garbage can lid and a nose looked like a baked potato. We call him the Slim Slam Man on accounta he be skinny and look like he slam ya if you look at him funny.''

''How do you mean like a baked potato?''

''Well, now how do I say it? You know how a baked potato is split up across the top with sour cream and some insides leakin' out? Well, that's what his nose look like. Musta got in a blade fight sometime. The Slim Slam Man done it. We pretty sure o' that.''

"So what happened?''

"Just what I was sayin'. The dead one be waitin' in the alley like he got some serious business to attend to, only he don't got nobody to attend with. The ole Slim come along and they talk for a little bit and then the dead man try to scoot away. Slim grabs him by the collar and yanks him behind that dumpster right over there. Slipped him the blade he did, just once or twice and then walks away real slow, like he just got done makin' a telephone call. I take a quick peak and see that the man is just about dead pretty soon, so I call the cops and they come clean him up.''

"You called the cops?''

"That's right. Me and them got ourselves a little deal where they don't mess with me and I let them know when there be some bad news brewin'. Course, it ain't like me to tell anybody everything.''

"Like what do you mean?''

"Like what the dead one say before the cops and the medicine wagon come by.''

The night turned still, as if the street itself strained to hear. "What did he say?''

Alex waited for a moment. "What you got for me? You got some money, for sure.''

I told him I didn't have a cent. He said he liked my coat. I said that would be okay.

"Riordan.''

"What?''

"I said 'Riordan.' That's what he say. He say 'Riordan' and it sounded real wet, like he talkin' into a glass of milk like kids do when they bein' bad at the supper table. That you, ain't it? You Riordan.''

"Give me back my coat and I'll answer your questions."

"That's okay. You keep the answer, I keep the coat."

"Which way did Slim go?"

"Down over there," Alex said, pointing toward the port. "You ain't gonna find him, though. Your best bet is stick around and let him find you, but I ain't so sure you wanna do that."

"What about the dead man? You ever seen him before?"

"Hell, no. He too pretty. Just like you, exceptin' he got two good legs and don't wear no tie. Alex only see rag men 'round here."

Alex doused the fire with a bucket full of sand he'd fetched from behind a pile of bulging Hefty bags. He disappeared around a corner and came back a moment later with a shopping cart filled with pillows and pots and clothes and odd pieces of wood and metal scraps. He woke up his three guests and they helped him load the grill and Naknek onto the shopping cart. Alex adjusted one of the pillows under his friend's head so it lay just right.

I walked with them a way. They took a right at F Street and headed down the bluff toward Steampipe Hotel. I waited at the corner for a moment and watched them trail away.

Alex turned back. "Hey Riordan! What's the rest of your name?"

I thought about it. Why not? "Prester. Prester John. My friends call me Pres."

The old man scratched an armpit while digesting the information. "That's a pretty weird-ass name, I got to say. Take care of yourself, Pres. Watch yourself out for the Slim Slam Man."

Chapter 6

I CALLED IN SICK THE NEXT DAY. PHIL DIDN'T MIND VERY much. Chena was downright thrilled. I cooked up a breakfast of fried eggs and bologna. She slavered over the leftovers while I worked the telephone.

"University records."

"Hi, ahh . . . my name is Pres Riordan. I'm a reporter with the *Herald*. I'm trying to get some information about one of your teachers, a Dr. Jeffrey Williams."

"One second, please."

The hold button oozed syrupy K-Tel renditions of classical movements turned into movie tunes. The 10,000 strings switched from Mantovani to Brahms without missing a stroke.

"Mr. Riordan?"

"Yes."

"You'll have to speak to the vice chancellor in charge of personnel."

"Great. Thanks. Can you transfer me?"

"I'm afraid that's not possible. He's not available."

"I see. And when will he be available?"

"Dr. Goode is on sabbatical for the term. He'll be back in the fall."

"In the fall? That's six months away. How about Dr. Neuman?"

"I'm sorry, sir. All inquiries about staff members must go through the personnel office."

"Who's acting in Dr. Goode's absence?"

"I am. Please understand that university personnel records are strictly confidential."

"And what's your name?"

"Sarah Worley."

"Please, Miss Worley. I have just a few simple questions."

But Miss Worley would not be moved. Chena had given up on the leftovers and fallen asleep. She stirred a bit from her reverie, letting out a mumbling bark that was almost a whine. Her forelegs started twitching. She dreamed she was young again and bounded over a dream fence. I tried the phone again.

"Deputy Chief Roland's office."

"Hi, Karen. This is Riordan. Is the Colonel in?"

"Well, hello, Pres. Hang on and I'll check."

Cop muzak: a country hit.

"Roland."

"Riordan."

"Hello, Mr. Riordan. Keeping out of trouble?"

"Well, at least I'm keeping out of jail. So far, anyway. How you doing, Colonel? I need your help."

"I'm doing fine. What's up?"

"There was a pug ugly out on the street earlier this week. The street people call him the Slim Slam Man. He's got big ears and a nose that looks like a baked potato. Ring a bell?"

"Pres, you're the only pug ugly I know. And I mean that with all sincerity."

"Thanks, Colonel. Could you check him out?"

"Sure. I'd be glad to."

"Thanks, Colonel."

"That it?"

"Yes. I guess."

"Bye."

Click. Click. He clicked first.

Chena had awakened. I could hear her sandpaper tongue scrape my breakfast plate. Before I could scold her, the plate and utensils tumbled to the floor. She was back to sleep before I could give her a piece of my mind.

"University records."

"Hello, my name is Rodney Wright." Rodney Wright sounded like Prester John with a finger up his nose. "I'm calling from Milwaukee, Wisconsin. I'm an adjuster with the Premium Life Insurance Company. I wonder if you could answer a few simple questions about an employee of yours: the late—let me see what's the name here—the late Jeff Williams."

"What can I do for you, sir?"

"Well, as you may know, Mr. Williams died the other day. Quite a tragedy. Double indemnity, in fact. But there's a problem with his policy. The chief beneficiary has moved away and we don't have a forwarding address. Like I said, there's a large sum of money involved and . . . well . . . Premium likes to be prompt as possible with payments in double indemnity cases. It helps to ease the pain. I'm hoping you might have a list of his next of kin . . . perhaps with some current addresses and telephone numbers. Most institutions require that sort of thing in case of an emergency."

This time Sarah Worley was more cooperative. Women love it when you lie. "If you'll hang on a moment I'll get the file."

The 10,000 strings labored to a crescendo. A nameless announcer came on to say, "This is beautiful music KOLD, the coolest sound in Alaska brought to you by the Greatland National Bank."

"Mr. Wright?"

"Yes, I'm still here."

Sarah Worley told me Williams had a sister in Chicago, a mother in Maywood, Illinois, and an uncle in Philadelphia. When she finished telling me their telephone numbers and addresses, I thanked her.

Then I tried my most conversational tone: "You know, this can be a funny business sometimes. I know where and when Mr. Williams was born and how much he used to weigh and how much he used to make. I even know what his lungs look like. But I don't know that much about the man, the person. Who he was and what he was like, or even what he did for a living. That's stuff's not on the fatality profile most of the time and we usually don't bother, except with stuntmen and acrobats and coal miners and the like. I assume that Mr. Williams was a teacher at your university."

"It's Dr. Williams, and that is correct. He was only here for a short time, but he had a very good reputation. He came highly recommended and was a nice man."

"I see. I see. This is a tragedy indeed. You know, life insurance companies get a bad rap. We really support our clients. We really hope that they all live a very long time. We're betting on it, in fact. And what, may I ask, did Dr. Williams teach?"

"He was a chemist. I believe his speciality was petrochemical research."

The icy membrane of the night before had melted back into the slushy puddles of spring. The air was crisp and clean. The front yards Chena and I passed en route to the car I'd bought from the assemblyman were made of a thick, brown sludge.

The assemblyman's car was a 1975 Pontiac with expired license plates and a driver's door so rotted with rust that I never dared open it for fear it would fall off. It needed a tune-up but moved well enough once it got going. Marked against it were more unpaid parking tickets than the car was worth. The warnings and warrants were delivered to the assemblyman's house because I never bothered to have the title filed in my own name. This was the cause of some stress to the politician, who had an image to maintain and an election to win. Someday someone would tow the car away, and I would never see it again. This made every trip a special one, like Sunday dinner with a close relative living on borrowed time. We drove against the grain of traffic, listening to easy rock on the radio.

The Alaska Institute of Technology was the living vision of a Presbyterian minister with a well-developed talent for extracting grants from state, local, and federal governments. He wanted Anchorage to be the "Petroleum Crossroads of the World." To this end, he stocked the place with brown beauties and yellow scientists from all along the Pacific Rim—the Philippines, Samoa, Hawaii, Korea, Taiwan, Australia, and, of course, Alaska, although the latter was deficient in both brown beauties and yellow scientists. I sat in a dark corner of the cafeteria and watched the girls go by, with their round Pacific breasts and taut Pacific bottoms and well-scrubbed Pacific faces.

The course schedule devoted but a single paragraph to Dr. Williams. This was his second semester at AIT. He hailed from the University of Texas and the Massachusetts Institute of Technology, where he received honors and a doctorate in molecular engineering. He taught chemistry and biology at AIT and had published scholarly papers in several obscure but prestigious journals. I wrote down the magazines, thinking to read his articles later.

I lit a cigarette and dumped the smoldering match in a discarded Coke can left on my table. I marked my target and headed for a clutch of girls gathered around a table littered with chemistry books. "Excuse me," I said, trying not to sound too lecherous, or at least too eager about it. "Do you mind if I join you?"

I remembered why I never liked college. College girls hadn't changed a bit in fifteen years. My gallantry was greeted with darting eyes and various laughs of uncertain timbre. "Have a seat," said the homeliest one. I wondered if girls ever hated college, too.

"What's wrong with your leg?" the prettiest one countered.

The last thing I want is for good-looking women to remind me of my affliction. It recalls all the pretty girls I've never had. "I got it cut up in a gang fight back in the old neighborhood."

The girls looked at me, then at one another. I couldn't tell if they didn't believe me or didn't care. "I'm a reporter with the *Herald*. I'd like to ask you a few questions."

There came another round of curious looks, and another surge of laughter. This time, their intent was unmistakable. "Did any of you know Dr. Williams?"

As if on cue, all eyes turned to the homely one. The other girls picked up their chemistry books and disappeared in a cloud of perfumed ignorance. "Goodbye, Genna. See you tomorrow—maybe," the prettiest called over her shoulder.

More laughter, then awkward silence.

The girl who remained behind was sturdy looking and had coarse brown hair tied back in a bun. Her nostrils flared like a filly reaching for the finish line. I bought her a Coke.

"Nice guy," she said when I returned from the check-out line. "But a little goofy. You know, different." She looked at me as if I was the most "different" person she'd ever met.

"How do you mean?"

"Well, he's only been here a little while, but you take this last term. Early November—just before Thanksgiving vacation. He gives us this big-deal assignment on electron interactions. We're supposed to diagram the production of nylon and vinyl from fossil fuels. Then it gets weird. He calls off classes for a whole week, he says, so we can work on the project full time. That's pretty weird to start with because we're only sophomores, but who's going to bitch? But then he disappears and leaves his graduate student in charge. And, of course, the graduate student doesn't know anything about electron interactions. Real weird."

"What's so strange about that?"

"Nothing. Except the Doc comes back on Monday and he never bothers to collect the papers even. Never says a word. Nothing. Doodily squat. It was like, 'Okay kids, I'm busy now. So you go out and play with petrochemicals.' But like I said, he was a real nice guy. He gave me a ride home one time when my brother's car broke down and he didn't even try to hit up on me. He just talked about politics the whole time so's I almost lost my lunch. But he didn't try any kind of moves. Like I said, a nice guy. But very strange."

"Was there anything else 'strange' about him?"

She swigged her Coke, letting some of it age in the pouch of her left cheek before swallowing. "Sure. Lots of things."

"Like what?"

"Like this was a chemistry class, right? But he was always going on and on about politics and economics and all sorts of stuff that had nothing to do with chemistry. He always said the scientists should always make sure their inventions are used right. So one time we spent all week talking about Einstein and the bomb and another time he spent two days talking about the Model T Ford like as just to about make me croak. He said that Henry Ford was a great man because he was the first to pay five dollars a day and made it so everybody could drive. But then he said that Einstein was a weenie even if everybody says he was a genius because he let the generals have the bomb.''

''What do you make of that?''

The girl drained her Coke and started packing her books into a knapsack. ''I don't know. Maybe he's right. But I didn't sign up for the course so I could learn the right thing to do. I need the chemistry if I'm ever gonna be a geologist for a big oil company.''

She stood up and put on her coat. ''If he wasn't so weird, I'd think the guy was hitting up on some lady that time he disappeared. But that guy . . . I don't know . . . Like I said, he never hit up on me.''

I worked the late desk on Friday. I don't remember what went into the Saturday paper, although I edited most of the news pages.

After work, I started my weekend with two quick shots and plenty of beer to wash them down until things got a little hazy. I crawled home to a long, heavy sleep brightened by a dream in which two Japanese stewardesses arm wrestled for the prize of my attention. I like aggressive women. They save me from the hazards of rejection. Just when we were getting to the good part, my nether world was split open by the sharp ring of the telephone. My head ached as if from an open wound.

''Mr. Riordan?'' She sounded nasal and distressed, as if a cold, prickly burr was lodged in one of her nostrils.

''Yes?''

"Please stand by for Hugh Smalley."

Say what? Chena hobbled into the bedroom and stretched herself over a pile of dirty laundry. She shook some sleep away, making a flash storm of old black hairs. She gave me that solemn look that meant she had to take a leak.

"Mr. Riordan?"

"Yes."

"This is Hugh Smalley. My, you are a troublesome fellow."

"How's that?"

"You can do so much damage with so little information. You may not realize this, but I've followed your career quite closely. I almost split a gut when I read that story about my secret petrochemical project. Hilarious."

"I'm glad you liked it. Why didn't you tell that to your public relations man? He seemed pretty annoyed with me."

"Henry Blaine is a silly fool. He's going to be reassigned. To Chad, perhaps. As a matter of fact, I've reassigned a number of people since your little story came out. I don't like to read about family secrets in the afternoon paper. It's bad for business. You can print that if you like."

"I may do that. Is there anything else? Or did you just call to say 'hello'?"

"I've got a proposition for you, Mr. Riordan."

"Really? What's that?"

"A story. A scoop, I think you fellows call it. I'd like you to come up to the Toyukuk and take a tour of this facility of mine you've been writing about. I think you'll find it most instructive. Much better than the half-truths you've been distributing at my expense."

Thank God for half-truths. So much for weird professors and tall killers with noses like baked potatoes. On

Monday, I announced to my associates in the newsroom that my exile to the copy desk was over. This was news indeed, especially to Phil.

"How's that?" he asked.

I didn't say. My only reply was to strut away with what I imagined to be a look of unbearable arrogance. I went upstairs and demanded an immediate appointment with the old man. Two hours later, I got one.

Chapter 7

THE MORNING TIDE KNOCKED SOME LEFTOVER SLABS OF winter ice against the shore as the train rolled into the station. Off to the east, the rising sun lent a thin, blue halo to the rolling peaks of the Chugach Mountains. I boarded the train with a hunting party full of beards and two aging tourists dressed up for the bitter cold they'd read so much about.

The husband said they were bound for the base camp of Mount McKinley, a seven-thousand-foot elevation accessible by light plane. The couple and I settled into our tattered Naugahyde seats and talked about the spruce and the moose and the Canadian goose while the bearded hunters drank from flasks and got rowdy. At 9:05 A.M., the train lurched forward with a jolt.

Ed Hadley loved the train, although not because it reminded him of the simpler, more optimistic America of his youth. He liked the accounts receivable.

"Fairbanks, huh?" he had said to me after I told him about the story which Smalley had offered us. "Can't you just interview him over the phone? We'll get the *Fairbanks News-Miner* to take some pictures.''

"I don't think so, Mr. Hadley. They might get wind of the story. Besides, Smalley said I should go to Toyukuk and take a tour of his plant. I guess my Chamber story must have struck a responsive chord.''

Hadley grunted and turned to the huge picture window behind his desk. The window provided a commanding view of Midtown, a part of the city identified in the negative. Everything that wasn't Fairview, Muldoon, Spenard, or the Hillside sagged in the middle and was called Midtown.

"Well then, I guess you'll have to go to Fairbanks," he said, still looking away from me. He turned around and yanked on an elephantine ear. "This had better be good, Mr. Riordan. The *Herald* didn't get to be a great newspaper by throwing money after wild geese.''

He paused. I nodded. This was most certainly so. Hadley turned back to his desk and sat down on his chair. He pulled a thick black binder from his top desk drawer. I waited while he paged through the binder and calculated the cost-benefit ratio.

"I see we have a bill outstanding to the Alaska Railroad. I suggest you take the Tuesday morning train to Fairbanks and then get Entco Investments to pick you up and take you to Toyukuk City. You can file a story for the Thursday edition. Your travel time will be off the time card, of course. We didn't get to be a great newspaper by paying people to lollygag around and look at scenery.''

As the train crawled through the mountain pass to Wasilla, I examined a full-color railroad brochure the conductor had given me when I asked him where the men's room was.

As a mode of transportation, the Alaska Railroad gives

eloquent testimony to the greater abilities of trucks and planes. It chugs between Seward and Anchorage, Anchorage and Fairbanks at a leisurely twenty-five miles an hour, stopping only for the occasional passenger and the unyielding moose. During the winter months, its progress is impeded by frost heaves, a local phenomenon which occurs when the ground freezes and expands, causing the tracks to buckle. Avalanches and moose are the other typical hazards. The moose, it seems, mistake the chugging of the train for the heavy breathing of a pack of wolves, their natural enemy. The huge beasts, not known for their intelligence, flee along the clearest path of retreat, which is, of course, the tracks themselves. On rare occasions, the train wins the race.

I tucked the brochure into my pocket and gazed out at Wasilla, a strip of fast-food restaurants, road signs, and liquor stores inhabited by people who will do almost anything—even live in Wasilla—to avoid paying property taxes. Wasilla is the northernmost edge of civilization as we know it. Beyond are puddles and bumps, mountains and lakes, puddles and bumps and Fairbanks. As we left the town, I settled into my seat and slept, dreaming of dead professors and fat guys from Tulsa.

By the time I awoke, the two aging tourists had themselves fallen into an unbothered sleep, their heads leaning against one another and their limbs woven into an intimate and complicated tangle. I envied them their weary affection and wondered if I too would someday run off on a last bold adventure with the woman of my life. I doubted it. After a while, the wife stirred and told me we'd whacked a moose just outside of Big Lake.

She nudged her partner awake when the train pulled into Talkeetna, a sleepy colony of about five hundred trappers, hippies, and welfare recipients located 160 miles due north of Anchorage.

THE COLD FRONT

During the short summers, the hippies guide sportsmen up and down Mount McKinley and up and down the Talkeetna River and get their pictures taken by tourists wishing to document their encounter with a real Alaskan. During the long winters, the men amuse themselves with hunting and trapping and drinking and gossiping while the womenfolk generate an income by waiting tables, teaching school, and fashioning artifacts for sale in the gift shops of Anchorage.

Half the town turned out to meet the train. A crusty gallery of men with nothing better to do followed our progress as we eased through the mud. I helped the old couple carry their bags from the train.

The street was a tunnel of frozen mud cut through snow banks piled higher than most of the buildings in town. A two-headed parking meter had been installed in front of the Fairview Inn where it served as a reminder of that which has left Talkeetna behind. The speed limit was posted at fifteen miles per hour, although the cars tended to move more slowly than the people.

The sun set over the place where the Susitna and Talkeetna rivers meet. Dogs and children charged up and over mountains of melting snow. Thin plumes of smoke full of dinnertime nutrition and fireplace warmth snaked from the chimneys of a dozen rough wood cabins. Old men with scarred hands and big, hard bellies gathered around a picnic table in front of the Fairview. They watched in silence as we trudged past the church and the one-room library and the general store.

"Evenin', folks," one man said through a ratty gray beard. "If you want some fine color picture-takin', be sure to go with Joe's Upriver Carrier."

I sent my companions on ahead while I went into the tavern to buy a pack of cigarettes. The people inside looked like a gathering of married cousins from the hills in town for a family reunion. They shared a cozy familarity and looked alike—men resplendent in their big coats and flowing beards, the women made wide and lush by the harsh winters and the hard-working summers: servants of the mountain all, their sustenance provided by the mountain, their water by the mountain streams.

The walls of the tavern were plastered with local icons carefully displayed: snapshots of Jeremiah Houston in his prime and a wood carving of a lost mountain-climber. Rafters hung heavy with the horns of moose and caribou. There was a long row of clumsy paintings that mean nothing to people who don't live in Talkeetna.

Everyone stopped talking while I purchased the cigarettes and started up again as soon as I was gone. The old couple were examining a menu when I stepped into the Roadhouse. I told them the restaurant was famous for pies and hospitality. They pestered each other about what to eat. Papa was feeling like a big hunk of steak. Mama didn't think that was a very good idea.

"Remember your digestion, George."

We sat under a bulletin board pasted with various public notices, hand-written advertisements, and a sign that read: "No swearing allowed." Our cook had a nice, Italian smile, a Brooklyn accent, and three small children with her dark eyes and the hair of three different men. One child fetched our silverware. Another stirred a pot full of something wonderful and the third sat on the counter and recited his reading lesson.

I ordered chili. My companions split a piece of pie àla mode.

"It's a pretty country," Mama said. "Thank your stars that you're lucky enough to enjoy it. Papa and I . . . well . . . it seemed like we never had the time ourselves. It seemed like we had so much to do when we were your age, but I can't for the life of me remember what it was we were so busy doing. I know we never had the chance to get out and about very much. There was the children and the business and I was active in the church. George sold cement. You're a lucky boy to be so young and free.''

Young and free. I kept my thoughts to myself. When you get right down to it, most men define freedom as the absence of a woman. I was free as could be. It's easy to live a life unbothered by the soft trouble of women. The secret is to want them in the plural rather than the singular, and to want them so desperately that when one draws near your eyes get wild with desire, your palms sweat, and your tongue becomes as thick as a ten-pound ham.

I was an easy target for that which lurked outside the Roadhouse. On the way back to the train, I spotted on the frozen mud street before me a small, waddling lump of humanity. A knot of light brown hair spilled out from the space between her collar and a fur bonnet perched atop her head. She wore a bulky coat that lent her the shape of a catcher's mitt with limbs. She walked to the train on careful, doelike legs. I stumbled after her, trying to catch up without appearing to do so.

I took a seat across the aisle from her and watched with furtive fascination as she peeled away layer after layer of clothing, until a slight, graceful figure emerged from the catcher's mitt. Her face was soft, round, and liberally sprinkled with freckles.

I smiled cloddishly at her and she looked away, her nose wrinkled with a twinkle that came from way down deep. She turned to me and it was my turn to look away. ''I love the train,'' she said, her voice quite full and deep for such a tiny person. ''Old trains like this become part of the landscape, like a river on wheels.''

''Me too,'' I grunted before my tongue became too thick for speech. With an earnestness that must have seemed absurd, I assured her that I loved trains, too. Then, compounding my cloddishness with buffoonery, I attempted to impress her with the detailed knowledge of the railroad I'd culled from the official brochure.

We talked about journalism and mushing. She wanted to run the Iditarod and listened with interest to my confused musings about dead professors, farming in Alaska, and other absurdities. She was worried about the toxic waste pit, and thought it shouldn't be so close to the Toyukuk River. I developed a curiosity about the care and feeding of sled dogs. She said one of her leaders was a gift from Susan Butcher, winner of the last three Iditarod races.

She said, "The important thing is to have a steady leader and strong dogs on the wheel. It's a battle of wills. They'll get lazy if you let them, and your dogs have to know that you're in charge. If you let them lie down without permission, they never run strong for you again. They'll plop down and go to sleep when you need them the most."

I couldn't agree more.

After a while, we ran out of easy things to say and our conversation slowed to that perfect pace where one says nothing when there's nothing to say. You can tell a lot about people from their silences. Ours were pleasant and natural.

When we passed under the great bulk of Mount McKinley, she said: "Denali. The Great One. That's what the Indians called it."

I tried once more to impress her with facts of dubious importance. "The white man who discovered it named it after his favorite president. Too bad it was discovered by a Republican."

Then we didn't say anything for a long, long time. We crossed the Alaska Range and all thought was swallowed by the void which passed by our window. We cruised through Sherman, Alaska, population three, without comment. None was needed. At Healy I pontificated on the great coal fields and their place in naval history. Then came Nenana, where the railroad meets the river and President Warren G. Harding caught the cold that killed him.

She said Talkeetna also takes credit for the kill. "Papa Paulie says he stayed over one night at the Fairview and that's where he caught the cold. He calls it the Presidential Suite and charges three bucks more."

I told her Nenana was famous for furs, gold, and a civic event called the Nenana Ice Classic. The Ice Classic is a game of chance having to do with the temporary victory of spring over Alaska. A prize of more than $100,000 goes to the lucky ticket-holder who predicts the month, day, and minute that the ice on the river cracks up and washes out to sea. An elaborate device is used to mark the magic moment.

"Ever buy a ticket?" I asked.

She looked out the window as the blue snow hills rolled by. "No. Gambling is a conspiracy of the rich against the foolish." Then she turned back to me. "What happened to your leg?"

"I lost it in a game of cards. I hate gambling, too."

It went like that for another fifty miles or so, as the train slowly lugged us over the interior plain. Now and then we exchanged meaningful looks when the other wasn't watching. We snoozed a bit and sometimes traded felt-tipped darts that didn't sting at all.

Chapter 8

WITH NIGHT CAME THE FIRST EVIDENCE OF FAIRBANKS. There was increased traffic on the road which ran alongside the tracks and a gradual thickening of the landscape, with more and more modest but sturdy houses and other oddities of city life—power lines, a gas station with a sale on studded tires, and a small shopping strip with a grocery store, a gun shop, and a pawnshop specializing in gold nugget jewelry. We inched past a traffic jam caused by the passage of our train. A snow machine raced us to the depot.

We said goodbye-it-was-nice-to-meet-you on the Fairbanks station platform. Her name was Rachel Morgan, by the way.

"And yours?"

"Prester John Riordan. My friends call me Pres."

"Prester John Riordan. That's a strange name."

"It's a long story. I'd like to tell it to you sometime."

She smiled with her eyes and walked away.

A man named Appleton Chambers grabbed me by the elbow and led me into a long limousine with the seal of

Entco Investments stenciled on the side. As we pulled away from the station, Chambers softened me up with flattery. I tried to steer our conversation toward more important matters.

"This is a pretty nice car. What's behind those sliding doors?" I asked, pointing my chin at a cabinet built into the panel separating us from the driver.

Chambers leaned forward and slid back the door to show a fully stocked liquor cabinet, complete with an automatic ice maker and swizzle sticks from around the world. I pretended a shrug of indifference.

"Would you like a drink?"

I looked at my watch. It was 9:30 P.M., about five hours past my cocktail time. "If you insist."

He made me a public relations school martini with plenty of gin and three olives speared with a swizzle stick from the Ritz Carlton Hotel. I wondered whose job it was to collect swizzle sticks for Entco Investments.

Chambers picked me up from my room at the Mush Inn North Motel at 4:30 the next morning. We rushed to the airport in the cool gray morning, drinking coffee from a thermos provided by the driver. A Lear jet carried us into a brilliant dawn lighting the biggest, flattest horizon I have ever seen. I do not like to fly, but I was still sleepy and the trip was too short to bother me much. Ten minutes after takeoff, we landed in Delta Junction, population 250.

Smalley was there with an old pickup truck. "Sorry about the early hour, Mr. Riordan. But we work a farmer's schedule up here."

He was dressed for the part in combat boots, a heavy leather coat, blue jean overalls, and the inevitable lumberjack shirt. The open collar of his shirt allowed his jowls to cascade down to the lower elevations of his neck.

Smalley said, "How about we go get a bite to eat and then we'll head for the farm? That okay by you?"

I nodded and Chambers smiled. He kept on smiling even when Smalley made him sit in the bed of the pickup all the way to Toyukuk City. The publicist looked ridiculous sitting back there on a bale of hay, holding his briefcase upright, with straw clinging to the cuffs of his $800 suit.

"Where you from, Mr. Riordan?"

"Chicago," I said, warming my hands on a fresh cup of thermos coffee.

He thought about it for a minute. "Chicago, huh? Chicago used to be a great city—a good place to make a bundle. Now it's a big, dying thing, an anachronism. That's why we let the blacks go there. So they won't be underfoot and so they can die along with it."

He paused to measure my reaction. I tried to combine the disgust appropriate to a human being with the detachment appropriate to a journalist. The result must have looked pretty silly because Smalley laughed. Not a forced, cocktail party laugh, but a full, big-bellied laugh. "I'm what you call a bee-got," he said, accenting the last word with a phony drawl.

We ate breakfast in Toyukuk City at a place called the Deadhead Roadhouse. The proprietor was a bow-legged man with an English accent and a two-day beard. He seemed to be drunk, although it wasn't clear whether his condition was left over from the night before or an early start on the new day.

"Yowattlitbeechems?" he asked, his cockney accent as thick as his breath.

"Try that again?" Smalley asked.

The Englishman steadied himself against the back of my chair and spat out the words one at a time: "I said, 'ello . . . 'n what'll . . . it . . . be . . . chums?"

85

Smalley ordered eggs and sausage and toast and home-fried potatos and pancakes to be washed down with two glasses of skim milk. I ordered coffee and an English muffin in honor of our host. I asked for cream. He thought I said Cremora.

"Do you like getting up at four in the morning?" I asked while using a spoon to mash up the last few blobs of creamlike powder.

He mixed together some potato, egg, and sausage and answered me while chewing it. "I was born on a farm, Mr. Riordan. Right in the middle of a dust storm bigger than most states. My pappy left me on his pappy's farm while he went off to get rich in the oil business. I grew up eating dust and watching my grandfather grow rocks and wheat. Rocks in the spring and wheat in the fall. The rocks are the hard part, of course. When my grandfather died they had to bury him in a special casket because picking up all those rocks made his back look like a question mark."

The impact of this revelation was blunted by the blob of egg yolk which dribbled down his chin.

"I suppose you'll be picking rocks yourself when the ground thaws."

He wiped the blob away. "Hell no, Mr. Riordan. I'm a rich man. If I want some rocks picked I just bring in some Injuns from Toyukuk City and they can pick 'em for me."

The Englishman cleared away our plates and refilled my coffee cup. A few other customers had filtered in. "You're a long way from Oklahoma," I said. "Why Alaska?"

He leaned back his chair and hooked his thumbs around the suspenders of his coveralls, in classic farmer style. "My market is the Third World, Mr. Riordan, and if you think about it hard enough, Alaska starts to be more like a Third World country than one of the United States. It's a big place, undeveloped, without much transportation to speak of. Why hell, there's no road into the state capital and it takes a week to drive to the rest of America. You've got a large native population with what's left of their own culture and the place can't feed itself no matter how hard they try.''

He paused. I filled the silence. ''And that's where you come in.''

He laughed so hard the table quivered. I looked at the other customers and saw them looking back at me. They ate in silence and were sullen, almost angry. It was as if they thought my host was laughing at them. Smalley said, ''Now, now, Mr. Riordan. Don't you be pissin' into the wind or you gonna get some on your shoes.''

A sullen, almost angry boatman ferried us across the Toyukuk River. He steered and I listened while Smalley expounded on the meaning of it all. His philosophy of life seemed to have a lot to do with Jews, Blacks, Masons, Catholics, and something called the Brotherhood of the Illuminated Ones. Their aim was to turn us all into Communist slaves. Journalists were their willing pawns. Smalley and a few close friends were the only people not infected by the disease.

The boatman dropped us off on a floating dock on Smalley's side of the river. Nearby was a gate with barbed wire and a tall blond man with a gun to tend it. Leftward from the gate extended miles of chicken-wire fence, behind which roamed the Doberman pinschers. To the right of the gate, the fence veered toward a black smudge which leaked into the river.

''What's that?'' I asked, pointing at the smudge.

Smalley bristled a bit before replying. ''That's the dump. We produce a little waste product here that don't smell too sweet. My neighbors across the river don't like it much but that's too bad. They can hardly feed themselves. I'm gonna feed millions with what you're gonna see right now."

The guard put us through an elaborate ritual before letting us into the compound. He patted me down and asked Smalley a riddle and took our fingerprints on an electronic device no bigger than an important man's beeper.

"Industrial spies," Smalley explained. "You can't be too careful in protecting your investment."

We walked along a dusty gravel road to a cluster of buildings. The place was laid out like half of a wagon wheel leaning against the river. At the hub were a house, a barn, and a pressed-steel refinery belching fire and smoke. Narrow gravel roads fanned out like spokes to the fields, the river dock, and the dump. The chicken-wire fence, crowned with barbed wire and charged with an electric current, followed the curve of the rim.

Men in moonsuits scurried about, getting ready for some big event. Some plowed the fields. Some painted the barn. Some repaired machinery or scooted between the house and the refinery. All of them averted their eyes when Smalley and I walked by.

The object of all this industry was a new synthetic fertilizer which Smalley had dubbed "ReapRight—the best thing for the right wing, get it?" Appleton Chambers was charged with developing a product logo under which would be inscribed a bastardized Biblical legend: "Those who Reap the Wind will Inherit the Earth."

"I have an apocalyptic bent, Mr. Riordan. My grandfather used to pray at me from dark passages of the Scripture—the Antichrist and all that crap. He was pretty sure that Roosevelt was the Antichrist."

"What's it made of?"

"It's got something to do with the nitrogen molecules. To tell you the truth, I don't know too much about that end of things. The important thing is that people need it and I've got it."

"Just what does it do?"

Smalley stopped walking and started kicking at one of the ruts the plows had made. "Think about this, Mr. Riordan. Chad has a famine and Australia has so much grain that it has to plow some of its overproduction back into the ground. Why doesn't Australia send its surplus to Chad?"

"Because Chad doesn't have anything to send back."

His kicking had loosened a pebble from the ground. He picked it up. "That's just another way of saying 'money.' It makes the world go 'round. In this case, 'money' means transportation—logistics. It costs one hundred dollars to ship fifty dollars worth of grain to Africa. It's cheaper to plow the stuff back under than it is to <u>deliver</u> needed food to starving children halfway around the world. Logistics. Money."

"Okay. So where do you come in?"

He held the pebble under my nose, like a priest dispensing the Sacrament. "How much do you think it would cost to deliver *this* to Africa?"

He tossed the pebble to me. I dropped it. He continued: "You take this much ReapRight and mix it with common dirt—good dirt, bad dirt. Just so it's dirt. Sand if that's what you've got. Mix it with water and spread it real thin over three hundred acres and you can feed a million people for a year."

I know nothing about farming, but I assumed that was a lot. I checked later and found that it was more than a lot. But I didn't know that at the time, so I faked it: "That's quite a trick."

Smalley puffed out his chest. "I'm quite a man. I'm going to change the world, Mr. Riordan. And you're going to help me."

* * *

We ate dinner with the field hands in a large dining room set up in the basement of the farmhouse. We ate ReapRight peas and ReapRight bread and steaks cut from cattle fed with ReapRight corn. It all tasted fine to me. The men listened politely while Smalley lectured them over ReapRight apple pie on the proper way to vote in the upcoming general election.

"The environmental lobby owns the U.S. Congress," he bellowed. "If they get their way, you'll all lose your jobs."

After dinner we drank whiskey made from the finest ReapRight grains before inspecting the refinery. There Smalley introduced me to a goose-necked man with thick eyeglasses and a painful stutter. He had a lot of trouble with "B's." His name was Bob Brown.

"G-g-g-good a-afterno-noon, M-M-Mr. Re-R-R-Riordan," Dr. Bob Brown said.

Smalley smiled. "Mr. Riordan here is a reporter with the *Anchorage Herald.* He's doing a very important story about our work here. Why don't you tell him about nitrogen molecules."

The lesson took a long time. He used body English and I used guesswork to get past the hard parts. I felt like we were playing a game of Password. I didn't understand everything he said, but the basic idea was this: raw petroleum goes in one end, travels through a bunch of vats and tubes and furnaces where it is blended with secret ingredients and ReapRight comes out the other end. The waste goes into dump trucks which carry it out to the pit every evening at eight P.M.

When Bob Brown was done, Smalley came over and put his arm around his shoulders. The man stiffened. Smalley said, "Now, Mr. Riordan. One more demonstration and we're done for the day."

He turned to the worker. "B-B-B-B-Bob," Smalley said. "I'd like you to get the f-f-f-f-fuck outta here."

The man turned red and cringed, as if he were trying to wriggle out of his own skin. Smalley wouldn't let him go. He leaned into the scientist's face and said, "But first, don't forget to say 'Thank you, Mr. Smalley.' Didn't your bitch mother teacher you any manners?"

It took him five minutes to say it, but say it he did. I averted my eyes in horror. Smalley beamed. After Bob Brown slinked away, Smalley said: "Painful, isn't it?" Before I could reply, he went on. "You have no secret source like you told Mr. Blaine. It's just not possible. Dr. Brown hates me like the devil, but he's very loyal."

"What happens if he decides he hates you more than he loves money?"

Smalley searched his neck with the fingers of his right hand, stopping at a hairy mole near his left ear. "But Dr. Brown doesn't love money at all. Appleton Chambers loves money, but not Dr. Brown. Dr. Brown loves his wife and children. The handicapped are like that, you know. They're so starved for affection that they cling to whatever love comes along as if it was life itself. But I suppose you know all about that. I'm most partial to family men. They have so much more to lose. And a family man with a speech impediment . . . well, Dr. Brown is a very loyal employee."

He let go of the mole and examined his fingers for mole juice. He wiped it off on the front of his overalls and said, "Do you have a family, Mr. Riordan?"

"No, not really."

"That's too bad. A man should have a family. Women and children are a civilizing influence, don't you think? That's why I stay away from them."

She came to me that night with a muffled tap on the door of my rented room in the Mush Inn North Motel. My eyes complained about the light from the hall as she stepped in like a warm shadow in a magical dream. I tried to ask her what was going on, but she said, "Be quiet," and shut the door behind her. We fumbled and fussed and laughed in the dark and afterward I tried to talk about love and other things denied me. But again she shushed me so we just lay there, my leg melting into her thighs, her head a part of my shoulder. Then I fell back to sleep if, in fact, I'd ever woken up.

The next day, she was gone, if, in fact, she'd ever been there. I daydreamed of musher love for an hour or so before stirring out of bed to call my story into the *Herald*. Phil asked me if I'd double-checked my sources. I told him that I'd done so. Then to the train.

I walked the length of the train several times, braving the cold wind between each car in search of Rachel Morgan. She was not to be found. This time, there was no laughter, and the plain was crisp and cold. The land crawled by at twenty-five miles an hour. The mountains were dark and foreboding, as they'd always been for me. They betrayed no hint of the swelling spring, or of Rachel, or of the miracle which Smalley had promised to perform.

Chapter 9

ANCHORAGE TREATED ME TO ALL THE ATTENTION WHICH a minor town accords its minor celebrities. Anyone who was someone knew I had done something that was somewhat important. Wherever I went, I was the object of the sideways glances and whispered comments which the masses employ when in the company of the slightly famous. More important, my Entco story—played under one of Phil's bludgeon headlines—earned me that most welcome token of public esteem: free drinks.

I made the rounds of every bar in downtown Anchorage, so that those who wanted to congratulate me would have the opportunity to do so. I exploited the moment shamelessly, although a little shame was in order. The facts of my story were scrupulously accurate, but the whole and the sum of my various articles on the subject of ReapRight were, in their most basic sense, lies.

Of lies, more later. For the time being, I'll confine myself to the facts. The cause of all this excitement ran as the lead story in the Thursday paper and went like this:

THE COLD FRONT

ENTCO SERVES UP MIRACLE MEAL

By Prester John Riordan
Herald staff writer

Three hundred million children went to bed hungry last night. While the silos of Canada, Australia, and the United States split at the seams with surplus grain, famished people walk the backroads of the Third World looking for a bite to eat, their ribs poking through translucent skin.

"Today—in the 1980s—famine is a problem of economics and famine is a problem of logistics and famine is a problem of politics," said Hubert Bartholomew Smalley, president and chief stockholder of Entco Investments, the international commodities giant. Smalley says he can solve all of these problems with a highly concentrated synthetic fertilizer called ReapRight.

According to Smalley, ReapRight can turn barren sand into lush farmland, cut the growing season in half and make one acre do the work of ten. It can produce food where it is most needed, in the impoverished countries of the Third World.

"We're talking about a return to subsistence agriculture on a national scale," Smalley said. "The free market simply cannot feed the people of the world. The prosperous nations grow too much food and the poor nations can neither grow enough nor afford the high cost of transportation. ReapRight will allow poor nations to become self-sufficient."

Manufacture of ReapRight has already begun on a huge experimental farm located across the river from Toyukuk City, on the ruins of the state's failed Delta barley project. Smalley chose Alaska as the site of his project because is resembles a Third World country.

"Alaska is an undeveloped wilderness with only a rudimentary transportation network. It has a harsh, unforgiving climate and a long record of failure in the business of agriculture," Smalley said.

The key to this new product is a biochemical process that forges an extra electron onto the molecular composition of nitrogen, a natural fertilizing element found in soil. "This vagabond electron causes some remarkable chemical bonding when combined with water and common topsoil," said Dr. Robert Brown, a biochemist working on the ReapRight project.

A test crop will be planted near Toyukuk City next month. Six weeks later, scientists, journalists, and political leaders from around the world will be invited to the Delta to watch Smalley reap the benefits of his experiment. The visitors will be invited to dine on ReapRight peas and ReapRight corn and ReapRight potatoes. Then they can buy the first batch of the new fertilizer, which will be made available next spring.

The rest of the article was devoted to the statements of various experts who were stunned or excited or concerned. A passing reference was made to Smalley's racist disposition. The last paragraph said something about the foul by-product which Smalley dumped into a smelly pit on the banks of the Toyukuk River.

The story had all the power and efficiency of a well-crafted Entco Investments press release, with the added advantage to Smalley that it was not readily identifiable as such. The Associated Press rewrote my story and scattered it across the United States like so much fertilizer. Reuter's Press Service of England picked up the A.P. rewrite and rewrote it for a European audience. Pravda denounced ReapRight as a fascist ploy and an Australian tabloid ran a photograph of a scantily clad young woman with red hair who claimed to have acquired her large breasts by eating ReapRight products.

The "NBC Nightly News" made a beeline to Toyukuk City, as did *Time*, *Newsweek*, the *Wall Street Journal*, and the *New York Times*. The *Washington Post* stayed home, contenting itself with a thoughtful editorial on the meaning of it all. Radio reporters who couldn't reach Smalley interviewed me instead.

Somewhere in there, Smalley made the cover of *Time*. The fourteenth paragraph of the third story mentioned the humble country reporter who got the scoop. They called me Preston instead of Prester, but my mother clipped the article anyway. She circled the important passage and mailed it to several dozen relatives who couldn't care less.

I started to get laid on a regular, if not exhausting, basis. A tax lawyer, a political consultant, and the supervisor of an oil drilling rig. Even Margaret the food reporter, that little bitch. The warm gentle memory of Rachel Morgan became but a soft, flickering glow that was soon extinguished by the floodlights of my celebrity.

My colleagues at the *Herald* complimented me with their envy. People who never used to return my phone calls started giving me hot tips which I was too important to pursue. I had hoped to parlay this triumph into a long period of idleness, but Phil insisted on a few follow-up stories so that he could use photographs of Smalley he had acquired at great expense.

Over the next few weeks, I wrote the same story again and again, with the bored tenacity of a pit bull gnawing on his favorite bone. I went to Toyukuk for the planting story. Seven weeks later, I returned for the harvesting story, which came off without a hitch under the caustic lights of television cameras from around the world.

Time passed. Holidays, too. On Easter the Pope prayed for peace. My mother called me on Mother's Day. Memorial Day was marked by picnics and automobile fatalities. I worked the copy desk on the Fourth of July and wrote the headline for a story in which the president summoned us to the flag.

I forgot about Rachel, and the way she'd made me feel, all jittery and crazy, ready to do it all. And I almost forgot about Jeffrey Williams, who died with my name on his lips. But every now and then, usually when I was sleeping, his head would flop around and lips that never moved would whisper "Riordan . . . Riordan . . . they killed me Riordan and it's all because of you."

But guilt can be overcome by fear and celebrity, by free drinks and congenial women and strangers who talked about how wonderful I was. Everything was fine, until celebrity begat boredom.

Summer stayed for a while. I convinced myself I had nothing important to do, and no energy left for unimportant things. If I couldn't always sleep at night, well, that was the price of fame. I couldn't help the dead, even if it was a last request. Just one more beer and brandy, and maybe he'll go away. Everything was fine, until boredom begat a restless heart.

Phil thought perhaps I should write a story or two. Free drinks and the attendant fame diminished, but just before my celebrity was extinguished altogether, I took up company with a woman named Monique Peterson, who was attracted to me by my reputation.

I met her while lost in a martini in the bar atop the Governor's Hotel. I was thinking about the Iditarod because Phil still wanted me to cover it. This got me to thinking about Rachel and all the women I have ever known. I realized then that I would do anything for Rachel—anything, that is except pick up the telephone and announce my affection. I had suffered so much rejection in matters of the heart that I came to prefer what-might-have-beens to the hazards of pursuing them.

It all started with Maria Guttierez. Then came Annabelle the Aging Hippie and Blanche the Barfly. Two lesbians from Milwaukee and an untold number of prostitutes. The only good to come out of all of this was Chena.

Chena's mistress was a perky person from Seattle. It was January and I was drunk again, paying more attention to my empty glass than to any of the other lonely people in the place. All of a sudden, a perky account executive from Seattle came up to me, her eyes all a-flutter and said "Hi."

That was enough for me. I talked about news and she talked about advertising agencies. She asked me if I liked dogs. I asked her if she liked movies. We made a date for the following evening.

"I'll pick you up about seven," she said.

I explained that I had my own vehicle. I didn't explain that it still wore the assemblyman's license plates and was liable for more parking tickets than it was worth.

"Oh please, let me drive," she said, her perkiness all a-flutter. "The advertising agents never let me drive."

I should have suspected something was wrong when she showed up at my front door with a graybeard black Labrador with arthritic back legs and a small bag of dog food.

"Poor Chena can't stand to be alone all night," she said with a perky wink.

I took this as an indication she planned to spend the night with me. My toes started to tingle, and I babbled nervously all the way to the movie house. I put my arm around her during the scary part, and sweated profusely during the love scene. Right after the chase scene she went to the ladies room and never came back.

When I got home, I discovered that Chena had helped

herself to my garbage and had made herself a bed of my
dirty laundry. From that day forward, my life has been
littered with wiry black hairs.

This incident should have served to warn me about the
hazards of tavern love and prepared me to resist the sweet
smell of strong perfume and the soft sound of stockinged
thighs rubbing against one another. But I was not prepared
and I did not resist. I looked up.

An abundance of makeup dramatized a plain face with
a thin mouth. She was blond and lean and at least four
inches taller than I. Her dress clung to her hips like a
queen-sized sheet on a king-sized waterbed. She walked
like she had a fire between her legs and was using her
bottom to fan the flame. By the time she sat in the seat
next to mine, my heart was racing like an engine with
valve trouble. She shook my hand, lingering on the thumb,
and said, "You must be Prester John Riordan. I admire
your work."

I admired her breasts. The blood surged out of my brain
and into my groin, leaving me ready, but dull-witted.

"Ahh . . . well . . . Hello. I mean yes, I am."

Her name was Monique Peterson. She told me that good
reporting was like an aphrodisiac and good writing like a
multiple orgasm. A guy sitting near us almost choked to
death on an ice cube. She asked me about my work and I
told her everything. Then she asked me about my work
again.

She was a Republican, and therefore had an insatiable
appetite for cunnilingus. Weeks passed. Her purpose in
my life was to cause other men to envy me and admire
my sexual prowess. I believed that my purpose in hers was
to offer evidence that she was neither empty-headed nor
shallow. We talked about the seventies in an eighties sort
of way, introspective yet detached, as if our mistakes had
been made by someone else. The lovemaking was some-

thing we did when other people weren't watching. Nothing more, nothing less. She asked me about my work again. My jaw ached a bit.

After a while, the nature of our relationship changed. People didn't buy me drinks anymore and my celebrity vanished altogether. She stopped fawning on me and I started fawning on her.

"How are things at the *Herald?*" she asked me one more time.

Things weren't going very well. Phil was fed up again and this time he meant it. He had assigned me to write a series of stories in anticipation of the Iditarod. I dreaded the one about the new crop of female mushers who'd been inspired to run by Susan Butcher.

". . . And now that prick Smalley won't return my phone calls."

She was sympathetic. "The ingrate. And after all you did for him. What are you going to do about it?"

I told her that I wasn't going to do anything, that I was going to start writing stories about the Iditarod. She smiled and said she had to go. It was several months before I saw her again under quite different circumstances.

Chena snapped me out of it. It was a Thursday. She smelled winter in the air, and wanted to go for a walk. I know it was a Thursday because I was stone cold sober. I define an alcoholic as someone who gets drunk every night of the week. To avoid this social stigma, I devote my Thursdays to sobriety. On this particular Thursday, I was sober and jittery and had been thinking about Rachel so much I almost picked up the telephone.

But Chena smelled winter in the air and wanted to go for a walk. Sad brown eyes hung low, she sighed a smelly dog-breath sigh and licked herself in the snatch. I felt as if all the women I have ever known were looking at me through Chena's eyes and were licking some wound my clumsiness had inflicted. Depression swelled up inside me like an oily sponge. The walls closed in.

"Okay, okay. I'll take you for a walk." I sometimes talk to Chena when there's no one else around.

It was late in the season and late in the day, the dying time of the northern sun. Chena busied herself with a brown, rotten thing as we walked to the Delany Park Strip. Once we were on the grass, she laid it at my feet, so that I could throw it. I threw the soggy stick a couple of times, until she tired of the game. I wiped the dog drool off on the seat of my blue jeans and let Chena run free—peeing here, sniffing there, and wagging her tail at the slightest provocation. She scooted among the kite-fliers and the Frisbee-throwers and softball players of all sizes and both genders hurrying to get in one more inning before winter blasted down from the north.

I settled onto the aluminum seats along the third base line of an all-girl's game. It took me about half an inning to fall in love with a left fielder with long black hair and a mouth full of fire: "Come on, batta! Come on, batta! Come on, batta, batta, batta! Batta up!"

Her thighs rippled with wild yearning every time she touched the ball. When at the plate, she crouched low, twitched her butt, and slammed a double into the alley in right center field. She took a long lead at second. I thought about approaching her after the game and telling her I admired her style.

"But you're overweight, crippled, and at least six inches shorter than I," she would say. I'd forgotten about that. I would promise never to admire her again.

I jumped up from the aluminum seats and went in search of Chena. At first, I couldn't see her among the other black shapes which slid across the park strip as the sun dipped low.

Then, I spotted her off in the distance, one black shadow lapping at another over by a clutch of trees two softball diamonds to the west. The second black shape was an old Native man wrapped in rags and clutching a bottle of pinkish wine.

As I approached, the old man jumped to his feet, made a sudden move to get away, and then fell down again, his legs too drunk for flight.

"Oh my God! Oh, please no. It's the Wobblin' One. Please don't hurt me. Please don't tell the Slim Slam Man. I didn't see a thing. Alex was the only one and you took care of him. He dead now. Please don't kill me. Please don't tell the Slim Slam Man. Alex was the only one and he dead now."

That would be Alex of Alex's Outdoor Salmon Bake and Alex's Steampipe Hotel.

The old man blubbered. Chena lay down. I just stood there, made still and silent by the shock of remembering. This was the same old man who'd been at Alex's Outdoor Salmon bake the night I'd gone down to the strip looking for information about the murder of Dr. Williams. I remembered Alex telling me how this quivering bundle of rags had run all the rivers and climbed all the mountains and seen all the things that can't be seen anymore. I remembered Alex and the others carrying him away in a shopping cart. Naknek was his name.

Alex had told me about the Slim Slam Man and how he'd sliced up the professor and walked away like he'd just made a long-distance telephone call. Then Alex got himself killed and now his good friend from Minto was full of terror. The terror was me, the Wobblin' One.

"It's okay," I said. But it wasn't okay. It was all weird and crazy. Alex had been murdered and this man thought I had something to do with it. Maybe I did. I tried to step closer, but the man ducked down and wrapped his arms around his head, protecting himself from the fatal blow he expected me to deliver.

I called Chena and started to back away from the poor, frightened man. He jumped three feet when she gave him a goodbye nudge with her cold, wet nose.

I didn't sleep at all that night.

Chena and I walked the late summer streets for hours. I thought about murder, Rachel, toxic waste, and more murder. Chena thought about food, sleep, more food, and more sleep. About two A.M. we came to our senses in front of Alice's All-Night Restaurant. I lashed Chena to a parking meter and stumbled into the place. Ruthie swabbed the counter with a grungy rag and plunked a cup of hours-old coffee in front of me. She shifted the cling of her grease-spotted dress from one ample hip to the other and adjusted her ill-fitting wig.

"Out late, Pres? How's work?"

"I'm in love."

"That's too bad. I hope it ain't contagious."

One of Ruthie's customers slipped off his stool into a floppy heap on the floor. She tapped him in the small of the back with the plastic toe of her left shoe. "That's it from you. Out! Right now. Out! Out!"

Then she delivered my order to the cook. "Chef cheese, hold the mayo, fries." The drunk ambled out into the night. Ruthie is one of my favorite people.

"So what's the real deal on this ReapRight stuff, anyway? I don't believe a word you write," she said, laying down my plate.

"I don't know, Ruthie. I don't know. What do you think? This guy says he's gonna save the world."

Her wig slipped back into its natural place, exposing some crinkly hair. "Yea, right. Save the world. I read a story once that your friend Ralph wrote in Ed Hadley's newspaper where this Smalley guy says, 'Buy gold.' That's it. Buy gold and get rich. So I buy gold and get poor, not that I wasn't poor already. The bottom falls out and I lose half my savings. Got some nice earrings, though.''

She fluffed up her wig so I could see a flat piece of gold in the shape of a moose. "So what do you think?''

"Real pretty. What do you think?''

"I think Hugh Smalley is an asshole. When guys like him start to talk about feeding the world, I put my potatoes under lock and key and start stocking up on canned goods. They ain't gonna fool me again. So what's the real story anyhow? You're a reporter. You want some more coffee?''

Phil cornered me by Anchorage Harold, a plaster-of-Paris newsboy who hawked plaster-of-Paris newspapers from the middle of a fountain in the lobby of Ed Hadley's newspaper. The caffeine made me twitch and sweat while he read me the riot act.

"You're on probation,'' he began. "Again. That's straight from Hadley through me to you. One more goof and you're out.''

Anchorage Harold smiled. He always does. "Now let's talk about the Iditarod. The sled dog race. I want profiles of all the foreign mushers. We've got them from Sweden, Italy, and Japan. The guy from Italy won some kind of game show. And I want a list of all the winners and their times and I want a map of the trail and a big Sunday spread about the original serum run back in the twenties. Find out all you can about the diphtheria epidemic and talk to anybody you can find who ever knew Leonard Seppala or met him or saw him. One of his sled dogs was stuffed and put on display in the Cleveland museum. Get the *Cleveland Plain-Dealer* to take a picture for us and get some comments from the Humane Society and see if there's anybody who wants to bring the dog back here.

Balto's the name, I think. Imagine that . . . the poor thing hauls medicine to Nome in the dead of the winter and all he gets for it is stuffed and sent to Cleveland. Are you listening to me? Say, you don't look so good.''

My ears were ringing from the speech, or the coffee or the lack of sleep. I turned away and headed for the door.

"Where are you going, Riordan?''

"I'm going out to get some news.''

"What about all the Iditarod stuff?''

I jerked my thumb at the plaster-of-Paris newsboy. "Get him to do it.''

Phil ate a Rolaids. I walked away. Anchorage Harold smiled.

Chapter 10

THE ANCHORAGE POLICE STATION HAD THAT LOOK OF seedy neglect which democracies prefer in their local government offices. Immaculate floors, polished counters, and stuffed cushion chairs serve only to advertise that the taxpayers' money has been wasted on frivolities. The Anchorage Police Station had none of these. The linoleum was peeling and any shine had been scrubbed away long ago. The counter where the desk clerk sits was riddled with cigarette burns and gashes cut by ten thousand keys slammed down in righteous indignation. I waited for the colonel on a folding chair which spilled stuffing out onto the seat of my pants.

The Colonel's secretary ushered me into his office. "Deputy Chief Roland will be with you in a moment, Pres. Make yourself comfortable. Can I get you some coffee?"

"No thanks. I've had enough."

A few minutes later, the door clacked open and the Colonel stepped in. "Prester John. You look like hell," he said.

"Thanks, Colonel."

The policeman sat down, scratched his weary jowls. He leaned forward, elbows on his desk, as if that were the only way to keep his shoulders from slumping. All unpopular orders at the Anchorage Police Department were carried out by the colonel. Likewise, all complaints from the rank and file filtered up through the same tired person. Most of this trouble seemed to have settled in his jowls, which had grown loose and heavy from the burden. He scratched them again and said, "What can I do for you?"

"Do you remember that professor who got cut up in the alley behind the Colorado Club?"

The Colonel nodded. He remembered.

"I think I've got a lead. I'm looking for a hired thug, a pro with a big nose who uses a knife. The street people call him the Slim Slam Man. You know any pug uglies like that?"

"Riordan, you astonish me."

For a moment, he left it at that. Then: "You get all hot and bothered for a case and think you're Sam Spade with a typewriter. Then you go off into this ReapRight bullshit like the poor sonofabitch never even died. Then you get bored or your editor gets antsy and you jump back on the case. Now you want to write the same story you should have written four months ago."

I looked down at my hands. They were folded neatly on the edge of his desk, like those of the penitent Catholic schoolboy I used to be. "Colonel, it's weird. Listen to this. Jeffrey Williams calls me, right? The day before he was murdered. He left a message for me at the *Herald*. I called him back and he sounded pretty scared. We were supposed to get together, but he never showed up and then he was killed. He said he had a story for me. I didn't think too much of it at first, but now . . . I don't know what to think now."

"You're right. That's weird."

"There's more. I went out on the strip to check it out and I talked to Alex. He said he thinks this Slim Slam Man did it. Now I find out that Alex is dead, too. Murdered, too." I paused a moment to gauge his reaction. There was none. "What do you think?"

Slowly, with tired legs that were ready to buckle, the Colonel got up and ambled over to a file cabinet bulging with paperwork. The colonel pulled out a thin manila folder. He trundled back to his desk, laid the folder down, and warned me not to touch it. I promised I would never do such a thing. Then he left the room. He said he had to take a leak.

The name on the yellow stick-em was innocent enough: Martin Parker. I cracked the folder open and riffled through its contents—four photos, a three-page biography, and a handful of newspaper clips.

I looked at the pictures first. Alex was right. His nose did look like a baked potato, ruddy and irregular, with a hairy mole that could pass for the eye of a potato and a poorly repaired gash that in the right light might even look like a smudge of sour cream. His ears were huge. His skin was rutted and splotchy from a bad case of teenage acne. His broad head seemed more like a bludgeon than an instrument of thought. The general impression was one of stupidity made dangerous by a certain animal cunning.

Martin Parker was also known as Michael Porter, Mack Phillips, Maurice Poucheaut, and the Slim Slam Man. His friends, whoever they were, called him Mick the Pick. He was born somewhere in New Jersey sometime in 1948. In 1966 he was arrested, charged, and convicted of armed robbery and extortion. After two and a half years in Attica State, he began his career in earnest, chalking up many arrests, few indictments, and no convictions for extortion, drugs, and a little bit of homicide, the Big 11-1: nine at the last count, which was probably incomplete. There were constant references to the garrote and the shiv, for which he used banjo strings and a French stiletto with a six-inch blade. The author of the report devoted an entire paragraph to the stiletto, pointing out that it was a particularly effective weapon because it was quiet and cut an X-shaped hole that no amount of surgical skill could close. Mick the Pick worked with tall white women or one tall white woman with the ability to disguise her features. On those few occasions when he required additional assistance, the additional assistants turned up dead. There were no arrests after 1979, although the anonymous author of the report suggested that Mick the Pick had become "a known associate of underworld figures." The only fact after 1979 wasn't much of a fact at all. It had to do with an unconfirmed report that a man fitting Mick's description was seen in Brussels in the company of a tall white woman on the night Roger Witherspoon was kidnapped. The biographer suggested that the kidnapping was just a cover for simple murder, the famous industrialist's ultimate fate. Of course, no one looking like Mick was around when Witherspoon's body was found bloated and stinking, floating face down in a Belgian canal. Now to the fact: his only wound was in the shape of an X.

Four of the newspaper clips were about the murder of Dr. Williams, my own brief account included. One longer story published by our competitor reminded me of something that bothered me a bit: Williams had been born in Maywood, a suburb of my native Chicago. I wondered whether I'd ever passed him on the street, or whether we'd sat on opposite bleachers at the same high school basketball game. We were about the same age. It could have been me. He'd called out my name and died.

The other news clips were rudimentary accounts of the death of one Alexander Longley, address and occupation unknown. Longley, known to his friends as Alex, had been strangled with a thin length of wire and left in a ditch outside of Steampipe Hotel. Friends discovered his body when they went there to stay for the night. Steampipe Hotel was shut down and Alex's Downtown Salmon Bake went out of business. It was as if Alex never was. I wondered if lonely old men would start to freeze to death when winter returned.

I was halfway through by second examination of the photographs when I heard some banging and a too-loud coughing just outside the door. I quickly put the documents back into their folder and put the file back on the desk. The Colonel came in. He checked to see that everything was in order and then looked at me in a distracted way, as if surprised that I was still around. He slouched into his chair and leaned back, his hands knitted together and resting on his paunch.

"So where were we?" he asked.

"What do you think? Why would a top-notch pro bother about a professor and a bum?"

The Colonel picked up an ivory paperweight carved into the shape of a seal. He placed it on top of the folder. "I don't know. Drugs, I guess."

"Spoken like a true cop. You guys blame everything on drugs."

He fretted his brow for a second, then smiled. "That's right. We use drugs like you use 'experts.' Whenever you don't know what to say, or are afraid to say what's on your mind, you call up some 'expert' and get him to say it for you. 'Experts' say this and 'experts' say that. Whenever we don't know what to say, we say 'It must be drugs.' "

"If it is drugs, then why don't you arrest him?"

He cracked a coplike smile, full of trouble and secret knowledge. "We have no evidence. Alex had some but I don't think his testimony would have stood up in court.

Besides, he's dead. We haven't placed Parker in Alaska yet. As far as we know, he runs a small import shop in Newark. You're the only person I know who makes him in Anchorage and you're the only person I know who thinks he knows what's going on. You tell me. What's going on? Why don't you write a story?''

''I can't.''

''How come?''

''Because I haven't any facts.''

''You see my problem.'' The Colonel was enjoying this.

The phone rang. He kept me on ice for five minutes while he sorted out some trouble having to do with the mayor. Teenagers had thrown a wild party in an abandoned condominium and the mayor wanted to knock it down. When the Colonel hung up, I asked him about the Mob.

''The Mob? You're kidding. Nobody calls them the Mob anymore. You must be from Chicago, right? Well, he used to be 'Mobbed up.' I underline the 'used to.' '' His voice underlined the ''Mobbed.''

He continued, ''It seems that Parker's moving up in the world. He only does special assignments now for an international clientele. The Mob might still run him, but he's too high class for the hamburger business. But you can read, can't you?''

His Uncle Joe didn't know anything, but it took him an hour to say so. Chena watched me nod into the phone as he told me about life in Maywood, Jeff's funeral, and the effect of oil price fluctuations on the used car business.

''So, eight years ago everybody's thinkin' small for the mileage and so I got a lot full of big cars that nobody wants so I sell 'em for a song. Now the price of gas goes down again so I got a yard full of Chevy Chevettes, it bein' what you call your Chevette Lag, get it? Come on, I'll sell you two and you use them for roller skates.''

My conversation with Jeffrey Williams's sister didn't take any time at all.

"Hello?" she said.

"Is this Evey Williams?"

"Yes, it is. Who is this?"

"My name is George Robertson. I was a friend of your brother's."

"Oh really? Well, I have nothing to say to you."

Click.

Chena pressed her nose into my crotch. It was snowing outside and she wanted to play. She settled down as soon as it became clear we weren't going anywhere. I tossed down a Diet Coke. Then I tossed down another one. Chena got all excited when I pulled a half-empty can of Primo Chili from the refrigerator. She drooled on the carpet. Her toenails clacked a dance on the kitchen floor. I heated up the chili and ladled it over some pasta. I let her lick the can so I could eat in peace. She eyed the greasy bowl as I picked up the telephone.

"Hello?"

"Miss Williams, this is George Robertson again. It's very important that I . . ."

"Look, I told you people to leave me alone. I have nothing to say to you."

Click.

Chena nudged the bowl with her nose. I put it away. When you're dealing with a dog, you've got to draw the line somewhere. I tried the third and final telephone number.

"Hello?" the mother said. Her voice was thin and delicate.

"Mrs. Williams?"

"Yes?"

"My name is George Robertson. I was a friend of your son's."

112

"Oh," she said. Long pause. "Did you know Jeff very well?"

"We worked at the university together . . . up here in Alaska. We were working on a project when . . . he . . . ahh . . . when he . . ."

"When he was murdered, George. That's what happened, isn't it?"

"Yes, ma'am."

"I didn't think Jeff had that many friends up in Alaska. He should have stayed home and he'd still be with us."

I waited for a moment. "Jeffrey always talked a lot about Maywood. I feel like I lived there myself sometimes. I can almost picture the railroad tracks running past the old can factory. We would listen to John Prine records sometimes. He used to call me Billy the Bum from a song that John Prine wrote."

Her huff filled the phone. "Oh, shoot. Maywood's changed now. It's almost all coloreds now. Jeff didn't mind, though. I remember when he was sixteen or seventeen or so. It was almost like he was black himself—going 'that's cool' and 'dig it' and stuff like that. He always said that black people knew how to have fun because they couldn't afford anything else. But Jimmy and I, well, we were old-timers and Jimmy especially didn't take too well to a mixing of the races—not that they shouldn't have their own, you know. We always wanted Jeff to be a banker or an accountant, but he didn't pay us any attention. He wanted to be a doctor so he could find the cure for cancer. Didn't find it soon enough, though, 'cause that's what got Papa. Guess Jeff won't save anybody now. The silly boy couldn't even save himself. I guess I'll die here just like Jimmy. Might as well. But it's tough on an old lady sometimes. Them little kids are just trouble on wheels and mean to me. An old lady shouldn't have to put up with that stuff."

113

"I know what you mean, Mrs. Williams. And how's Evey doing? Jeff used to talk a lot about her, too. He loved his sister."

"Oh, she's still teachin' in the Catholic school and still stayin' far away from the boys. She shoulda been a nun like me and Papa wanted. Now, I don't know. If she gets married before I die, this old lady'll dance the jig again. Probably have a heart attack, too, but that'd be worth it. What's an old lady to do anyway, without a man at home? Used to be Evey and Jeff'd come over sometimes and play canasta with me, but now we don't play because it takes three and my heart's not in it anymore. I worry about Evey. If she was a nun at least she'd have other nuns around all the time and she wouldn't get lonely like most old maids. It's a bitch to get old, George. Take it from me. And it's worse to be lonely, too. But what'm I gonna do? Jeff's dead and the only kinda kids Evey's gonna have're the ones shoot rubber bands in her arithmetic class . . . You ain't married are you?"

"Yes, I am," I lied. "Listen, I hate to bother you, Mrs. Williams, but I need your help. Jeff took some time off from school, just right before Thanksgiving it was, I think. I think he had some papers I need for the project we were working on and I think maybe he didn't bring them back because I can't find them at the school."

I held my breath. The lie took hold.

"Papers? What kind of papers?"

"Well, they had to do with the work we were working on. It's pretty hard to explain to somebody who doesn't know biochemistry, but it's a spectroscopic analysis of the proteum anomaly paired with the refractory calculus of the basic elements. We were trying to deactivate the polar modules and reconstitute a refractive membrane so that it would work a little better. He didn't happen to leave anything like that lying around the house anywhere did he?"

"I'm afraid not, Mr. Robertson. I think you should talk to my daughter Evey. She might be able to help you."

"Gee, I don't know about that, Mrs. Williams. I don't think Evey would be much help."

"I see. And Bob didn't know anything about it?"

"Bob?"

"Of course. You must know Bob Brown. Bob and Jeff went to school together. They were the best of friends. The poor boy has such a cross to bear with that stutter and all. First time I met him, it took us five minutes just to say 'hello.' "

We talked for another ten minutes about sons and daughters and Maywood. I eased off the line by telling her that Jeff had always said the nicest things about his mother. She said, "Well, you're real sweet even if you are a big liar. You play canasta?"

I hung up the phone. Chena was fast asleep. The sun was gone and the city sparkled with snow, which is death's way of looking pretty.

Chapter 11

THERE IS NO EASY WAY TO GET TO TOYUKUK CITY. THE railroad is cheap, but takes a long time and once you get to Fairbanks you still have a long way to go. There are no commercial flights, and a charter was way beyond my means. It was all up to the assemblyman's car.

The frost lay thick on the windows of the assemblyman's car, and on the scrawny trees, and on the hills and on the rivers and on the road itself. And on a roadside fireworks stand that had been locked up and left until spring. The assemblyman's car chugged up through the Chugach Mountains at a troubled thirty miles per hour, but I dared not stop for a rest because momentum was its only friend. Once through the mountain pass, it eased down into a low passage between the Wrangell Mountains and the Alaska Range. It was a long, boring drive relieved only by the gospel-rock music of KGOD and by the trans-Alaska pipeline, a marvel of engineering which crossed my path at Glennallen.

There I filled up the tank and checked the oil before heading north up the Richardson Highway, which runs parallel to the pipeline for a few hundred miles. At Gulkana, I plugged the assemblyman's car into an electric outlet to keep it warm and stayed overnight in a prefabricated motel that cost too much. I started early the next morning and made good time through Isabell Pass and down into river country. Shortly after noon, I arrived at the Deadhead Roadhouse in Toyukuk City on the banks of the Toyukuk River, a tributary of the Tanana.

The owner was already drunk and anxious that I should join him. "What'll it be, mate? We got burgers and we got jars of beer," he said in a thick English accent, with a hopeful emphasis on the beer. "And we got plenty of both."

I settled onto a stool halfway between the bar and the grill, waited a bit for dramatic effect, and said: "A bit of both, I guess . . . and I hope you'll join me for the beer."

He slapped his hand on the counter and then dragged it across a grease stain on his apron. "Leave me cook your food and then I'll do just that, me boy-o. What'll it be?"

I thought about it for a moment before deciding in favor of a Deadhead Mooseburger with Canadian bacon and cheese. He said, "Now the moose is just a name, you know? Can't sell that when the law's around." He added a wink, as if to say "You know what I mean?"

I didn't know what he meant. I looked around while the Englishman hunched over the grill. I hadn't noticed much when I'd been here with Smalley during my first visit to Toyukuk City. Now I saw how the place had gotten its name. The wall opposite the counter was ladened with the horns of dead animals—a moose, a caribou, a buffalo, and a dahl sheep. The skulls were small in proportion to the horns and arranged in no particular order. They didn't look disgusting if you didn't look too close.

Another wall was dominated by a large photograph which showed a satellite view of the thin silver thread of the trans-Alaska pipeline. The legend below described the pipeline as small compared to Alaska, "like a long hair stretched across a football field," but big compared to the rest of the world: "The Great Wall of China is the only other man-made object that can be seen from such an altitude."

A third wall featured shelves stocked with a strange variety of dry goods: canned corn, Hamburger Helper (but no sign of any hamburger), sardines, potato chips, the economy-size box of Kotex, toothpaste, Kool-Aid (but no sugar), and socks—five large boxes of white tube socks.

"What kinda beer would that be, chum?" the Englishman asked. There was something strange in his speech— besides the thick cockney accent—that I couldn't quite pin down.

It took us two beers to get around to the subject of Hugh Smalley. After describing his adventures during World War Two and his winter ascent of Mount McKinley, the Englishman said, with absolutely no prompting: "How'd you like it if some bloke pissed in *your* drinking water? That's what he's doin' to us for certain."

I was just about to eat my last bite of Deadhead Mooseburger with Canadian bacon and cheese but no illegal moosemeat. I set the morsel down and took a sip of beer. "Who's that?"

"Mr. Hubert Bartholomew Smalley, that's who. The chap you came up here to see. The one I seen you with a couple of months back."

He stared me down with hard eyes set in deep, wrinkled folds. I thought of three different lies and rejected them all. "You don't like him, do you?"

He didn't say a word and he didn't move a bit. He kept staring. I said at last, "Well, I don't like him either and I'd like to kick his ass."

At this, the Englishman cracked a crooked smile and set up another round of beer.

His name was Reggie Moore. He'd worked in the textile mills of his native Manchester until he was called to duty for the Second World War. He caught malaria in Burma and was shipped to a hospital in Calcutta to sweat it out while his chums got killed. He never forgave himself for surviving that bitter struggle for the jungles of South Asia. After it was over, he moved to Alaska to forget about things because it was the most remote corner of the English-speaking world. He climbed Mount McKinley to prove a point.

"The hot death is like a poison in your belly. It starts on the inside and spreads out in a fever. The cold death goes the other way—starting at the toesies and the fingers and working its way in, first to the feet and hands, then the arms and legs, while all your heat retreats to the belly and the brain. The body'll be smart that way, chum. It'll give up your feet to the cold so as to save all them interior parts of the body what you can't do without."

In his middle years he took to drink and was elected the mayor of Toyukuk City, population seventy-three or seventy-eight, depending on the season. Technically, the mayor was supposed to be a United States citizen, but the native voters of the village kept electing Reggie Moore anyway. He was *their* white man, their buffer against other white men with more hostile natures and less delicious sandwiches. He talked funny—full of "blokes" and "chums" and "right-o's"—because he was a loyal Englishman who hadn't been to England in almost forty years. Old black-and-white movies were his only link with home.

"Right-o, chum. Now I know a likely lad with a quick snowmobile and a right snappy dog what knows all about gray ice and whatnot."

"Gray ice?"

"That's right. Best step away from any gray ice or you can fall through and get wet. Bloke that does that is pretty dead soon enough, I'm afraid. Cold like we got'll freeze you up good. Rickie Peters and Chuka'd be the way to go."

Chuka was a lively Malamute lead dog with three legs. The fourth had gotten wet after he stepped on gray river ice one bitter cold night. Reggie Moore had to cut it off to stop the gangrene from killing him. Chuka never forgave Reggie and he never forgot about gray ice.

"He's been real smart about the gray ice ever since," Rickie said. And Rickie was smart about Smalley. His wife and his sister had both had miscarriages in the past year. His neighbors had never even heard of miscarriages before.

"It's the water. Got to be," he said, his breath blowing up clouds of smoke.

We waited for sunset on a ridge high above the river valley. Beneath us lay the frozen Toyukuk River, blue and white mostly, with spots of gray here and there. The scene had the aspect of a photograph: the river was distinctly a river, with banks and curves and such; but it was still and made strange grinding sounds. Great blocks of ice were frozen in place, their headlong rush downstream captured in an instant that wouldn't let go.

Across the river were the farm, with its great silent fields, and the petrochemical plant, with its tubes and surly shapes and columns of fire and smoke. Between the plant and the river was the dump, a festering wound which the cold couldn't heal. Even at ten below it steamed and gurgled and oozed, a black smudge on an otherwise glistening panorama of white and blue and gray.

Sunset came about 1:45 P.M., full dark an hour or so

120

later. Our plan was to cross the river under cover of night. Rickie would wait behind while I inched around the toxic pit and sneaked through the gate at 8 P.M., when the dump truck came to dispose of the day's sludge. My hope was that dark and boredom and the unlikely prospect of someone sneaking through the stink would work to my advantage.

A bitter wind kicked up and the dark dropped the temperature another five degrees. It was twenty below but felt like thirty. My cheeks were numb and a light glaze gathered on my eyelashes. My nose dripped and every breath seared my lungs.

While Chuka danced at the end of a line attached to the nose of the snowmachine, and while I sat down in front covered with furs and tucked in low against the wind, and while the wind blew and the temperature plunged another ten degrees, Rickie Peters stood tall and straight, as if the elements were but a minor inconvenience. A lumpy coat made of plastic and down disguised his form, but he seemed to be in good condition. The hood of his parka hid most of his face, but his eyes betrayed a certain mischievous charm. He fancied himself a ladies' man and bragged about sneaking over to Delta Junction on a Saturday night and "having all the girls in the world, you know."

All that stopped when his wife had the miscarriage. After that, he had to be a man. Anger filled his heart and Smalley was its target. I was his first chance to do something about it.

"Ready, boss?" he asked.

I nodded, although I wasn't all that ready.

Rickie stepped onto the back of the snowmachine and worked the ignition until a sickly, halting start built up into a fierce, metallic complaint. He turned the headlight on and a narrow funnel of black ink became a shadowy blue. The moon danced out from behind a cloud, lending a sinister aspect to the river gorge.

"Hieeeeeee!" he screamed. Chuka tugged on the towline and we followed him down to the river in low gear. The moon slipped behind a cloud and the world was dark again. We bumped against the night. The moon came back and gave us a brief glimpse of the frozen riverway. Rickie hit the brake, and Chuka yelped as the towline yanked him to a halt. He jumped to his feet and danced around, anxious to make tracks.

The frozen river wasn't as flat as rivers are supposed to be. Downstream in a straightaway, the frost had heaved up into great smooth ripples of ice which Rickie said were too steep to navigate. "The treads'll never take hold of that. Chuka might make it, but we never would."

Upstream was a river bend crammed with chunks of ice which had slammed against the shore and couldn't make the turn. Frozen slabs bigger than a house were piled into a weird confusion of holes and peaks and gullies. If I held my breath and kept very still, I could hear these great ice blocks grind against each other like the unoiled hinges of creation's biggest door.

"Even Chuka won't go there," Rickie said. "He too smart for that. You go down a slippery hole and you don't come out 'til you melt." The dog looked up at the sound of his name and gave Rickie a curious look, wondering what trouble he had in mind.

Between the two ice formations—between the smooth ripples and the frozen slabs—was a low, flat place where the river ran deep and fast and had left spots of gray behind it. Rickie gave the command and Chuka started to lead us through this narrow pass—his ears and his nose working hard. He walked with a light, mincing step that he could take back if he wanted.

We zigzagged through the pass, avoiding the gray

splotches. The moon disappeared. We stopped and waited. The moon came back and we started up again. We stopped and started three more times before we reached the other side.

Rickie dropped Chuka into my lap. He turned right and we started to pick up speed, following the bend in the river. The ice jam looked even bigger as we passed near it. When we stopped to wait for the moon, I could feel the ice rumble through my toes.

The dump smelled of ammonia, smog, rotten meat, and something else—something worse. It maintained a somewhat fluid consistency despite the bitter cold. Chuka shied away from the pit, seeming to prefer the hazards of gray ice and the ice jam to the sticky toxins which Smalley had dumped into their river. If the earth could get syphilis, the open sores would look like this—dark, full of puss, immoral and corrupted.

"Don't ya fall in," Rickie had said as I began to work my way around the pit.

I couldn't see much by the light of the moon. But from my first visit to Smalley's plant I remembered the layout of the farm, the refinery, and the pit. The farmland was spread all along that side of the river—still now, waiting for spring. At its center were the house, the barracks, and the refinery, which could be seen as an orange glow where a smokestack spat fire into the sky. Wedged between the back gate and the ice jam and unprotected by anything but its own putrid stench was the pit—five hundred yards deep and a quarter mile wide. The ice jam made a great dam separating the black pit from the white river. In the spring, the ice jam would melt and the black pit would spill a nameless horror into the Toyukuk, killing things downstream. If Smalley had his way, this would happen every spring until his bank notes were paid and the wide basin of the Toyukuk River became his own special dead place.

Except for the smell, the first leg of my journey was easy enough. I kept the pit on my right and the chain-link fence on my left. The ground was brown and some of it stuck to my shoes.

As I neared the back gate, the space between the fence and the pit became more narrow, until I was wedged into a thin path no wider than my shoulders. I leaned toward the pit a bit, for fear of getting a deadly jolt from the electrified fence. The pit was about thirty degrees warmer than the air. My eyelashes thawed out and the tiny icicle which had formed at the tip of my nose melted into a drop and fell off.

Fifty yards short of the back gate, the pit butted against the fence and my path disappeared altogether. Fortunately, from that distance I could see by the light of the moon a crescent of high ground on my side of the gate and a shadow where I might hide if I was able to successfully cross the fifty yards of poison sludge.

I put on the rubber hip waders which I had borrowed from Reggie Moore for the purpose and plunged into the pit. It was slow going. The muck was shallow enough, coming to just below my knees, but the stuff was sticky and thick, like 40-weight motor oil.

The odor rose to my nostrils and sank into my skin. I can't describe it, but I'll try anyway. Maybe if you took No Man's Land from World War One, littered with bodies dead for three days, diverted an open sewer onto the carnage, and put the whole thing in the middle of Gary, Indiana, you might come close to the aroma produced by the pit Smalley had made on the banks of the Toyukuk. I threw up the Deadhead Mooseburger with Canadian bacon and cheese and dry-heaved the rest of the way.

One time the moon dipped behind a cloud and I had to

stop and wait for the light. Another time I lost my balance after bumping into a rotten something that used to be a tree. I plunged my gloved hand into the stuff to brake my fall. The glove was ruined and my wrist burned where some of the waste had touched it. I threw the glove away and tucked my hand into the pocket of my coat.

I reached high ground before the hip waders melted away from my legs. As I peeled them off, I noticed that the stuff had burned a hole in the left toe. The boot beneath was frayed a bit, but otherwise undamaged. I threw the hip waders into the muck and sat down low in the shadow cast by an old Chevy van which had been left to rust just on the other side of the chicken-wire gate. I had an hour to kill. I spent most of it blowing hot breath into my ungloved hand.

Right on schedule, at 8:05 P.M., I heard an engine rumbling my way. I peeked around the shadow and saw headlights bobbing up the road. The gears complained as the driver did a Y turn and backed the dumpster up to the gate. A second worker dressed for a moonwalk unlocked and opened the gate. If he came my way and started looking around he would probably discover me. But he kept away from the pit, leaning against the headlight on my side of the truck while his partner flipped a switch and started dumping more putrid waste onto Earth.

The truck groaned and the sludge sloshed and the air became even more foul. I made my move, diving under the truck and crawling on my belly to the front end of the passenger's side. I watched the moonwalker's feet. They pointed away from me. I hoped the driver wasn't looking my way. He wasn't, I guess, because I made it clear to another shadow on Smalley's side of the fence. I worried some about the dogs, but then decided that I was about the last thing they would want to sniff.

Chapter 12

I SPENT THE REST OF THE NIGHT IN A HAYLOFT WHICH seemed to have more to do with Smalley's nostalgia for Oklahoma than the business of this particular farm. A nostalgic rooster started the dawn and I spent hours peaking through a splintery knothole. Bob Brown, his gooseneck bobbing, passed by three times before I was able to catch his attention. To work. To lunch. Back to work. After work, he took an aimless little walk that brought him close enough for me to hit him with a dirt ball.

My first throw was long, my second wide of the mark. My third almost clipped him in the ear and my fourth cracked him dead center in the chest. He looked up, more curious than injured, and analyzed the situation for a second. I threw another dirt ball that missed him by a wide margin but caught his eye.

I waved and beckoned, yelled without making any noise. He thought about it for another second and then came my way.

"Hey, Doc! Up here!" I said in a stage whisper.

He hesitated. Then he remembered. "Pr-Pre-Pr-Pre . . . what are you do-doing here?"

"I've got to talk to you—about Jeff Williams."

It took the scientist a minute or two to explain that if he didn't eat dinner with the rest he would be missed, but that after dinner we could talk.

I told him his friend had been murdered by his boss. He didn't believe me at first and said I smelled pretty bad.

"You've got to believe me, Bob. It's the only way. You can put the two men together. You worked with Williams, right? That's what his mother said."

The word "mother" seemed to startle him, as if it had some mystical power. He nodded severely and picked up a handful of straw. Selecting a fat piece to chew on, he said, "Ye-Ye-Ye-Ye-Yes. Tha-That's right."

"Then help me. Tell me what you know."

He knew a lot, and it took him a long time to tell it to me. Bob Brown and Jeff Williams had been friends for many years, ever since MIT. Together they did all the things that young students do. They drank beer, played touch football, and studied the biology of young women and the chemistry of petrochemicals. On Bob's twenty-first birthday Jeff paid a woman to forget about his stutter and relieve him of his virginity, "which was like a Scarlet Letter 'A' upside down, without the crossbar." (Bob Brown wrote this down on a scrap of note paper, because it would have taken forever to say. He seemed very proud of what he'd written.)

They graduated from MIT in the same year and went on to the same graduate school: the University of Texas Program of Petroleum Science. Jeff's dream was to follow in the footsteps of the great American agronomist Dr. Norman Borlaug, who received the Nobel Peace Prize in 1970 for starting the Green Revolution. Borlaug had fed millions. Williams would feed billions. Bob Brown went along for the ride. They collaborated on many projects, including the early development of a synthetic fertilizer to be used with Borlaug's super seeds.

"Bu-Bu-Bu-But we co-couldn't get e-enough mo-money to finish, so Je-Jeff looked around f-for a gr-grant."

They got one from Smalley, who wrote a blank check in exchange for market rights to the formula that the two young scientists proposed to develop. They moved to To-yukuk City and went right to work. But somewhere along the line, Jeff started to change. A pretty girl from Tal-keetna became his "friend" and opened his eyes.

How many pretty girls can a place like Talkeetna have? I thought I'd met the only one on the Alaska Railroad. There couldn't be another. "What do you mean a 'friend'? What kind of 'friend'?"

"I d-don't know. A f-f-f-friend. D-D-Don't you have a-a-any fr-friends?"

I ignored his question and asked another one of my own. "So then what happened?"

"Re-Re-ReapRi-Right. Je-Je-Jeff said it wa-was di-dirty and h-had to be-be-be-be cleaned up s-so t-the waste pr-pr-product w-wouldn't p-poison the r-river. B-B-B-. . ." He spent thirty seconds trying to say a word with "B." He seemed to be wrestling with his rebellious tongue. The tongue won and he tried another word. "H-However, Smalley re-refused t-t-to w-wait."

Smalley's creditors wanted money right now. Dr. Williams wanted to wait until ReapRight had been cleaned up. They had a big fight. Smalley won and Williams walked off the job.

"Je-Jeff s-said he wa-was gonna b-b-b-." He paused, took a deep breath and summoned all his strength. "Gonna b-b-b-. . ." Gulp, close your eyes, relax. "B-B-Burn Smalley."

He blew out all that air and fell back against the pile of straw he'd been sitting on. He was exhausted. I said, "Did he say how he was going to burn him?"

Dr. Brown shook his head. "Je-Je-Jeff would d-do it though. H-He's t-that way. R-R-R-R-R-ReapR-Right w-was his w-work and he wanted it t-to be g-g-good not b-b-b-b- . . ." He bit his lip. "B-B-B-B- . . . Oh f-fuck it."

I tried to help him out. "Bad?"

Dr. Bob Brown nodded. Then he told me how sorry he was. Sorry he couldn't talk and sorry that Jeff was dead and sorry that he loved his wife and kids and that he still worked for Smalley and sorry he couldn't just quit and sorry that he couldn't do more to help me. Smalley was quite insane, and Dr. Brown feared for his family. I told him everything would be forgiven if he would find me a thick pair of rubber boots.

Chapter 13

CHUKA STRAINED AGAINST THE TOWLINE. THE WIND kicked up a blinding fury of snow. All other sounds and sights were washed out by the primeval turbulence. The world will die in ice, not fire.

After commenting on how badly I smelled, Rickie Peters packed me into the carriage of his snowmobile like too much dirty laundry in a small shopping cart. It was too cold for small talk, and the wind was too loud for anything less than a shout. We headed down river, the ice jam now on our left.

The snow had covered up the gray ice and the wind had clawed snowy ridges into the frozen river bank. For a couple of hundred yards, we moved against the grain, bouncing over the rock-hard bumps like a bowling ball over corrugated tin.

We turned left to cross the river, in low gear and at a slower pace. Chuka went to work—sniffing and listening and testing the ice with his remaining front paw. I kept my eye on the towline, looking for signs of slack that indicated gray ice ahead. After three or four detours, I got to the point where I could sense trouble just as Rickie hit the brake.

Slowly, slowly we inched across the river for what seemed like forever. Then, without warning, Rickie hit the brake of his own accord. Chuka snapped back like a yelping yo-yo. The dog scrambled to his feet and pulled on the line again, as if waiting for his master to realize his mistake. But instead of easing up on the brake, Rickie threw out the anchor and buried it in a shifting ridge of drifting snow.

He shouted into my face, "Wait here!" He sounded worried. I asked him what was wrong, but the wind carried my question away.

The guide disappeared into the wind, crouching low and moving on tiptoes, as if anyone could hear anything in the chaos of the storm. After a few more tugs on the line, Chuka gave up and jumped into my lap, falling right asleep. My breath had frosted my nose and chin. I buried my face in the smelly warmth of his flank. Man and dog. What a team. I thought about Chena and wondered if my friend Andrew was keeping her water dish full as he had promised to do. Chuka stirred from his slumber long enough to lick my face. The drool froze to my cheek.

After a while, Rickie came back. He pressed his face close to mine. "We got trouble up there, Pres. Somebody's burning stuff right in the middle of where we want to cross back over. It's like they're waitin' for us."

There was no other safe way to get back to Toyukuk City. The snow had made the rolling ridges downriver even slicker than before and the ice jam would kill us for sure. Going back to Smalley's farm was out of the question and the storm would kill us if we lingered too long. "What do you think we should do?" I screamed.

He screamed back that we'd better move along.

For a while, I couldn't see anything but Chuka's rear

end, the towline, and a tiny beam of storm illuminated by the headlight as we inched through the storm. Chuka led us around a couple of spots that looked okay to me. She smelled our fear, shared it, and stopped tugging on the line. After a short while that took a long time, I saw in front of us the distant glow of a nightlight in a theater, a glow worm in a cave. We moved closer and the fire split in two. Spaced about ten yards apart, in the narrow passage at the foot of the ice jam, were two oil drums filled with something that blazed golden heat like the gateposts of hell itself.

"Hey ho! Up there!" Rickie screamed.

As we came closer, we could distinguish the crackling of the fire from the greater noise of the storm. When we were too close to turn back, the dark spat out two shadows. One shadow seemed thin and girlish and didn't say a word. The other one had a nose like a baked potato, ears like garbage can lids and yelled into the wind: "You're late."

Rickie laughed, but he didn't mean it. He said, "Yes, man. Right. We went ice fishin', man. It's great. Mr. Riordan here is a big-time city reporter and he always heard about the ice fishin' on the Toyukuk River and how good I am as a guide 'n' stuff. One of these days, I'm gonna ice fish me a trophy-size fish, so I said I'd take him out and now here we are, you know. There's a real good spot out there. I'll show you, too, if you want."

"Ice fishing," the big shadow said, as if learning a foreign phrase.

"Yea, the fishin's great. We caught us a bunch, but then we had to get lost in the storm and so we dropped 'em. That's how come we're comin' in so late, 'cause we got lost, you know. Well, you know, we been out here a pretty long time and my fingers are feelin' a little thick, so if you don't mind we'll come on through now."

"Come on through now," the big shadowed mimicked, a bitter edge in his voice.

The girlish shadow's arm whipped up. It spat out thunder and a flash. Rickie blew off of the snowmobile and backflipped into a gory pile on the ice. For a few seconds, the trail smoked into a sickly pink mist where his blood spilled out. All was still and quiet but the wailing of the wind and the crackling of fire in the two oil drums.

"Now it's time for you to die," the larger shadow said.

I said, "Martin Parker. Mick the Pick."

"Very good," he screamed. "For that correct answer, you win the knife. Have you ever seen somebody take it with a knife? It's the one kind of killing where you can watch yourself go. The blade makes just a little hole, not much of a hole at all—just about as big as a dime." The wind paused, but he kept on shouting. "If you do it right, you go flush into an artery. I always do it right. You can see yourself die. The blood starts squirtin' real hard—like a water fountain, only it's a deep, rich color and it comes in spurts. You can watch it spill outta you and you know you're gonna die and it squirts out because that's your brain pumpin', only instead of pumpin' the blood to your brain, it's pumpin' it on the floor. Ain't that right, Monique? And then you're almost dead. About then it gets to feel like you got an icicle in your belly. I wonder what it feels like at twenty below. My stiletto's pretty cold."

The girlish one—did he really say Monique?—watched closely as Mick the Pick stepped toward me. I remarked to myself how clever Alex had been to describe his nose as like a baked potato. The mind sets strange priorities at moments like these.

The body does strange things, too. Suddenly my hands and my nose weren't numb anymore. I wasn't crippled either, or maybe I was just crippled enough. I vaulted out of the snowmachine and ducked behind it while Chuka danced at the end of his tether. My knees wobbled and my heart raced and a bead of sweat crawled down my forehead and froze into a diamond droplet at the tip of my nose. I thought about Rachel and my mother and my father and my dog and my first grade teacher in half a second. In the other half I thought about the time I was a street corner patrol boy in the Catholic school and had a bright orange patrol belt as the symbol of my authority until one day a first grader who was faster than I ruined everything. Mocking me while just out of reach, he said: "Prester, Prester. Shame on you. He hits you with his brace and you go boo-hoo."

Boo-hoo.

Boo-hoo.

Mick the Pick pulled back the heavy hood of his coat so I could see his face while he did it. I recognized the broad, bent nose with the poorly mended scar and the flat features from the photographs the colonel had shown me. Rough trade. Two years in Attica State. A known associate of underworld figures. A bloated and stinking body found floating face down in a Belgian canal. I stepped away from the snowmachine and dug in with the heel of my good left foot. I curled my toes for more traction and waited. Ten feet. Seven feet. Five feet. Four. Chuka made his move, snapping at our attacker's feet and clawing at his ankles with a paw he no longer had. Before he was able to shake off the dog, I dipped my head, rolled down my left shoulder and dived to the ice—spinning desperately at him like a human pinwheel with lots of soft, besotten, overfed, squishy parts and one heavy, unyielding, metal-bound leg that whipped around like the spoke of a wheel and caught him flush on the knee.

There was a crisp and certain explosion, like the crack of a single kernel of popping corn.

Mick the Pick squeaked in pain, grabbed the offended knee, and bounced briefly on his one good leg. Chuka pestered him some more. The killer hopped twice before slipping on the ice and crashing down into the circle of gray melting out from the flaming oil drums they had positioned to bar our way. Watch out for the gray ice, Reggie Miller had said.

Mick the Pick's armed fist made a nice, neat hole in the thin, gray ice—not much of a hole at all, just a jagged one about the size of a softball. He screamed and rolled back toward me, sat up and looked with horror at his dripping fist. It took about fifteen seconds for the dripping to stop and the soaking to congeal into an attractive frost. He tried to remove the stiletto, but the cold, dead knife was frozen solid to his cold, dead hand.

I don't remember the rest too well.

While the thin shadow helped the bigger one—did he really say Monique?—Chuka led me away. We fumbled through the wind and the snow and the strange calmness which accompanies the certainty of death. It took me a long time to get the snowmachine going. My brain was failing and I'd never driven one before.

I think I remember the flaming oil drums hissing and sizzling as they sank into the puddles they'd melted in the ice. I knew they were behind me, but I didn't know which side of the river we were on.

Chuka and I were left alone on the dark river. He pulled on the towline, leading me into the wind and the snow. I retrieved a glove from the frozen splatter of Rickie's body and tied it around my face to protect it from the numbing attack of the wind. For a long time or a short time, we wandered through the ice fog and the storm and around and around gray splotches and heavy mounds of jammed-up ice which had been trapped for the winter by the paralyzed river. We followed the river bank for a while, until the river itself was swallowed by the storm.

Then we wandered, just wandered, with no place to go.

The lame leg that had saved me lost all feeling as it gave its failing life to the rest of my body. The hand-stitched glove slowed but did not stop the destruction of my nose. If I lived, I would spend the rest of my life with only one leg and half a face. But I wouldn't live. I'd spend an eternity frozen solid in my thirty-fifth year, like one of those prehistoric mastodons they uncover from time to time. In warm places, me buck-o boy, death starts in the belly and spreads out in a fever to the limbs. In cold places, it starts at the body's outer edges and creeps inward, chasing life's warming glow to the sanctuary of the gut.

And the snow swirled and the wind ripped.

In my dream, I climbed out of the snowmachine and cut Chuka loose, so he could escape my fate.

In my dream, I fashioned a fuse from his towline and dipped one end into the gas tank.

In my dream, I sparked the fuse with a quivering match and dived away as the explosion boomed a desperate cry to a lifeless void. I crawled next to the blazing plastic and, for a while, it was very warm. And then, for another while, it was very cold. And then I didn't feel anything at all, as blood abandoned brain and flickering life retreated to the last sanctuary of my gut.

Chapter 14

THE HINDUS WERE RIGHT AFTER ALL. DEATH REPAIRS ALL things, transforms them. The slug becomes a man after death turns it to rot. A plant grows from the rot. A bird eats the plant. A man eats the bird. Death repairs all things.

This time when Eugene and I ran into the ravine, we ran like the wind because I didn't have a leg brace to slow us down. This time, we vaulted over the thin stream of sewer water that had etched a gully into the tired soil of Willow Springs and this time I didn't slip as we scrambled up the crumbling bank on the other side of the gully toward the graceful smile of Sally Schroeder, age eight. And this time Mrs. Schroeder didn't greet me with an ugly look and ask, "When was the last time that dog had a bath?" because this time Eugene was clean and fresh and didn't bark too much. This time, Mrs. Schroeder called me a fine young man and told Sally and me to go splashing in a little aluminum pool that leaked chlorinated water onto her flower patch. This time, Mrs. Schroeder poured a mixing bowl full of water for Eugene and gave him a meaty pot roast bone to chew on. And this time, Sally didn't laugh when I tried to kiss her because this time she tried to kiss me. This time, Mrs. Schroeder didn't whisper to Sally that perhaps I should go home, because this time she asked me to stay and served a dinner of pizza and ice cream, my favorite. But this time, Mrs. Schroeder grabbed me by the throat while Mr. Schroeder hacked away at my good-as-new polio foot with a hot butter knife.

Death repaired all things, and then released me into the cozy warmth of an upstairs room in the Deadhead Roadhouse of Toyukuk City. My ears came back first, humming with the twangy jive of some country singer whose name escapes me. Next my nose flared alive with the aroma of frying fish. My eyes popped open, but I couldn't see much.

"That right-o, chum . . . Come along slowly now."

Something cool and wonderful passed across my forehead and I heard the woman of my dreams say, "How did you find him?"

"Heard a big boom, miss. Then come Chuka here fulla beans to lead me where he was. He was only about fifty yards down south of here, but I couldna' see him at first it was so blowed up outside."

"Pres," she said while stroking my cheek. "It's me, Rachel."

I couldn't see her, but I could smell her well enough and she smelled like the best thing there ever was. I eased back onto a pillow and slept for a long, long time.

My polio foot was wrapped in thick bandages and propped up by a rope suspended from a hook in the ceiling. Reggie Moore informed me, with a great measure of pride, that he had amputated three of my toes, but had been too drunk to remember which ones.

"It were all fer the gangrene, chum. Mighta killed ya otherwise. If you're feelin' up to it, we can take a little peek to see fer sure that I cut the right ones."

My big toe and the next one were a little banged up, but still intact. The other three had been replaced by tender scabs. When I was done feeling angry and sorry for myself, I found consolation in the realization that I could now tell a bold and glorious story about what had happened to my leg without going to the trouble of fabricating one. Fights on the ice and amputation sound more courageous than polio, more likely to impress other drunks during storytelling time at the local pub.

"Yer nose were near in trouble, too, chum, but I didna cut it off. Purple at the tip, you see, so I plugged her all up with a wet, warm rag 'n' rubbed her till she be okay. You'd be pretty ugly wit'out no nose."

"Where's Rachel?" I asked.

Her voice was behind me. "I'm right here, Pres."

She had a lot of explaining to do, but it all boiled down to this: "Jeff Williams was my friend, Pres. Hugh Smalley has to pay the price for killing him."

My mind did a triple somersault and landed with a splat. What kind of friend? Is that friend, or "friend"? I asked myself, hoping Rachel would provide the answer. Reggie slipped downstairs and started banging pots together.

"Why didn't you say something? Let me know what was going on?"

She sighed as if she meant it. "I didn't know what to make of you. When I met you on the train the first time, I was checking you out and I thought you were a good man, but then when I read that story you wrote I thought you were on Smalley's payroll or something. Now I see you here all banged up and now I don't know what to think. But I think maybe I was right the first time and you're a good man after all."

I told her about my conversation with Dr. Brown and she told me about her friend's ("friend's"?) efforts to cleanse and perfect ReapRight after he walked out on

Smalley. I told her about the Slim Slam Man and she told me that another girl had had another miscarriage in Toyukuk City. I told her that Jeff Williams must have been a pretty good "friend" for her to go through all this trouble, and she told me that he was a good friend without giving me any clue as to what kind.

"It's not just Jeff, though. It's bigger than that. ReapRight is nothing but bad news the way it is now. It works okay, I guess, but it's too dirty. If Smalley gets his way, the whole river valley will turn into a big pit just like the one you went through. He doesn't care about anybody's drinking water or anybody's unborn child and the only way he'll stop is if we stop him."

I was going to agree, but before I could Reggie Moore came upstairs with a tray piled high with potatoes and fish. Reggie said he bought his fish from Delta Junction now because the fish from the Toyukuk River were weird-looking now and might kill you. We made plans for Talkeetna while eating our fill.

Chapter 15

RACHEL'S CABIN WAS LOCATED AT THE END OF A LITTLE-traveled path piled high with snow and guarded on either side by frosted branches which poked me whenever I walked by. The path was made more treacherous by a network of frozen roots which made the footing slick and uneven. A copse of trees protected the place from the wind and the more adventuresome moose.

She'd built the cabin herself from lumber pirated from a pile of trees cut down and discarded by the builders of a road between Talkeetna and a hunting lodge on the out-skirts of nowhere. While without electricity or running water, the place had a cozy, wood-stove warmth. It was a pleasant refuge, though she allowed neither alcohol nor cigarettes.

On several occasions during my stay there I suggested, in language vague enough so that I could deny my inten-tion should it be necessary, that perhaps, all things con-sidered, it was time that we made love. In language that wasn't vague at all, Rachel insisted that I save my strength for my convalescence and trials yet to come. When I inquired as to the nature of these trials, she shrugged her shoulders and said, "Who knows?"

Because of the prohibitions against lovemaking, cigarette smoking and beer drinking, breakfast became the most dynamic aspect of my stay in Talkeetna. After years of solitude, the sight and smell and taste of flapjacks fried on an open stove by a freckled woman in a flannel nightgown was too much to bear. My bones softened. My marrow leaked.

Rachel indulged me in all sorts of delicious, female attention. She rubbed my back and cleansed my wound and tended to my ailing body. She nourished me back to full strength with flapjacks, milk, reindeer sausages, cookies, pork steaks, moose steaks, onion rings, stew, fried eggs, scrambled eggs, boiled eggs (hard and soft), apple cider, and more flapjacks. She soothed me with such sympathy that I came to hope I'd never recover.

I paid attention to her, too, and flattered her as much as I could, although not enough for her taste. When I told her she was pretty, she denied that it was true so that I could say it again with more enthusiasm.

We laughed a lot.

Every morning after breakfast, her dogs would howl for the trail, as if the aroma of biscuits and peanut butter triggered in them some unnatural appetite for exercise. One of my tasks was to hold the sled while she tied the dogs to the lines. My other task was to then jump aboard and serve as dead-weight ballast during long, galavanting jaunts through the countryside. All this was in training for the Iditarod, the biggest sled dog race of them all—1,049 miles from Anchorage to Nome. Rachel had entered. She wanted to win. My useless bulk helped her dogs develop stamina.

On the return leg of our exercise, we'd swing through town where the big news was that heavy snow had driven hordes of moose out of hiding and onto the tracks of the Alaska Railroad. The trains were slaughtering the beasts in alarming numbers, a tragedy that had filled every meat-locker in Talkeetna.

To teach discipline to her dogs, Rachel would always stop three miles from home and cook them up a pungent stew of Gravy Train, lean moose meat, and natural vita-mins. The dogs drooled patiently until she gave them the signal to eat. Coffee and Cream, her two half-breed Mal-amute leaders, always got first pickings. After the team wolfed down lunch, she hitched them back up again and made them finish the run home. This is contrary to a dog's natural inclination, which is to take a nap after dinner. She was teaching them to eat and run, which is required on the Iditarod trail.

Once the exercise was done, the dogs would file into their kennel, clustering into a warm, furry heap. They snoozed while Rachel and I went into the cabin and clus-tered into our own warm, furry heap, which she agreed to do only if I agreed not to become excited. We snoozed. We talked. We cuddled together until the next day, when we cuddled, talked, and snoozed. I was at great pains to hide any evidence of arousal.

We lived for a week or so in the hot glow of an old wood stove, our shadows made large on the ceiling by the light of a kerosene lamp. Rachel did most of the talking and as the nights passed on she moved from the general to the specific, slowly leading me down the dark roads of my own soul, picking me up when I stumbled. She taught me about myself and she taught me about dog mushing.

All in all, mushing was the more interesting topic. Her dogs had a limited vocabulary. Here it is:

1) ''Gee'' means ''right turn.''
2) ''Good boy'' means ''nicely done.''
3) ''Haw'' means ''left turn.''

4) "Hieeeee" means "let's go." "Mush" does not mean "let's go," no matter what Sergeant Preston of the Yukon said to his lead dog King. "Mush" is too soft a syllable to provoke dogs to labor. The word comes from the French word "march," which means "to run across the tundra with a dog sled full of furs stolen from gullible Natives." If Sergeant Preston of the Yukon really knew his stuff, he'd have said, "hieeeee," with a screeching accent on the "eeeeeee."

5) "No" means "no."

6) "On by" means "move along. Do not stop to sniff the assholes of the slower dogs lingering up ahead."

She talked about the Iditarod, toxic waste pits, and growing up in Idaho. Her fondest memories were of working on a ranch in Nebraska and of Dr. Jeffrey Williams, her good friend ("friend"?). She was an anachronism. Her politics dated back to a more hopeful time, to before she'd been born. She was a card-carrying leftist of the 1930s variety, thanks to her parents, who believed in class conflict because they were too intelligent to be as poor as they were.

Her efforts to keep alive the fires of their failed revolution were in pointed contrast to my own cancerous cynicism. Sure, I'd been in a demonstration once and had talked at length one night about the Beatles, Jesus, and the systematic exploitation of the masses by the sordid manipulators of Wall Street. But I stopped all that when I got my degree and forgot about it when I started looking for a job.

Rachel had forgotten nothing. She'd enjoyed the political ecstasies of the sixties and had stoically endured their subsequent degradation. She was now keeping the fire alive until saner heads prevailed. Now she made a private war on mindless corporations that gobbled up the ozone, made acid rain, and dumped poison on the Earth. That's how she met Jeffrey Williams.

"How come you never say anything?" she asked me one time while warming herself in front of the stove. "You sit there and nod and say, 'Yeah, uh-huh' and sometimes I'm not even sure you're listening to me. I'll talk for hours and bare my soul and you won't say a word. Then, if I'm lucky and the stars are placed just right, you might say something. But it's always a one-liner, like a joke that only you understand."

"I'm a writer. I edit my thoughts."

She leaned forward on her haunches and peeked through a gold crescent crack in the old wood stove. Satisfied that the fire was still burning hot, she rolled back into my arms.

"I met an old woman once," she said. "She was seventy or eighty. She'd been around a lot, married a couple of times, and she'd been a WAC in the war. Her name was Matilda and she ran a little candy store in Nebraska, before I moved to Alaska. Import candies and fresh fruit, nothing but the best. Right after work every day, I'd go to Matilda's and treat myself to a piece of chocolate— Cadbury nut bars mostly. I was in a self-awareness phase and that was part of the therapy. I realized that I really like Cadbury nut bars, even if it's a multinational and candy isn't always so good for you. So I'd eat my Cadbury and we would talk about the weather and the price of beef. That's what people talk about in Nebraska. Anyway, I go in there one time and Matilda starts asking me about work, and I told her how I started out as a cook and then got to ride the range because I'm pretty good on a horse.

"So she looked at me real funny-like. With a big question in her eyes and says, 'But are you true to yourself, girl?'

"I said I thought I was, that I always try to be. So then

she goes on to tell me about this theory she has about people. It has to do with the jobs they take—at least those people who can pick and choose. Matilda said she always thought that people pick jobs that'll fix them up—improve themselves. You know, compensate for their failures and shortcomings. It's like, the lawyer is really a crook at heart and maybe a doctor is in love with death deep down and a fireman likes to see things burn.''

She paused, waiting for me. I said, ''Yeah, I know. And writers can't communicate.''

''Unless it's on paper where nobody can talk back.''

I thought about this for a minute, then said, ''Okay. Fair enough. I want to communicate to you—face to face—that I think it's time we made love.''

She laughed to disguise her annoyance. ''I think you need all your strength for more important things.''

I wanted to tell her that nothing in the world was more important than making love to her. Instead, I said, ''Tell me about Jeffrey.''

''Jeffrey was a good man, Pres. And a good friend ['friend'?]. It's just not right.''

They met during the second round of the Fur Rondy Cribbage tournament. ''He was getting all the cards, so I had to peg my way to victory.''

A few days later, they had dinner and a movie. Jeffrey was proud of his work and talked about it at length. Rachel was worried about the pit. Jeffrey hadn't heard about any miscarriages, but he was sure that Hugh Smalley would understand. He told Rachel that he would take care of everything.

I interjected, ''But Smalley took care of him instead. What did Jeff do after he walked out?''

''I don't know,'' she said. ''I was in Talkeetna then, in training for the race, and I never heard anything until I heard he was killed. I looked for you on the train because I thought you could help—that you knew something.''

"I don't know anything. So what did you guys do after the movie?''

She answered me by rolling over and falling asleep without another word.

In the morning, she greeted me with that bitchy, razor's-edge temper which women employ when men have pissed them off. Her "good morning" smile was thin and insincere. U-shaped wrinkles of agitation rippled up her forehead. She banged the breakfast pots a little too loudly for coincidence. When I complained about the pain in my missing toes, she coughed politely, as if I had just farted in public.

"You okay?" I asked. The question only aggravated the situation.

"Fine," she snarled.

I made a clumsy attempt to diagnose her malady. "Are you sure you're okay? You look a little off. How are you feeling? Maybe you're getting the flu or something."

Glare.

"Look, I'm sorry about last night," I said, although I didn't know why I should be.

Her anger bubbled over. "So, I suppose you're just going to sit here and fiddle around while Hugh Smalley does God-knows-what to God-knows-who."

Oh, that. I rubbed the stump of my foot for dramatic effect. She ignored the gesture. We ate breakfast in awkward silence. When the dogs started to howl for their morning exercise, she jumped up and laced on her boots. I moved to do the same, but she shook her head, her mouth puckered with disappointment. "No. You stay here. I'd like to be alone right now. With my dogs. *They* understand things."

THE COLD FRONT

I watched from the front porch as she tied her team to the sled. They rushed away without looking back.

I felt pretty sorry for myself and sorry that the well of her sympathy had run dry. The cabin became still and silent and cold, a sterile reminder of the difference a friend can make, with or without the quotation marks. No companion, no TV, no glass of beer to tell my troubles to. I checked her bookshelves, but her reading was all about heros and how to improve the world.

For the first time in years, I was alone, awake and sober, with no easy distractions from the guilt and the disappointment, and no more fragile hopes of the sort that had helped me go from day to day like a thirsty man chasing phantoms in the desert. Papa left me and I left Mom and the polio bug knocked me off my feet. Sally Schroeder and a dozen others made sure I stayed there. I was tormented by the cruel remarks of nasty children who were half my age and twice my speed. The Jesuits taught me to think, but they didn't teach me to live. I started writing news because the daily bylines were a reminder that I was still alive. But then I learned that cheap fame is like a bad drug because you need more and more to feel less and less. But I maintained the illusion of vitality until my unlimited appetite for attention smacked right up against my very limited ability. The game was all up and there was nothing left to do but fold, until Rachel came along with freckles and brown hair and a gap-toothed smile and important things that had to be done. She told me I was okay and she told me that I could write a big story that would actually be true and would mean a lot to a lot of people.

All things previously denied me could be gotten if I could just stop feeling sorry for myself. But that, of course, was the rub. If I didn't feel sorry, no one would. I had learned to live off pity.

The sun disappeared and the walls closed in, compressing me until I reached a critical mass; until a new idea was distilled from all of the old ideas. I was still alive. The same child who'd been humiliated by unpleasant first graders had walked away from death in the form of a sadistic killer with a nose like a baked potato. It suddenly occurred to me that once, just once, I'd been a very remarkable man. I became quite pleased with myself. It was a new sensation. I liked it.

Midnight came and another day. When she came back the next morning, her cheeks were flushed and her dogs exhausted. I told her I would do what I could do, but I didn't think I could do very much.

She smiled a smile of uncertain meaning. "Okay. Then let's go."

I helped her put the dogs away. The long run had made them grumpy, and they were reluctant to move until it became clear we were going to the kennel and not back to the trail.

Over coffee, Rachel said, "Now let's think about this. Bob Brown says Jeff was going to burn Smalley somehow. So he keeps quiet for a couple of months and then he tried to talk to you. That must mean that he had it figured out and he wanted you to do some kind of story that would hurt Smalley real bad. So now all we have to do is figure out what the story is and then you can write it."

Of course, I probably didn't have a newspaper to print it anymore, but at the time this seemed like an unimportant detail. I drained my coffee cup. She said, "Okay. Once more. Tell it to me again, and with all the details."

I told it to her again—how he called me at the *Herald* and how he missed our meeting and how he died with my name on his lips. I told her about the trip to Fairbanks, about the way Smalley humiliated Dr. Bob Brown, about my conversation with the Colonel and about going to the strip to look for a story about the dead professor. I told her how I wound up at Alex's Outdoor Salmon Bake and how Alex had seen Mick the Pick stick a stiletto into Jeffrey's gut. I told her about my big scoop and about how Alex was murdered, too. I told her how I lied my way into the confidence of Jeffrey's mother by pretending to be a friend of her son. Then I told her how Jeffrey's sister wouldn't talk to me no matter how many lies I told. Finally, I told her about the ice pass on the Toyukuk River and what it feels like to die and live again.

Rachel poured us another round of coffee and then looked me right in the eyes. "Why did you lie?"

I shrugged my shoulders and sighed, a bit embarrassed by a difficult question. "It's easier that way. A lot of people don't like reporters. They don't trust them. They don't like their personal problems splashed all over the front page. So what's the family of a murdered man going to do except cry a lot and tell me to go to hell?"

She reached across the table and took my hands in hers. She squeezed tightly and spoke slowly. "That must be it."

"That must be what?"

"Don't you see? Jeff wouldn't leave anything for a phony insurance adjuster or a phony friend. He thought he was dealing with a reporter, not a confidence man. He died with your name on his lips, not some stupid name you made up. He had something that was just for you that night that he never showed up, and whatever it is must still have your name on it. Prester John Riordan, boy reporter. You've got to make the same calls again. Only don't lie this time."

We drove to town in a big pickup truck that smelled of dog. At the Roadhouse, I exchanged a five for a fistful of quarters and stepped up to the telephone, which was situated under a sign that read: "NO SWEARING, PLEESE."

Rachel bit her lower lip when the phone jumped away from my ear. That was Jeffrey's mother hanging up on me. Next I tried his sister, who had always refused to talk to my imaginary insurance adjusters.

"My God! Where have you been? It's been months. I thought you'd never call. What took you so long? I'd given up. It's been months. How many months has it been?"

I mumbled something incomprehensible. She took a deep breath and continued, "I've got something for you. Jeff sent me a letter right before he died. He said you would call me and that I should give it to you right away if anything ever happened."

"Oh, great! What is it?"

Rachel smiled like a little Goodie Two-shoes who had told me so. I congratulated her with a wink.

"I don't know what it is," the sister said. She had the thin, harried voice of a quickly aging grade school teacher.

"What do you mean you don't know?"

"I mean I don't know. It's an envelope. It's sealed. It had your name on it, and I'm not in the habit of opening other people's mail. And besides, I think I probably don't want to know."

"Okay, then send it to me. Hang on a second and I'll give you my address."

"No. I'm sorry, but I can't do that. Jeff said I should give it right to you directly so I would know for sure that it's you. You're the guy with the bad leg and Jeff said I should look for that. He was very clear with all of his instructions, and then he got killed."

Chapter 16

I DO NOT LIKE TO FLY. FOR ONE THING, THE WINGS WOB-
ble. A number of airline stewardesses have assured me
that wing wobbling is some sort of aerodynamic necessity,
but I don't believe them. I fully expect that if I fly too
much, some day a wing will wobble loose from its moor-
ings and I will be a vindicated smudge of smoldering goo.

I do not like to fly for other reasons. The drinks are
watery and the food is rubbery and the stewardesses are
pretty but unavailable. Every time I walk through the official airport hijack weapon-detector, the metal super-
structure of my leg brace sets off the alarm and security
guards with fat hands and body odor pat me down in full
view of the other passengers, who seem thereafter to re-
gard me as some sort of criminal.

I do not like to fly, but flying is the only way out of
Alaska that takes less than a week. The wings wobbled all
the way to Chicago.

Chicago is . . .

The 'hood, short for neighborhood, where Maria Guttierez used to be. Where Sister Angela Marie beat the

devil out of Patrick Davis for teasing me about my leg. The 'hood is where I was adopted by a Puerto Rican street gang, the members of which admired me because I was crippled and tried to play basketball anyway. Or was it because I was even worse off than them, because I was the one white boy they wouldn't gladly trade places with? The 'hood was where Steady Eddie Crawford took a carp he'd fished from the Lincoln Park Lagoon and beat it against the supports of our basketball hoop until the pole was slimy with blood and mashed fish guts. The 'hood was where Rickie Richards started sniffing glue and suffered a peculiar side effect that froze one half of his face and made the other half twitch like a bag full of bumble bees. The 'hood was where I drank my first beer.

But most of all, the 'hood is where Maria Guttierez used to be and where I discovered in myself a wild craving as painful and exhilarating as life itself. She used to tie up her blouse into a loose knot that made cloth bunny ears beneath the proud swell of her pubescent breasts, exposing a tantalizing patch of lean, brown tummy. In the company of her little sister and a bratty cousin named Freddie, she paraded before me all summer long, oblivious to my undying love and thankfully unaware of the things I did with her in my sweet Chicago dreams.

And Chicago is . . .

The rhythm and blues of Sam and Dave. When suburban teenagers were buying Nehru jackets and listening to any music with an English accent, we wore grease and leather. We tried to be black because black was cool. It was the summer of 1967—one of those magical summers when you're too young to work and too old to be in bed by nine. We tied on our combat boots, rolled up the cuffs of our baggy pants and put on our Puerto Rican tuxedos, those strapped undershirts which the Puerto Ricans call Dago-Ts. We rode the bus to the Chicago Stadium, where we tapped the cleated toes of our combat boots to the cappella harmonies of The Persuasions. The music settled in my hips and my heart yearned for some legendary black diddly-do. Someone's eyes must have fastened on the wrong pair of ebony breasts, because after the show our small band of white toughs were surrounded by a larger band of black ones. I watched in horror as they beat the shit out of everyone but me. You see it's taboo—unmanly— to beat the shit out of a crippled boy. Lucky me. That's the sort of useful lesson one learns in Chicago.

Rivers of humanity wearing thick coats over Hawaiian shirts or anonymous gray business suits coursed through the channels of O'Hare Airport. Fishing for customers along the channel were the usual pimps and dealers and hookers and hustlers and gnarled shoeshine boys with tobacco juice dribbling down their chins. With my limp and Talkeetna beard, I looked more like a shoeshine boy than a source of ready cash, so no one molested me as I followed the flow of people to a taxi stand.

My cabbie was a Puerto Rican who knew just enough English to carry on a one-sided conversation.

"This town's all gone to the gangs, man, you know? I seed them comin' all 'long, but now they got they scag and they reefer and they ladies with the clap. Small-time punks, you know? Spray cans so as they put their chickenshit names all over the place and it gets so you can't walk down the street without some little dude that ain't got no hair yet callin' you out with a knife to check out your action. Got so I can't even drive my own cab in the 'hood 'cause the 'hood stinks up from the Devil's Disciples jammin' on the Panthers who be jammin' on the Meyer Boys who be jammin' on the Tornados 'cause everybody jams on them. We do okay, though, my cousin and me, 'cause my cousin works, too, but we both gotta drive beat-up old cars 'cause if you drive a pretty car they slash you tires if you don't pay them up five bucks a week, unless you got a Caddy, which is five bucks more.''

The cabbie continued to babble as we fought our way into the fast lane of the Eisenhower Expressway, the only road in town named for a Republican. He dropped me off in the parking lot of the Melrose Inn, a dark cloistered motel tucked between a bowling alley and a small west suburban shopping center. I paid for my room with a check that was almost certain to bounce guaranteed with a charge card against which all purchases had been stopped. I drank shots in the bar of the bowling alley until the buzz of the bowlers and the thunderous claps of their strikes chased me to my room. I fell asleep on a queen-size bed that smelled of Lysol and mothballs.

Late the next morning, I hopped on a bus which stopped right across the street from the motel. It was long past rush hour and the bus was empty except for myself, the driver, and two old babushkas with overflowing shopping bags, sagging arms, and white socks bunched down to the ankles of their elephantine legs. The babushkas clucked away in the seat closest to the driver while I sat in the back-most seat, feeling conspicuous and just a little bit guilty, like a man without a job or a student playing hooky. In Chicago, able-bodied men do not ride the bus in the middle of the day unless they've committed some antisocial act.

The babushkas eyed me warily and clutched their bags tightly when I stepped off the bus in Oak Park. There I transferred to the Lake Street El. The battered train yanked me into the city with a series of jolting starts and grinding, metallic stops.

''Austeeeeeen Boooolabard Auusteeeeeen,'' the conductor complained. Then ''Kedzie, Kedzie. Transfertoda-BeetrainKedzie.''

THE COLD FRONT

The sky was clear of clouds, but the city haze made the sunlight thin and ill-defined. The air smelled like used underwear.

The city looks better at a distance, like an old hooker with potholes. Her complexion became worse as we pressed into the West Side, the scene of a riot after the assassination of Martin Luther King. On the east side of Kedzie, the city was made of crumbling brown bricks, broken windows, and a barbed-wire factory or two pasted together with gang graffiti in bright, fluffy pastels. The people were packed into plain brown boxes of three hundred apartments each. The buildings were still, as if waiting for death. Hope was laundry strung up to dry on the cage screens which protected the windows from angry rocks.

Metal complained against metal as the dilapidated train snaked around the broad curve at Laramie Street. Then, like magic, we passed Halsted Street and were suddenly in that stylish no-man's-land known as The Loop. A joke from my childhood:

LADY: "Does dis bus go to da loop?"
DRIVER: "No lady, it goes beep-beep."

I got off the El at Lake Street and walked around for an hour or so, slipping into nostalgia and drifting through the fringe area of pawn shops and liquor stores where the night people wait for the day people to finish their business and leave. I trundled into Joe's Best Sandwiches and took a seat at the counter.

"Whaddaya need?" asked a Joe-like person with hairy tatoos lacquered to his arms.

I treated myself to an Italian beef sandwich, floppy French fries, and a watered-down Coke. After the grease settled, Joe changed me a dollar and I plugged a Canadian quarter into his pay phone.

Her "hello" implied deep suspicion.

"Hi. Is Evey there?"

"Who's this?"

"Pres Riordan."

"From Alaska?"

"Yes. That's right."

"This is Evey. Where are you?"

"I'm downtown. Where are you?"

She was uptown. We agree to meet someplace in my old neighborhood, which was roughly halfway between us.

The Near North Side of Chicago has a venerable history which is the source of a great deal of local pride. You can still see a movie at the Biograph Theater, where the Lady in Red fingered John Dillinger for Melvin Purvis of the FBI. The feds gunned him down in the alley out back. Local rumor has it that Dillinger's penis was so long that it was pickled and kept in a jar in the basement of the Smithsonian Institution.

A few blocks southeast of the Biograph is the site of the old Clark Street Garage, where Bugs Moran's men were gunned down by Al Capone's men in the St. Valentine's Day Massacre. Michael Buchovich, a childhood friend, always insisted that it was Capone who had the pickled Big One. He would bet anybody a million dollars that he was right, but he was unable to prove anything one way or another despite several calls to the Smithsonian, which denied the existence of any such exhibit.

Finally, the Near North Side was the scene of my own brief career as a gangster. I hung around with the Puerto Ricans for most of the summer of my fifteenth year. Then one night, two cops rousted me out by Mary's Candy Store. They pointed their guns at me and demanded that

I drop my trousers. I was neither Capone nor Dillinger. They seemed disappointed.

"Sorry about that, son, but we saw you limping with your leg all straight. We got a report here that a young man about your age was walking around with a shotgun in his pants. What happened to your leg, anyway?"

"A burglar stole it. How come you guys are never around when you're needed?"

This remark was followed by a squeal of girlish laughter from Maria Guttierez, who had just emerged from the alley next to Mary's Candy Store. I don't know if she was laughing at my clever remark or the fact that I was standing there with my pants around my ankles. I do know that my entire body turned bright red, which caused the cops to start laughing too. I spent the rest of that summer swimming in Diversy Harbor with Michael Buchovich, and have avoided street gangs and Maria ever since.

The history and the memories and the 'hood itself are all gone now. The Clark Street Garage was torn down and the Biograph shows classy foreign films to the sort of people Dillinger used to rob when he was a national hero. The Puerto Ricans have moved uptown, forced out of the 'hood by bands of roving Yuppies who keep their music to themselves by means of Walkman radios.

The meeting place I selected was a bar called the Concrete Overcoat. It is just the sort of thing that Yuppies do to tradition. The lights were dim and the unvarnished walls were laden with tommy guns, garrotes, plug and shivs, and the inevitable lacquered reproductions of *Chicago Tribune* front pages from Prohibition and the Depression. The pages were neatly frayed and air-brushed with genuine-looking yellow spots of age. The bartender wore a red pin-striped shirt lashed to his trunk with sleeve garters and a bow tie. He had a little nameplate that said, "Hi, I'm Louie the Lug."

THE COLD FRONT

I ordered the special—something called "Louie's Bathtub Gingerale"—and went to the phone while Louie poured. Evey wasn't home or didn't answer, so I settled into a booth to wait for a bit. The drink was delicious—an alcoholic variation on Italian ice. After sucking three down, I tried the phone again.

She said, "Fine, I'll meet you there in twenty minutes."

I said, "Just look for a guy with a limp."

Then, for no good reason that I can recall, I took a booth under a newspaper headlining the Crash of '29 and tucked my leg out of sight. I waited.

She was a thin, anxious woman. She clutched a crisp, plain tan coat tightly to her busom, as if it were the only garment she had on; clog shoes, baggy corduroy slacks, and brownish hair tied tightly enough to anchor her ears to her head. She had the aspect of someone who equates pleasure with sin and avoids the near occasion of both. I watched her make one pass through the bar, looking at the feet of a half-dozen or so men who had nothing better to do than drink away the afternoon. One of the men, a hipster with gold chains and a hairy chest, said something that made her run to the bartender for help. Louie the Lug sent her my way.

Her cheeks showed a hot red rash of embarrassment. "Mr. Riordan?"

"Hello, Miss Williams. Glad to meet you." I lurched up and extended my hand in greeting, in the process spilling half a glass of Louie's Bathtub Gingerale onto the seat facing mine. Her blush disappeared as mine rose. "Have a seat," I said, pointing stupidly at the puddle I'd made.

"Thank you. I'll get my own. Do you drink very much, Mr. Riordan?"

"Only all the time," I replied.

"Let me see your leg."

I banged my brace against the table. It sounded like an aluminum baseball bat. She relaxed a bit.

I offered to buy her a drink, but she declined. She thumped the table with well-chewed nails while I went off to refill my glass. As soon as I sat back down, she reached into the side pocket of her coat and pulled out a greeting-card-sized envelope. She nudged the envelope across the table with a ringless left hand.

"There you are, Mr. Riordan. Now, if you'll excuse me . . ."

"Wait. Hold on a second, please. What is it?" I stammered.

"I'm sure I don't know. As I told you on the phone, I'm not in the habit of opening other people's mail. Now, if you don't mind, I've got a lot of things to do. I really don't care to . . ."

I feigned anger. "Now wait a second. He's your brother. He's not my brother. I don't care who killed him. I'm just looking for a story. If you care who killed him, just sit still for fifteen minutes."

She reluctantly held onto her seat, as if the padded plastic were alive and possibly hostile. I examined the envelope. It was sealed with Scotchguard Clear. A message was scrawled over the front in an uneven hand:

Dear Ev,

I don't have too much time, so I'll get right to business. If anything happens to me, a newspaper reporter with the Anchorage Herald will probably contact you. He's got a bad leg and when you hear from him, give him what's inside. You MUST give it to him in person because there are some people who shouldn't have it. I'd tell you about it, but that would just mean trouble for you. Tell no one. If anyone else calls you about me,

tell them we stopped talking to each other years ago,
and you don't know anything about me.

Love, Jeff

"Did anyone else ever call you—call you and ask about your brother?"

She bit her lip and worried. "Sure, I got a couple of calls. Mom did, too. Always liars. One guy said he had a business deal with Jeff and another said he was some kind of insurance man with a bunch of money for us, but Jeff didn't have any insurance. He spent money faster than he made it."

I contemplated confession but thought better of it. "This one guy—the guy who said he was Jeff's partner—what else did he say?"

"Nothing, because I hung up on him every time he called. He called me a dozen times, I bet, and Mama, too, but we always just hung up. Was Jeff dealing drugs or something? I can't believe that."

"Where did you get this?" I asked, pointing at the envelope.

"He mailed it to me from Anchorage. That's what the postmark said, anyway, and that's where he was at the time. It was just before he got killed."

I sliced the envelope open with the sharp end of a plastic swizzle stick molded in the shape of a switchblade knife. A stubby key slipped out. I poked my finger inside, but that was it. No note. One side of the key's turning nob was engraved with the number 563. Five-six-three. It could be for a padlock or a footlocker. It wasn't for a house or a car.

"Where did you get this again?"

"Like I said, he mailed it to me right before he got killed."

"And the postmark said Anchorage?"

"That's right. Was Jeff dealing drugs?"

"No, he wasn't dealing drugs or anything like that. It was

something else. I'm not sure what, but it was something else.''

I asked her again if she wanted a drink and this time, to my surprise, she consented. The Happy Hour tightened around us. We drank Louie's Bathtub Gingerale and talked about other things for a while: the mayor's heart attack, the resurgent Cubs, and the lamentable condition of the Chicago River. Eventually we came upon a subject which generated its own natural warmth: Catholic school. I began with a brief account of Jesuits I have known, followed by an anthology of their methods of punishment: Father Joseph exacted fingertip push-ups while Father Raymond made me stay after school to memorize one of Shakespeare's sonnets. I recited for Evey: '' 'When, in disgrace with Fortune and men's eyes,/I all alone beweep my outcast state . . . For thy sweet love rememb'red such wealth brings/That then I scorn to change my state with kings.' ''

The subject of Catholic school struck a responsive chord in this strange, harried woman. There is to be found in the deepest nooks and crannies of this country a community of fallen Catholics well schooled in the careful contradictions of the Dutch Catechism. They share a wealth of stories about burly nuns and their laughter is akin to the nervous giggling of young children who've just escaped the boogeyman. Fallen Catholics usually return to the fold with the advent of parenthood, when it suddenly seems to be a good idea to suppress the more primitive urges of youth.

Evey never left the fold. She said, ''I had this one teacher, Sister Rose Marie, it was. She was about five feet tall and about eighty pounds and a hundred years old. But rough and tough and mean enough and quick sometimes. A nice lady, though, when you got right down to it. She taught the eighth grade because she was the only one tough enough and smart enough to keep the older boys in line. She used to hit 'em in the head with her geography book. She didn't worry too much about the girls, of course, because we were always angels.''

She drained her glass. ''You know, it's funny. I used to think back then that I'd never want to be like Sister Rose, but the older I get, the more I get like her. Mom wanted me to be a nun, too, but I guess I just wanted something more out of life.''

I walked her home. The sun had set and the Near North Side had been given over to the nightwalkers—the straights and gays and cops and criminals, all of them on the make in one way or another, drifting from neon promise to neon warning.

Her block looked like it was trying to decide between trendy rejuvenation and honorable decay. The east side of the street had a proud, glitzy gaslight, lots of wrought-iron fencing and bright windows cluttered with doo-dads hanging from a vine. The west side—Evey's side—clung to the memory of better days with ratty curtains and thick brown shades. The windows were darkened, as if the buildings themselves were ashamed of their shabbiness.

I spent the night in something called the Near North Delux Hotel 50 Rooms Transients Welcome Vacancies Pay-TV. The clerk seemed surprised and a bit suspicious when I asked for the all-night rate.

All night long the other guests annoyed me with their drunken laughter, their desire, and their clumsy bangings up and down the hall. I tossed and turned until the noise subsided and all was quiet except the painful coupling of the people in the room next to mine.

Business to do.

My foot still tingled where my toes used to be. My brace had taken quite a beating. Time for the leg man, one Franz Kruger, a German who claimed to be an Austrian. Many of the leg men in America are German because the two world wars which that nation has inflicted on our century gave the Germans lots of practice in the construction of artificial limbs and such. In America, they apply their engineering genius to the aftereffects of the great polio epidemic of 1952, the one that struck me down. I've been dealing with German leg men ever since I was old enough to pee standing up.

Franz Kruger untwisted the bend my brace had suffered while galavanting around the Toyukuk River. He asked me what had happened and I told him the truth. He didn't believe me. I knew he wouldn't. We dropped the subject. I paid him two hundred and fifty dollars.

"Well, you might want to start thinking about getting a new one. Plastics are the new thing now. These new alloy metals don't take too well to bending. Once they get out of whack they start to lose a lot of strength. If you don't watch it, she'll bust up on you when you need her most."

More business to do, the hardest part of all. She was shrinking fast and had taken to wearing a heavy wig dyed an aristocratic gray.

"How are you feeling, Mama?"

"How do you think I'm feeling? I'm sixty-eight years old. If you were sixty-eight you'd be dead already with the way you live. Do you have a girlfriend yet?"

"Yea, sure Mama. Lots of them."

"That doesn't count. Well, you'll stay for dinner then."

"Yes, of course. But first thing tomorrow I've got to go. I've got a plane to catch."

Chapter 17

I HAD MY HAIR CLIPPED SHORT AT AN OLD-STYLE BARBER-shop with a candy-cane pole and the smell of Brylcream. The barber clacked scissors against comb with the easy skill of a maracas player while complaining about Republicans, fancy hair salons, and the mess I'd made of his floor. Tumbleweeds of my rough brown hair rolled over a scattering of cigarette butts.

I tipped him two bucks for an eight-dollar cut. He recommended Fritz's Finest Toupes, where I purchased a dark red piece from Fritz's handlebar collection to replace the mustache I could never grow. I rounded out my disguise at the downtown Chicago branch of the Army-Navy Surplus Store with combat boots, khaki trousers with the cuffs turned up, a tan workshirt with button-down pockets, mirrored sunglasses, and a wide, floppy hat of the sort worn by robust Australians who have absolutely no trouble at all growing bushels of facial hair.

My walk was a little more difficult to disguise. My crippled leg does not bend at the knee. When I step forward, it swings to the side so as to avoid scraping against the ground. This sort of gait does not readily lend itself to masquerade, but I did the best I could. I took a page from my shotgun-toting youth and adopted what the Puerto Ricans used to call "The Pimp." The Pimp is a stiff-legged tough-guy strut in which the fists are curled into the wrists and back behind the hips while the shoulders lean forward and rock to the motion of each measured step. The effect was like that of an inebriated flamingo, which is okay in flamingos, but unsettling in human beings and positively sinister when combined with the suspicion that I might be carrying a shotgun in my pants.

My disguise failed its first crucial test. As I moved through the arch of the Chicago airport security station, my brace once again set off the alarm, summoning a matronly black guard who looked strong enough to subdue a bull. The Pimp aroused her suspicions. She withered Fritz's Finest Mustache with a hot glare as she ran a hand-held metal detector up and down my leg. She regarded me with a careful look and seemed ready to dismiss my usual explanation of what had set off the alarm. But then a baby in an aluminum carriage sounded the alarm again. This distracted the guard, who grunted that I should move along. The baby chuckled as she frisked him for a weapon.

All this was observed by a sour-pussed man in a gray pin-striped suit. As luck would have it, he sat next to me on the plane. He read the *Wall Street Journal* from cover to cover and back again and told me he was saving the Standard Oil Company some money by traveling coach as part of a company-wide austerity program that had something to do with the price of Saudi oil. I looked out the window and watched the wing wobble.

When the stewardess delivered to us a meal that tasted like deep-fried carpet, he put down the *Journal* and asked me about my leg. I told him it had been blown off in the

Vietnam War. I asked him about Alaska and he lectured me about current economic conditions.

"The pipeline days are over, son. Alaska's got one of the highest unemployment rates in the country. You can still get a job and you can still make some good money, but these days you've got to have a skill."

I told him I had a skill. I told him I was very good at killing Vietnamese. "Standard got any openings along that line?"

Our plane touched down shortly after ten P.M., Anchorage time, Thursday March 4th. Rachel had started light training in preparation for the start of the Iditarod, which was only a week and a half away. She was resting her dogs for the long haul to Nome. When the race was over, spring would come to the northern part of the northern hemisphere and with it, planting season for the farmers, huge profits for Hugh Smalley, and some sort of trouble I couldn't figure out.

The trouble was all about key number 563.

While waiting for my luggage, I told myself there must be a lot of locks numbered 563 in a city the size of Anchorage. Footlockers, padlocks, and safe-deposit boxes. I tried the key in airport locker number 563, but it didn't fit. One down; dozens to go.

The guy who answered the phone at the Fairview Inn said Rachel wasn't around. He hadn't seen her for a couple of days and sure, he could take a message but the race was coming up real soon and he probably wouldn't see her. I tried my friend Andrew at his condo, but there was no answer. I went into the airport bar in search of more reliable comfort.

I scanned the faces there, looking for the one Smalley had paid to kill me. Maybe it was the big guy with vodka on the rocks and fingers as thick as pepperonis. He looked strong enough to strangle a moose. Or maybe it was the little guy with weasly eyes who munched nervously on a swizzle stick. Maybe he was packing a hand grenade, or maybe he used a stiletto, too, just like Mick the Pick. He looked snaky quick, just like the stiletto type. Or maybe the bartender? Maybe the waitress? Maybe the angular pimp who held court by the jukebox in the corner? Maybe they'd nail me as soon as I stepped outside? Or maybe there was a sharpshooter nestled in a shadow on the Minnesota Extension? Maybe I'd already been marked and it was just a matter of time? Maybe he was waiting for my taxi to hit the stoplight at the intersection. Cab stops, finger squeezes, head explodes. Maybe I'd better hop on a plane and go back to Chicago. Mama would take me in, and Evey I would take to the movies. I could get a job editing the community calendar for the *Skokie News*.

Thompson's Always Elegant Airport Limousine Service carried me into town. I sat low in the middle seat, hoping the other passengers might provide protection or witnesses in the event of a sniper attack. Three college coeds up for the race whispered and giggled and guarded my rear. A tourist couple from Iowa, in town for the same event, protected my left flank while a lobbyist up from Juneau protected my right.

Since the lobbyist was easily the most expendable of us all, I sidled close and engaged him in conversation. "I hear Senator Gambell's trying to bust up the Railbelt Coalition."

This set the lobbyist off on a lengthy dissertation about power politics and insiders and outsiders and knowing the ropes and calling back chits. Lobbyists talk like that because they worship power and are insiders who know the ropes and collect chits. I listened carefully, cocking my ear at odd angles so that his head was always between mine and the Minnesota Extension. I neglected to mention that he might be called on to intercept a bullet meant for me. In this case, both the bullet and the lobbyist would be performing a valuable service.

Thompson's Always Elegant Airport Limousine Service chugged beneath the yawning sky and toward the city's glow. As we approached the Extension, I leaned closer, egging him on: "But what about the Bush Caucus?"

This evoked more pontifications about trends, committees, oil revenue, and public-opinon polls. If there was an assassin on the Extension, he forgot to pull the trigger.

Thinking myself safe, I ignored the lobbyist and listened to Thompson instead. He was a garrulous black man full of inside tips for his tourist customers. The Downtown Deli served the best sandwiches and the Fly-By-Night had the best band. Mount Alyeska had the best ski slope and the Calista Native Corporation ran the best hotel. Portage Glacier had the bluest icebergs and the Kenai Peninsula the biggest salmon. Thompson's Always Elegant Greatland Tours had a package deal that hit them all. I asked him to drop me off in front of the Governor's Hotel. The coeds giggled and the lobbyist droned on about the most efficient way to suborn senators by means of strategically placed campaign contributions.

My disguise fooled the cocktail waitress, but not Andrew. She was busy. He, of course, was not. We sat in a shadow by the green olives. My friend took a big suck on his Rooseveltian cigarette holder and regarded me through the cloud of smoke he disgorged. "And so, a great thirst forces the fugitive out of hiding," he said in the grandiose tone of a funeral orator.

My hair stood on end. Word had got around fast. Andrew's expression changed from mock sorrow to genuine concern. Our eyes connected. "What do you mean, 'fugitive'?"

"Phil Norwood has been looking for you for the last

two weeks. He wants to fire you in front of witnesses. He's a bit put off by some of the rumors about you."

"Which are?"

The actor took charge again. This time he tried a pompous official, a role to which he was well suited. "Well, I have sources of information that are usually reliable that you walked out on the poor fellow—left him standing in Mr. Hadley's lobby with his mouth hung open. He hasn't quite closed it since. I, of course, have been giving these reports the widest possible circulation. But now I suspect there is more here than meets the eye. By the way, that mustache has to go. You look like you're auditioning for a comic book."

"How's Chena doing?"

Andrew had taken a chunk of New York City and wedged it into the hillside of the Chugach Mountains. His condo was white, airy, lofty, and papered with enlargements of some political cartoons which have withstood the test of time—Mauldin's Weeping Lincoln, MacNeely's Two-faced Nixon, and McCutcheon's Injun Summer. Above an elegant imitation fireplace with gas-fed flames was a shrine to FDR—candles, incense, and an enormous photograph of the great man with the famous, confident chin, his teeth clamped tightly on a cigarette holder which pointed upward like a robust gross national product.

A full picture window provided a commanding view of the city—white smoke billowing from a thousand chimneys by day, rectangles of sparkling light by night. Beyond the city, an early sunset dropped into Cook Inlet while to the north, mountains snored away the last weeks of winter.

My dog Chena had added a profusion of wiry black hairs which thawed some of this chilly elegance and gave the place a soft, homey feel. In the month since I had placed her in Andrew's care, she had come to love him as dearly as her next bowl of food. His white couch was turning gray, and the scent of dog breath lingered in the air.

"My cats think she is the second coming of mother," Andrew said, fetching a bottle of brandy from the kitchen.

I talked about Rachel and the Iditarod and Mick the Pick and Smalley and the price of wheat futures. Andrew talked about my dog's sleeping habits and the upcoming state primary elections, for which he had been hired as a consultant by three Democrats, five Republicans, and a long-shot Libertarian candidate for governor. By the time he was done, we were quite drunk and he launched into the inevitable imitation of FDR:

"And though the dark clouds gather over Toyukuk City, and though Prester John is consumed by love for a woman who prefers the company of dogs, stand straight before the whirlwind, my fellow Americans, and rest assured in your heart of hearts that the only thing we have to fear is that the liquor stores are closed."

After that, I showed him key number 563, but he was too drunk to make much of it. The next morning he said that it probably had to do with banks.

Banks are contrary to my nature. To me, they are the means by which those who already have too much money profit from my mistakes. Consider the $10 penalty for bouncing a $5 check. Then there's the Canadian quarter. It's worth about twenty cents and makes the typical American vending machine gag. Banks are Canada's way of sneaking these unwanted coins into my pocket. My petty revenge has been to become a master of the kited check. And I spend my money as quickly as possible, trying to keep the balance in my checking account between plus and minus one hundred dollars.

But these ploys of the insolvent are little help when dealing with safe-deposit boxes. There were seventeen banks in Anchorage. Most had a safe-deposit box numbered 563. I sought the counsel of a wiser head.

"Andrew, we've got a problem."

He, of course, had the perfect solution. The next day, I rented safe-deposit boxes in each of the seventeen federally insured banks. That night we compared each of the seventeen keys against the one Evey Williams had given me. Three of the keys were of the same style and color as number 563.

Andrew examined the bank brochures I'd collected along the way. He instructed me in bank procedures, which were pretty standard. Each bank required the filling out of forms with the proper signature. All safe-deposit boxes had to be opened with two keys, the second held by an officer of the bank. Since these safeguards tend to discourage casual mischief, we developed a two-man plan of operation.

"Let's start with the First Bank of the Far North," Andrew suggested, and the next afternoon, after rehearsing our lines and synchronizing our watches, we did just that.

We marched into the bank just before closing time. It was Friday, March 8th. The start of the Iditarod was only eight days away. Spring would follow shortly thereafter. Time was on Smalley's side, though time had also repaired my foot from the surgery performed by Reggie Moore. Down south in the rest of America, the first hush of a new season slipped through a crack in the Earth.

Meanwhile, our fellow Alaskans withdrew, deposited, borrowed, and lent at a furious pace with bankers anxious to close their accounts and begin their bankers' weekend. Andrew stepped to the end of the shortest line while I hobbled over to a gathering of mahogany desks situated beneath the huge oil portrait of some lord of commerce.

I dawdled until Andrew was only two turns from the teller, then approached a harried-looking young woman who'd been left to hold down the fort while her superiors attended to other things. Her nameplate said, "Christine Adams." Her face was a mask of reluctant patience designed to make people feel guilty about retrieving their own money.

"May I help you?" she asked, not bothering to look at my face and fully certain the ledger she was working on was more important than any business of mine.

"Yes. I need to get into my lockbox," I said meekly. Andrew and I had agreed that I should be meek, unthreatening. Meekness and timing were important parts of our plan. I looked over at the row of tellers. Andrew was next in line. Christine Adams made an entry in her ledger.

"Name?"

"Pres Riordan. Or rather, Prester John Riordan. That's how I signed it. Yes, that's it."

"Number?"

I dug out the key I'd rented the day before and recited the number etched on it. The card I signed warned that fraud and theft were serious offenses punishable by imprisonment or fine or both. I watched Andrew's progress as Ms. Adams examined my signature and checked it against a card I'd signed the day before. It was Andrew's turn now. He leaned against the teller's cage, chatting easily as we had planned while Ms. Adams led me through a maze of desks and sober faces to a heavy door protected by electric eyes and a big guy who looked stupid.

Ms. Adams asked me for my key.

"My God! This is an outrage!" Andrew boomed in his most Rooseveltian voice. The teller winced. The other customers whispered and gaped, as if witnessing an indecent but interesting exposure. Playing to his audience,

Andrew turned away from the teller and roared: "I demand to see the owner. I want my money and I want it now. I'm being cheated. Don't tell me the check hasn't cleared. I want my money! This is a crime." He sounded like a bad actor in a bad play.

The eyelids of Ms. Christine Adams dropped slowly, blotting out the scene for a second while she prepared herself. I watched while courage and anger and patience and loathing jambled against one another until they got all clogged up in the tip of her nose, which turned bright red and quivered a bit from the strain.

"Excuse me," she said softly. She gave a signal to the guard and turned away from my outstretched hand with the wrong key in it.

The act was played as pantomime, beginning with Ms. Adam's stomping approach, a charge which I found reminiscent of a chase scene in the Lon Chaney version of the *Hunchback of Notre Dame*. Andrew replied with a windmilling gesture of outrage and disgust to which she nodded severely. She lectured him. He lectured her. Then she and another guard ushered Andrew out the door with the stoic courtesy one normally reserves for someone else's ill-bred children. By the time it was all done, the bank had been cleared of all wrongdoing. The few remaining customers and the hired help were well into the business of sweeping up and counting down. Ms. Adams returned to me almost as an afterthought.

"I apologize," she said with as little feeling as possible.

"That's okay." I tried to force some annoyance into my voice, but it sounded more like I had dropped something heavy on my toe. She either didn't notice or didn't care.

"Well, where were we?"

"We were going to open my safe-deposit box."

I handed her key number 563 and started twitching

about, as if in a great hurry. As we'd hoped, she didn't bother to check the key against the number on the card I'd signed until it became clear the key didn't fit the lock. She looked at me with a bitchy suspicion, but she didn't know what crime to accuse me of.

"Sorry," I said.

"Yes?" she said. Her nerves were frayed, her weekend already ruined by the unpleasantries Andrew and I had contrived for her.

"Yes . . . well . . . I'm very sorry. Must be the wrong key. That must be the key to another box I have at First Alaska. I guess I'll have to come back on Monday, unless you wouldn't mind waiting until I come back with the right key?"

"I'm sorry, but that's quite out of the question."

Of course, of course.

Chena and I holed up in the condo while Andrew spent most of the weekend in the bar atop the Governor's Hotel. On Monday, we perpetrated a similar scam on an ulcerating vice president of First Alaska. This time things went quite smoothly, although the vice president was a little confounded by the obscenity I uttered when lockbox 563 spat out a tube of paper wrapped in greasy rubber bands.

Chapter 18

THE LAST WILL AND TESTAMENT OF DR. JEFFREY WILliams contained a lengthy preamble. He began with a flowery tribute to Norman Borlaug, the Nobel Prize winner mentioned by Bob Brown during our conversation in Hugh Smalley's hayloft. Then came a strange and elaborate discussion of events in the Sahel region of equatorial Africa. He talked about slash-and-burn farming methods in Chad, Niger, and Mauritania and the fate of Lake Chad, which has lost ninety percent of its surface area in the last fifteen years.

This part of the preamble was written in a high rhetorical style which so exicted Andrew that his face became as red as his hair. He nagged me for pages of the manuscript which I was looking at and became so engrossed in his own reading that he allowed himself to run out of cigarettes. When he had smoked all of mine, too, he began rolling the tobacco which remained in a large pile of butts into makeshift cigarettes wrapped in newspaper and glued with spit.

The preamble rambled on for more than a hundred

pages. The gist of it was that the Sahara Desert will swallow the nations of the Sahel unless science comes to the rescue. He described the Sahara as a horrible place and noted that a precinct of Libya once registered a temperature of 136 degreees Fahrenheit. He talked about ergs and regs. Ergs are the rolling sand dunes used as background for stories about the French Foreign Legion. Regs are the broad, moonlike plains left behind when the winds have blown even the ergs away.

I quote him here: "This is where the thin membrane of life on Earth is being peeled back, revealing the hard core of infertile stone which makes up 99 percent of our planet. Seven thousand years ago, a microsecond in geological time, the Sahara was the size of an aggressive European nation—France before Napoleon or Germany after Bismark. Today, it is larger than the United States, but unlike the United States it is growing bigger. Every year, another one hundred square miles of fertile soil is peeled back by the relentless trade winds. It is as if the Dance of the Spheres is over and God is rolling up the carpet, leaving behind barren stone from which not even the hardiest weed can grow."

He concluded the preamble with a discussion of primitive farming methods in Brazil which he feared will make another Sahel out of the great tropical rain forest which ecologists call "The Lungs of the Earth."

Andrew lit one of his homemade cigarettes. He took a puff and started poking the hot end at a pile of denuded cigarette filters. He said, "It's a brilliant piece of work. Such compassion and anger. It seems he meant this to be read out loud—at the United Nations or some such international forum. Listen to the cadence of his sentences. This is not a manuscript to be read, but a speech to be heard."

The second half of the manuscript was almost as long,

but less highfalutin. It was written in the precise languages of the scientist and the lawyer. It started out like any other will: "I, Jeffrey Williams, being of sound mind and body, do hereby declare this to be my last will and testament."

The body of the will was a dense, incomprehensible jumble of mathematical equations and unpronounceable words arranged in convoluted sentences. He described these as instructions for the manufacture of a brand-new synthetic fertilizer. He said this new product would do all the good things that ReapRight could do without poisoning the Earth with a toxic by-product. His will bequeathed the formula to "The People of the Sahel, Africa."

Rachel Morgan was named executor of the will.

Now it was my turn to light a homemade cigarette and look astounded. By then we were smoking the butts of butts. The taste reminded me of Smalley's dump. Chena howled in her sleep and the cats rearranged themselves around her.

"Now *that's* a story," I said.

Andrew said, "You're right. It's a great story. What are you going to do about it?"

I thought about it for a second while I snuffed out my cigarette. Andrew snatched up the butt and started to squeeze out the charred tobacco tailings. I said, "Well, I guess I'll write a story and then see if Hadley wants to print it."

I waited in the lobby by Anchorage Harold, wondering if the plaster-of-Paris newsboy had spilled the beans about my walking out on Phil Norwood. Phil refused to look at me when he walked by. Some of my other colleagues poked their heads out of the newsroom to see if it was true that I had returned. Jamie said hello. Margaret walked by, but refused to talk to me, the little bitch.

After a half hour or so, Hadley's secretary came into

the lobby. She led me upstairs, quiet as a mouse, and sat me down on the refurbished pew reserved for Hadley's waiting guests. The circulation manager went into Hadley's office to witness a magnificent tirade that reverberated though the entire second floor of the *Herald*. I fidgeted with the hard copy of a story I'd written on Andrew's computer. The secretary attended to her work as if nothing was amiss. After another half hour—during which Hadley's long screams were interrupted by several apologetic silences—the circulation manager came back out looking like a cat that had just been pissed on. The secretary indicated that it was now my turn.

Hadley was in an expansive mood, invigorated by his conversation with the circulation manager. He asked me if I wanted to play a game of darts. I declined. He asked me if Phil could sit in on our conversation. I said that would be okay. We shared a nervous silence while Hadley's secretary summoned the city editor. Phil arrived flushed and out of breath, as if he had run upstairs, which he no doubt had.

"How's it going, Phil?"

"Prester John Riordan." He said this while gulping for air, which made it sound like "Ester On Ear."

Hadley adjusted his tie. "You have the floor, Mr. Riordan. What can we do for you?"

I laid the story on his desk. Phil looked over his shoulder while he glanced through the pages. He set the story down and rubbed his fingers together, as if feeling for scum. "What is this?"

"It's a story, Mr. Hadley. A big one. Print it and we'll blow the lid right off of Smalley's operation."

Hadley played with the lobe of an elephantine ear while I described my return trip to Toyukuk City and the various events which led to the discovery of Jeffrey Williams's last will and testament. I explained as best as I could what was in the will and talked about the plight of the millions of Africans living on the edge of ergs and regs.

When I was done, Hadley let go of his earlobe and said, "Riordan, you are a goddamn lunatic. You want me to shit on a man who has a long record of service to the community and who will create thousands of jobs for Alaskans. Get the hell out of here before I call the cops. I'll have you arrested for trespassing you . . . you . . ."

Phil used a phony cough to suppress a chortle. Hadley scanned his vocabulary for the worst available noun.

"You . . . environmentalist."

In Hadley's demonology, environmentalists are worse than communists, homosexuals, and Texans, but better than investment arbitragers. I picked up my story and started to walk away. I turned when I reached the door. "One other thing, Mr. Hadley. I never did get my last paycheck."

The old man picked up the telephone.

I tried to call Rachel from Andrew's condo, but the bartender at the Fairview Inn said she'd already left for Anchorage with a pickup truck full of dogs.

I called the other newspaper. In his own brilliant but bombastic way, the Skeptic from Baltimore also told me to take a hike. Smalley's promise to feed the hungry was popular with local liberals. And then there was the Porcupine caribou herd.

Andrew was delighted by these setbacks, as they helped confirm his dearly held opinions about journalism. "You can't be too shrill in defense of the environment when you're in the middle of a circulation war," he said.

This was unfair. The Skeptic was nothing if not intellectually honest and excessively proud of it. I defended him by changing the subject. "So much for my friends. Do you have any?"

THE COLD FRONT

Andrew walked over to the picture window. The setting sun left an afterglow on Mount Susitna, The Sleeping Lady. "We go East, young man, where the newsmakers are. We go to New York and we hold a press conference. Rachel should be there, as she is the executor of the will. We'll start with the networks and the *New York Times*. The rest will fall in line."

I tried to imagine Rachel addressing the world from a podium, with hot light on her freckles and a flower in her hair. I'd never seen her in a dress. I'd never seen her legs, unless you count . . . Andrew interrupted my reverie.

"You call the airport and make reservations," he said, then pointing at Williams's will. "I'll take care of this."

I didn't understand. Andrew explained. "We need a safe place for this until we get out of town. I think I know a place that will do well enough."

I nodded. He was right, of course. As he put on his coat, he said, "Let's talk about it later over pizza and beer. I'm feeling like a working-class hero tonight."

Chapter 19

I ORDERED AN EXTRA-LARGE PIZZA WITH SAUSAGE, MUSH-rooms, and double cheese. Chena watched the leftovers closely, drooling on the rug as Andrew's half cooled into a rubbery smudge on the coffee table.

The local late-night news was all about oil money, property taxes, and the community of Mountain Village, which was having trouble with its sewer pipes. Apparently, the Seattle firm which installed the pipes didn't use the proper insulation. When the temperature dipped to fifty-five below, the sewage froze and the pipes cracked like a bottle of Coca-Cola left in the freezer. The TV camera captured close-up pictures of brown ice covering main street. The TV reporter stood on a sheet of frozen excrement and said engineers had been called in to investigate. Doctors were worried about the spring thaw.

The last story after the weather (dark and cold, with a chance of snow flurries) was about a legal scuffle between two neighbors. One neighbor had turned his backyard into a temporary dog kennel for one of the Iditarod teams. The other neighbor didn't like dog shit all over his sidewalk or

howling in the middle of the night. The mayor promised
to submit an emergency ordinance, although it wasn't clear
who's interest the emergency ordinance would protect.

Then I switched to cable channel six, WGN in Chicago.
Chicago. I wondered what would happen to Evey Williams
as I watched *The Glass Key,* an Alan Ladd version of a
Dashiell Hammett story about the trials and tribulations
of a pair of corrupt but lovable politicians. After the movie,
it was time for Bert Barkley (or was it Bart Berkley?) and
the late-night edition of WGN News. Bart said a mistrial
had been declared in the tax-evasion case against Tony
"Two Scoops" Spumoni, a local thug. His sports headline
was about how the Cubs were getting ready for spring
training. It looked like they meant business this time.

After the weather (low to mid-forties, with a chance of
rain), I grabbed a beer and settled next to Chena for the
late, late movie. But the combination of Barbara Stanwyck
and too much alcohol proved too strong and I slipped off
into a troubled sleep full of mushers and killers and starving people living on the edge of the moon.

I awoke with a start.

It was three A.M. and Barbara Stanwyck had been replaced by Abbott and Costello. Chena's legs flayed the
floor. She uttered a guttural glow, as if dreaming that she
was young and tough again. Abbott and Costello fled before Frankenstein into the clutches of Dracula and then
took a short pause while Len Burton sold some Bert Wein-
man Fords. Abbott and Costello escaped from Dracula
with the assistance of Lon Chaney, Jr. But the full moon
popped out from behind a cloud and Lon turned into the
Wolfman. Frankenstein burst into the room and the two
chuckleheads slipped away while the monsters did battle.
Costello said "Ababababooooooooooooooott!" Len Burton came back to sell a new batch of Fords and the latch-
key clicked.

THE COLD FRONT

Andrew was home.

No, he wasn't.

Two figures darkened the door. The taller, thicker one had a nose like a baked potato and a black leather glove on his right hand. The shorter, thinner figure had rich red hair, a small handgun, and a penchant for oral sex. Her name was Monique Peterson. She seemed to be in charge.

"Hello, Pres," she said.

I offered them a slice of pizza. Monique pointed the gun at my nose and said, "Put your shoes on."

I put my shoes on.

"Get your coat."

I got my coat.

"Where are the papers?"

The papers? I shrugged. Chena disappeared into the bedroom as Mick the Pick peeled the glove off his right hand. The hand which had punched a hole in the ice of the Toyukuk River had been replaced by something like a hand made of plastic and chrome. He pressed a button on his cuff and the artificial hand closed into a fist. It hit me in the stomach. I threw back some half-digested pizza.

Some hours later, I awoke in a room that smelled of unwashed feet and antiseptic, like a hospital for people who don't need doctors anymore. The glare of an uncovered lightbulb broiled my eyes. My head felt swollen, yet soft, like a basketball in need of air.

"Good morning, Pres," said a voice I couldn't see. It sounded like Monique Peterson. I guess that was her name.

I tried to sit up, but every muscle in my body complained about it, so I fell back down. I was strapped at the ankles and hips to a leather bed with paper sheets. I turned my head in the direction of her voice and saw that my paper-covered pillow was sprinkled with wrinkled brown specks—probably dried blood, probably mine.

THE COLD FRONT

She said, "You should tell us where the papers are. We'll find them, anyway, and the sooner you tell us, the less it will hurt. I'd rather not hurt you, Pres."

For some reason, I doubted that. She sat backward on a plain wooden chair, her chin resting on the back support. Now she looked like a motorcycle queen. She wore a loose white blouse, tight black leather pants, and boots with high-heeled spikes. This time, her hair was platinum. Her eyes looked bigger than I remembered and were blue instead of green. Her face didn't seem as round, but it was the same woman who had shared my bed for a month or so. A put-up job, I suppose. She'd put the gun away.

"Whaddaya say, Pres?" Now she even talked like a motorcycle queen. "You give me the papers and then we'll let you go."

"You look great, Monique. Just great."

Her smile was thin. That hadn't changed. "Well, you look like hell. You gonna give me the papers or not?"

I said, "I don't know what you're talking about."

For a few seconds, she rocked back and forth on the hind legs of the chair. Then, with the animal grace that I remembered, she dismounted and brought the front legs down with a crisp bang. She shot out the door. Moments later, Mick the Pick came in. For a few minutes, he just stood there looking at me—still as a stone, hardly breathing. I started to sweat. He took the glove off his artificial hand and walked toward me. I strained against the straps. He leaned over me and put the chrome and plastic hand in my face. He pressed a button on the cuff and the fist closed. He pressed another button and the middle knuckle popped open and a six-inch stiletto slid out. He thought this was the funniest thing in the world and started laughing about it. When he regained control of himself he said, "I'm gonna stick this in your eye, motherfucker. It's gonna take you about a week to die." His breath stank.

THE COLD FRONT

He slipped the stiletto under the straps and cut them loose. My knees wobbled and my head floated as he walked me down a long beige hall made of plaster and linoleum to a large metal door. Mick the Pick tapped three times. The door clacked open of its own accord and he pushed me through.

"Welcome to my little hideaway, Mr. Riordan."

Smalley wore reading glasses and a billowing, tentlike Hawaiian shirt that flattered his enormous girth with plenty of room. He sat at a reading table littered with stacks of loose-leaf paper. His hand danced in a light which had made a gray beam of the cigar smoke gusting from his mouth. The rest of the room was dark and ill defined, shadows without substance.

He saw the question on my face and answered it. "It's a bomb shelter, Mr. Riordan. We've got our own power supply and enough food to last a year. If there's a nuclear war in the next few hours, you will be one of the only survivors. You would be one of the Lords of Creation, Mr. Riordan. But please, sit down. There's a chair over there. I'm counting Ethiopians right now. It won't take long."

He scribbled with the disciplined enthusiasm of a born accountant frowning at this number, smiling at that one. Every now and then he paused, tapping the eraser of his pencil on the furrows of his brow, feeling for a soft spot that might open a passage to the brain. He turned and bent over the glowing screen of a computer, tapped out a command, and then scribbled some more. After about ten minutes of this, he threw the pencil down. It was a gesture of neither victory nor defeat, but resignation. No matter how he crunched the numbers, two plus two equaled four.

"It's not very pleasant, Mr. Riordan. I wish it was, but it's not. The truth is simply not very pleasant. Have you ever heard of Malthus?"

I had, but said I hadn't. "Is that the guy who beat the shit out of me?"

"No, of course not. Malthus was a genius, the great social prophet of his day."

"No kidding."

"I most certainly am not kidding. I'm not allowed to kid. I'm too powerful for kidding. It wouldn't be right. He was a clergyman, you know. The Rev. Thomas Malthus prayed to a kind, orderly Anglican God and then looked down from his pulpit on an unkind and disorderly world. He wanted to know what went wrong. Why is there misery? Don't blame God. Why are so many people so poor? It's not God's fault. Why is the world in such a mess? There's going to be a bigger mess if I don't do something right now."

"What are you going to do?"

He ignored the question. "In 1798, the Reverend Malthus stared the Devil in the eye. He shattered our most precious illusion by pointing out that man is still but a carnal beast, still rutting around in the muck like a sow in heat."

"How's that?"

"Population, Mr. Riordan. Population. There's too much of it. Too many people and not enough food. Malthus knew that. He knew how to count, and he wasn't afraid to say that the numbers don't add up, that man the carnal beast cannot control himself. If he has food for five, he breeds six. If he has food for five billion, he breeds six billion. The more food we grow, the more we starve. Malthus saw the problem, but he was afraid of the solution. He left that to me."

"Enter ReapRight."

He licked down a fresh cigar and lit it. "That's right. The best thing for the right wing. ReapRight can feed the world, Mr. Riordan, but only if the world behaves itself.

You, sir, are a very strange man. I've never met anyone quite like you.''

He sucked in a great cloud of smoke and blew it in my direction. ''You have no great cause. Maybe your Rachel Morgan does, but you don't. Your ego is pathetic. You need a daily headline to establish your importance. As far as I can tell—and I am an astute judge of human beings— you're quick-witted but lack the will to make much of yourself. You blunder along and blunder along, but your blunders cause me serious difficulties. Where are the papers?''

I checked my lip for sweat. It felt like deep dish pizza dough. My clothes were soiled and I needed a bath. ''Papers?''

Smalley picked up the phone and said, ''Send Michael in here, please.''

The door clacked open and the killer came in. His stiletto was still unsheathed. He stood next to me and awaited further instructions.

Smalley said, ''I believe you've met Michael. His friends call him Mick the Pick. I am not his friend. I am his employer. If I tell him to stick that knife up your ass he will do so. Would you like a demonstration?''

I said, ''By 'papers' do you mean the last will and testament of Jeff Williams?''

Smalley nodded. ''That will be enough, Michael.'' He watched Mick the Pick leave, then said, ''Of course, you're more than a job as far as Michael is concerned. He's very angry with you. He wants you and he wants that little girl of yours. You can imagine what he would do if I let him have his way. He's quite crazy ever since he lost his hand. All he does is talk about what he's going to do to you and that little girl of yours. Now, I don't generally approve of such things, but Michael is a good worker and a good boss takes good care of good workers. Of course, if you co-operate you'll be a good worker, too. I'll even pay you.''

If I was a cartoon, a bell would have sounded and a light bulb would have appeared above my head. "You don't have to worry about the formula. It's safe enough. And it's all yours for five million.''

Smalley's smile froze in place. "Excuse me?''

"That's five million dollars. In cash, small bills. To be delivered by me. In person. Unharmed.'' I sounded like an old George Raft movie, the kind WGN plays after the late-night news. "Actually, Scoops doesn't care if you slice me into pimento loaf after the deal goes down. He just wants the money.''

Smalley picked up his cigar and tapped away a chunk of ash. He tried to pull some smoke, but the fire was out. He put the cigar back down. "Scoops? I don't believe I know him. Who is this 'Scoops' person?''

"Tony Spumoni. His friends call him 'Two Scoops' because his trademark is that he's always eating two scoops of spumoni ice cream. His name used to be something else but he changed it to Spumoni because in Chicago all of the big-time gangsters have nicknames that have to do with food. Giovanni 'Johnny Apples' Apelonia and guys like that. Those Italians like to eat. Spumoni's a funny guy. He runs drugs and some protection out of Chicago. Homicide, too, some guys say, if the price is right or the need is there. We're partners. He's got the formula and I know what it means. What do you pay these clowns for anyway? Why do you think I went to Chicago? To visit my mother?''

Smalley relit his cigar. The blue cloud passed into the light and was captured by the beam. "Get your friend Scoops on the phone. I want to talk to him.'' He pushed the receiver to my side of the desk.

I pushed it back. "Sorry, but Scoops doesn't do business over the telephone. There's FBI wiretaps. You can understand. He doesn't want to see you and he doesn't want to talk to you. He just wants the money with no complications. If you don't like it, you can kill me and he'll go sell the formula to somebody else. I don't like it, but that's the way it is. I'm sure he can find another buyer if you don't want to deal."

Smalley sucked in a big puff of smoke. It made a hissing sound as he let it out. "Yes, of course. Now I see. I thought you were too clever to be a newspaper reporter. And just what are the logistics of this transaction?"

I made it up as I went along. A trip to Chicago, a meeting at the corner of 35th and Halsted. Hand signals and a secret word.

Smalley smiled. Extortion made more sense than journalism. "Certainly. And after the deal is consummated, another copy of the document surfaces. This time it's Milwaukee and it's a nigger pimp named Marcel. He's your partner, too, and you both have dreams of wealth and glory which your bank accounts can't support."

"Maybe. But it won't matter much by the time spring planting comes around. You'll have enough advance orders to pay off all those bank notes and if you insist on long-term contracts you'll have a captive market. Then it won't matter what we do. It's the next two months that you have to worry about. Scoops knows that and so do you."

I don't think he bought it, but he sure pretended to. He picked up the telephone. "Michael, if you would please show Mr. Riordan to the shower. He's stinking up the place. Oh, and send Miss Peterson in here, please. You and she are going to escort Mr. Riordan to Chicago."

Chapter 20

AN AIRLINE BAG FULL OF MY CLOTHES AND SOME TOILET-
ries were stacked neatly on the counter next to a trough-
style sink that ranged the length of the room. Mick the
Pick stood by the door and sucked on his teeth. The long
mirror behind the sink followed me as I walked to the
showers. My face was a smudge of welts and scratches,
sprinkled with brown bloodstains.

The showers were at the far end of the cavernous room,
which featured dozens of cracked and stained urinals and
toilets. Everything was neatly symmetrical, if a bit worse
for wear. Although the place was obviously arranged for
the mass production of hygiene, filth had triumphed in the
end. There were no windows and the air was rank.

Mick the Pick laughed when I plopped down on the
floor and began to disengage from my leg brace. He got
a big kick out of the way I hopped to the shower on my
one good leg. The spray helped cool the welts on my face
and wash the beating away. I used the rinse cycle to con-
coct a plan of escape.

Mick the Pick laughed some more when I hopped from

the shower to my clothes. My lame leg flopped about like a slack rubber band. I made a great commotion of lashing the brace back on, swelling my chest with a pride I did not feel to ease the indignity of the moment. After dressing, I splashed my face with a handful of cold water and blotted the sore spots dry.

A freight elevator lifted us into a reinforced concrete bunker which opened onto a sprawling mudflat fed by the glacial silt of Eagle River, a wild young river which spilled down from the Chugach Mountains into the northern part of Anchorage. We were in the dead of night, but I didn't know which one. I might have been unconscious for hours or days.

A cold wind pushed against the bunker. We waited in silence until a pair of headlights started to wind toward us down a neglected gravel road.

The car eased to a stop. It was a Lincoln Continental and Monique was at the wheel. She had changed back into the young Republican I thought I knew a couple of months back. Her face was plainer and her hair was brown and tied back in a pillowy bun. She wore high heels, stockings, and the sort of manish overcoat popular with lady lawyers. She told Mick the Pick to take the wheel and sat down in the back with me.

The traffic got thicker as we pressed into the heart of the city. Fourth Avenue was already blocked off for the start of the race. I ran a quick computation in my head and figured it was Thursday night.

Mick the Pick had clamped his artificial hand to the steering wheel. I took an educated guess that I hoped would soften him a bit. "Hey, Mick. The boss lady here says you got a little dick. That right?"

There was a grinding sound as his chrome and plastic hand crushed the steering wheel. I had guessed right: Monique used sex to keep him in line. The other part was easy. American men tend to fuss about the size of their tools. This is the dark side of the big breast fetish. I looked at Monique. She was laughing inside.

"Isn't that like her, though? Boss you around all day and then laugh about you and talk a bunch of shit behind your back. It's not your fault you've got a little pecker. I'm sure you do the best you can."

The steering wheel made a dull snap and a piece came off in his hand. He pressed a button on his cuff and the twisted crescent of plastic fell to the floor. He clamped the hand back on the wheel, just under the gap he had made.

Monique wasn't laughing inside anymore. She said, "Take it easy, Mickie. He's playing a game with you."

Mick the Pick turned on the radio. After a few songs and a few commercials, a woman with a throaty voice announced that the race would start tomorrow. That would make it Friday. I'd lost a day somewhere. The news lady said Susan Butcher was favored to win again.

Traffic picked up on the airport side of town. Most of it was going the other way as visitors crowded into town for the start of the sled dog race. After the news, the dee-jay yelped for a minute about the Big Song Money Give-away Game and then spun some Bruce Springsteen. We eased to a stop at the tail end of a knot of cars under a bank clock which read 9:48—8 degrees."

Monique said, "Smalley says you're great friends with Tony Spumoni. That's a pretty rough crowd. How'd you meet him?"

I spun a wild yarn about a story I'd written while work-ing for the *Chicago Post*. It had to do with the tow-truck business on the Near North Side and the horrible things that happened to fancy cars which parked in the wrong place.

I was talking like George Raft again. "Tony's nephew

Lou ran the operation and I got a tip that sometimes the cars would get used for running numbers or robbing an all-night Stop 'n' Go food store. So Two Scoops calls me in and says that I better not write about that and that I should stick to cigarette burns on the upholstery. I say that that's okay, but what's in it for me?''

We arrived at the airport before I could explain what was in it for me. Mick the Pick retrieved a large footlocker from the trunk of the Lincoln. I imagine it contained some kind of powerful weapon. I didn't think Smalley would take any chances on me or Scoops or a pimp from Milwaukee named Marcel.

I made it a point to walk very slowly through the airport. Monique stayed at my elbow while Mick the Pick carried the footlocker to the ticket counter and arranged our seating. A large man with a red beard rolled by with a cart stacked high with small cages containing dogs yelping for the race to begin. I walked even slower as we approached the domestic terminal. This would help create the illusion of speed when I finally made my move.

I made some small talk as we waited in line at the security station. "Talk to the guy who made your hand," I said to Mick the Pick. "Maybe he can make you a decent-size pecker, too. Get one that vibrates. Your boss lady would like that."

Before he could answer, I stepped through the security gate. The alarm went off and I was approached by the security guard, a compact black man with wide shoulders and bandy legs. He took me off to the side and started waving a hand-held metal detector at me. The alarm went off again. That was Mick the Pick with his chrome and plastic hand. I made a break for it.

"Hey!" said Mick.

"Wait!" said the guard.

It was more of a hop and a skip than a run, but it worked

well enough. A commotion started behind me. I got about ten feet before Mick the Pick pulled me to the floor. There was another commotion as a ring of guards surrounded us and began to pry us apart.

The police watch commander was tired and had better things to do. He kept us on ice in separate cells before bringing us into a soundproof room for questioning.

I said, "I'm sorry I ran away, but I had to pee real bad. You know how it is."

"And what's your problem?" the watch commander said to Mick the Pick.

Mick the Pick thought about it for a second. The effort seemed to cause him some pain. "I want to see my lawyer and I'm not gonna say anything."

The watch commander fiddled with his badge. A lawyer was the last thing he needed. He said, "Okay, boys. I'm gonna let you go. I don't have time for chickenshit like this."

I said, "Officer, before you do that there's something you ought to know."

"What's that?"

"That man is carrying a concealed weapon."

The watch commander thumbed through a clutch of papers. "There's nothing in the report about a weapon."

"No, I mean he's still got it, as in right now."

The watch commander trained his gun on Mick the Pick while I explained the situation. He called another policeman into the room and told him to fiddle around with the buttons on Mick's cuff. The plastic middle knuckle opened up and a stiletto popped out.

Dozens of campfires and the gamey smell of boiled dog food gave the Buttress a pungent glow. The dogs were

195

uneasy. They smelled a race in the air and were anxious to get out of the city.

I couldn't find Rachel in the confusion. I heard the occasional clatter of cooking pots and the laughter of the mushers, but there were too many campfires and too many questions and too many strangers with secrets and guns and nothing to lose. I turned heel on the Buttress and headed for the dark places of Fourth Avenue.

A light snow dusted the street, which had been fenced off and packed down tightly with snow trucked in from the mountains for the start of the race. I wedged into a cranny between the Fourth Avenue Theater and the five-and-dime, clinging to a shadow and shivering while waiting for dawn.

Chapter 21

TRUCKLOADS OF DOGS BEGAN TO FILL THE STREET LONG before the sun came up. The yelping of the anxious beasts lent a festive mood to what was otherwise a late and gloomy day. The gusting snow thickened into a furious vertical descent.

From my sheltered place, I watched for Rachel and I watched the door of the Frontier Club for some sign of life and warmth within. As soon as the bartender flashed the "Open" sign, I made straight for the door. By the time I negotiated some slippery footing and the two barricades of chicken-wire fencing which flanked the street, a half-dozen other men had already entered the place and were settling onto their barstools and into their drinks.

They'd come here to drink hard liquor and cheer on their own, the Frontier Club being a bastion of that same Alaska manhood which had been dealt crippling blows by the last four Iditarod champions. When Libby Riddles became the first woman to win the race in 1985, these old sourdoughs were able to dismiss her victory as a cruel fluke having to do with the fierce storms which stopped the race at Rainy Pass and stopped everyone but Libby at Shaktoolik.

But no one could dismiss the results of the next three races, which were won by veteran musher Susan Butcher under close to ideal conditions: cold, crisp, and clear. She set one course record in 1986 and another in '87 and again in '88. Now the other mushers talked about Butcher as if she was one of the storms brewing in the Bering Sea. How's the wind? Where's the trail? What about Susan? How many dogs has she got left?

The Alaska manhood which gathered in the Frontier Club was disconsolate and seemed to hold little hope that these indignities would cease. The man closest to the door was neither young nor old. As far as I could tell, he was just drunk and seemed like he'd been that way for years. He'd already downed a Jack Daniel's on the rocks and gave me a funny look when I ordered black coffee—no cream, no sugar, no hair of the dog. His name was Jim. He liked to talk and had that special sourdough way of sounding grizzled and graveled and hundreds of years old, although he was several years younger than I. He said:

"It just ain't right. I read once someplace where now they don't even have to need men for babies so much anymore. Get some sissy scientist or quarterback to squirt his jiz in a mayonnaise jar and then they just pass the jar around. Gonna have a whole generation what looks like Mick Jagger. Just ain't right. You got lady lawyers and lady cops and ladies workin' up at the Prudhoe Bay oilfield. Now they win the goddamn Iditarod, too. Just ain't right. They should maybe just shoot all us men and be done with it."

"Hey, I'm with you," I said.

"Never happen to Len Seppala. He the one that started it all back in 1925 when they had that dipsytherium plague in Nome, you see. They had nineteen mushers—every one a man—runnin' a relay to get the medicine to Nome. That's when men had a usual purpose, other than the squirting of jiz in a mayonnaise jar. Seppala run the hardest leg, so Randy Hearst made him a national hero and then they stuffed his dog and put him in the Cleveland museum. I seen that in the *Herald* the other day."

The coffee warmed my stomach and made my scalp sweat and my hands quiver. "Think Butcher'll do it again?"

Jim was so excited by the question he almost fell off his barstool. "Hell no! My money's on the Bohemian Express. He runs a smart race, the 'Hunk does. Let's Mad Dog cut the trail at the start. Then the Mad Dog tires out and somebody else like Ingnukluk or Butcher takes the lead. The Bohunk, well he still hangs back—two, maybe three hours. You can't stay too far back or the bad weather might shut you in and let the leader run free all the way to Nome. I figure he's gonna make a move at Koyuk, after the rough part of the trail's been patted down by the early leaders. Pretty smart, the Bohunk is. Comes from the Gypsy blood. He lets somebody else cut the trail so his dogs don't have to work so hard—savin' 'em for the stretch run. Thing is, Butcher's dogs're so goddamn fast, she gets any kinda break and she's gone. Whaddayooo think?"

"I don't know that much about dog sled races," I confessed. "I'm just a salesman here in town on business, so I thought I'd check it out. I heard you get a good seat here at the Frontier Club. I'm just a salesman out to make a buck. Want to buy a forklift? You look like you could use one."

The drunk looked at me, not sure if I was joking and not caring really. "Hell no. Not me. I just want to get together enough money to buy a cabin on the Kenai so I can get the hell out of Anchorage. Anyway, it's a sled dog race."

"Say what?"

"You called it a dog sled race. Well, it's a sled dog race. The dogs do the work and the man does the thinkin'. The sled doesn't do nothin', at least not much. So it's called a sled dog race."

"Thanks. I'll remember that."

Jim's third Jack Daniel's on the rocks numbed him into silence. The tavern began to fill up with the gruff chatter of old-timers with beards and stories to tell. A dozen regulars sat near the pool table and talked about their ex-wives, their memories, and their unpaid bills. I eavesdropped on these aging retainers, who had worked for the railroad, survived the Big Quake and worried about the fading glow of the good old days, when women were stout, if scarce, and strong enough to pull a boxcar full of ore.

My barstool provided a clear view of both the street and the bar TV. I could watch real things happen outside and then see how television made them small. Channel Five, I think it was.

I looked outside. The street was becoming crowded with light and noise. The snow had slowed down to a light dusting. Rugged men pampered rugged dogs all jittery with the will to run.

The TV guy was a blondly confident local newsman. I knew him from press conferences and light plane crashes, the bread and butter of Anchorage television news. The dogs howled in harmony as he romanced the camera with sincere brown eyes while reporting that unseasonably warm weather had made a slush bath of the trail between Anchorage and Eagle River. He said if the warm weather continued, it would be a slow race with many exhausted dogs.

"And again this year, a few dogs will die," he added with the unreal sobriety fashionable among television reporters. "The death of dogs is the public relations soft spot of the Iditarod. But Channel Five News has obtained a study commissioned by the Iditarod committee that proves that in a two-week period, just as many house pets die of natural causes . . ."

And so forth. The TV guy also said the warm trail gave the edge to Fred Tunny, who trained his team on the warm summer beaches of Homer. He said the slush bath was bad news for teams that had drawn late starting positions. He said the heavy traffic of the early starters would make the slop deeper and harder to navigate.

Then he said, "We'll be right back after this commercial message." But something went wrong and the commercial never came on, so he just stood there smiling a lot and trying not to look too foolish. Channel Five, I think it was.

I weaved through the race fans and the old geezers to the men's room, took a leak, weaved back. The telephone was tucked in a corner by the old men. As I fumbled for change, I heard a railroad conductor complain that he had lost his job to something called "The End of Train Device."

I counted the rings of the telephone. Three, four, five. The conductor said, "Fuckin' bullshit End of Train Device. I don't wanna work for no railroad that don't have a caboose."

Eight, nine, ten. Andrew picked up the telephone. "Hello?"

"Andrew. It's me. Pres."

"Where've you been? I've been worried about you."

I described my capture and escape. "I'll get Rachel and we'll leave for New York right away."

"I don't think that's such a good idea, Pres."

"How come?"

"Well, I went to the airport this morning and who do I see but your lady friend Miss Monique Peterson and a couple of guys who looked like they ate ugly for breakfast. I'm afraid they're waiting for you.''

''Shit. So we drive out.''

''On the Alcan Highway? You're kidding? That would be worse. You can drive that road for five hundred miles and not see another human being. Hugh Smalley could drop an MX missile on your head and nobody would hear it.''

''Okay. So I'll just sit here and drink coffee until they come to take me away.''

Andrew laughed. ''Well, you could do that. But I was talking to Rachel last night and she's got a better idea. Are you still friends with Ralph the Obit Man?''

We had to shout out the last part of our conversation thanks to an argument which had brewed between the railroad conductor and another old geezer who'd staked a small gold mine just outside of Hope. The miner said that if an End of Train Device could save the state some money, then that was okay by him.

''Oh, yeah!'' screamed the conductor. ''Well, how would you like to get punched in the nose by an End of Arm Device, you asshole.''

Their tempers had been aggravated by alcohol and the crush of young people who'd invaded their sanctuary to wait for the start of the race. The fight seemed to be for the benefit of a chesty redhead who kept bumping her round denim bottom against the gold-digger's wrinkled ear. I hung up the phone and fought my way between his ear and her bottom, through the crowd, and out into a day which was turning bright and crisp.

In the blink of an eye, that which was television became a howling, panting, real-life chaos of dogs with their tails held high. They sniffed each other's assholes and bared their teeth at the slightest provocation. Their masters adjusted harnesses and packed provisions into the carriage of their sleds.

The Channel Five TV crew presided over the confusion from a scaffolding erected in front of the Fourth Avenue Theater. Two thousand racing fans buzzed and chattered behind chicken-wire fences. Traffic cops held up crosstown traffic while the first few teams cruised through the intersection of Fourth and C Streets. Over by the bleachers, the mayor shook hands with everyone who had them. His public works department had done a fine job of trucking in a street full of fresh snow from the foothills of the Chugach Mountains. They'd laid it in a foot-thick blanket down the middle of the city's main drag. Tomorrow, they'd have to clean it up. By then, the snow would be spotted with yellow stains, frozen turds, and eight million paw prints.

Rachel had drawn the seventeenth starting position. The TV guy had told me so. Herbie Ingnukluk, the fifth musher, and a favorite of the folks from his hometown of Bethel, climbed aboard and mushed away, carrying a dog handler in his sled for extra weight. The TV guy, who knew a lot for a TV guy, had said the practice of towing an extra body along helped slow down the dogs. He said it's smart to start easy, especially in slush, because the dogs are so anxious to get out of Anchorage they want to sprint at a madcap pace, causing tie-ups and collisions.

The sixth musher was a man by the name of Gino DeVino. Mr. DeVino was the winner of an Italian game show with an unpronounceable name. Or so said the TV guy. The rules didn't survive translation too well, but the basic idea of the show was this: persuade the judges that your adventure is a magnificent gesture in a troubled world and the sponsors will pay for it. DeVino had made a good case for the Iditarod. His prize was a round-trip ticket to Anchorage, mushing lessons from Joe Harrington, a thousand pounds of Italian dog food, and twenty thousand dollars to rent and supply a first-class team. Italian flags were pasted to both sides of his sled. An Italian TV crew filmed the magic moment when the master of the race called their hero to the starting line. The cameraman held the shot as DeVino sped away. As soon as he was gone, the crew packed up their gear.

I looked for Rachel among the confusion of the starting gate. I saw a high school marching band frozen in place. Their instruments leaked clouds of hot air as they accompanied a tenor wearing furs in the Alaska Flag Song:

> Eight stars of gold on a field of blue . . .
> Alaska's flag, may it mean to you . . .

I saw Jamie Farrell of the *Anchorage Herald* interview Susan Butcher, who had drawn the twelfth starting position. I saw an ABC Sports crew scurry among the dogs with a microphone trying to capture barks on tape. I saw Ed Hadley and Brad Swanson and the man who owned the bar atop the Governor's Hotel and thousands of other spectators huddled together for warmth.

And I saw Hugh Smalley, Mick the Pick, and some of their associates propped up against the grandstand. Smalley waved at me. I waved back with my middle finger.

"Hey, Pres. Prester John Riordan." It was a rich, gentle voice. Rachel's voice. I turned toward it. She wore snow pants, a heavy coat, thick gloves, and a Cossack hat. A nose with freckles on it. She ran so fast she couldn't stop and almost knocked me down. I crushed her with a hug. She crushed back.

She said, "You okay? Where were you? What happened?" Her nose leaked a sniffle.

I told her all about it. I asked her about the manuscript. She told me she had one copy in her sled and that Andrew had mailed a dozen more to newspapers across the United States. I said, "You're crazy. This will never work."

She said, "It gets awful lonely out there on the trail."

"Lonely enough to get us killed?"

She shook her head. I wasn't sure whether she was responding to my question or commenting on the magnitude of our predicament. She bent down and scratched Coffee behind the ears. His tail was high. He was ready to go.

"I'm going to slow you down," I said. "People will think it's pretty strange that you're hauling all this dead weight around."

"You'll have to get out and walk when we get to the checkpoints."

"I'll slow you down."

Her smile had all the warm wisdom of womanhood itself. "That's right. You will. So are you ready to go? My number's up."

I settled into the sled and tried to look confident. Smalley and Mick the Pick applauded when they called us to the starting gate.

Her plan wasn't all that crazy. Smalley had planes and cars and killers and guns and money and everything that money can buy. But these things are of little use on the Iditarod Trail or in the untouched wilderness that yawns on either side for thousands of miles. We, on the other hand, had a fast sled, two frisky lead dogs raised by Susan Butcher, and a copy of the last will and testament of Jeffrey Williams. All we needed were the eyes and ears of the world, so we headed for Nome, where journalists from a dozen countries would soon gather for the finish of the Last Great Race.

The first leg of our journey was more like an obstacle course than a race. We zigzagged around cops and cars and through intersections all the way to Eagle River. Beyond that suburb were the frozen gray mudflats of the Knik River and beyond that the plywood and plastic swell of Wasilla.

Beyond Wasilla is an older world unlike any place I have ever known—quiet and full of life, the City of God. In the times of long, cold quiet I was struck by the strangest thing: frozen moments from long ago. It seemed that nothing had happened before or after these memories. They meant nothing and were related to nothing, but they came back to me with a sensual clarity much greater than that of more important incidents. I'd forgotten names and places and lost whole years of my life, but as we raced through the mountains I could remember a bridge in Milwaukee on a sticky summer day when a cool wind from Lake Michigan suddenly blew under the sleeves of my short-sleeve shirt. And I recalled a basketball hoop which filled my life in the lush confusion between boy and man and how the flattened goo of discarded gum made my sneakers cling to the asphalt, and how the ball made a hollow sound when it banged against the backboard. An instant on a train, a feeling in the morning. These things came to me in a real, touchable way, unlike more useful memories. I rediscovered them in the long, cold dark of the Iditarod Trail and came to believe that when I become old and senility has destroyed everything else, these images will stay with me until death, entertaining me with their pointlessness.

The blue silence of the trail did this to me. And it turned plastic bags full of frozen seal meat into leaky pillows which cushioned my feet with their icky softness.

The musher's camp at Knik looked like some depressed Hooverville, although surely a gathering of the unemployed would have had more men than dogs. Jamie Farrell was among the reporters eager to be insulted who gathered around the Bohunk in search of quotable remarks. The

'Hunk got more good ink from despising the press than a convention full of politicians got from flattery. They called him a "crusty curmudgeon" or a "sarcastic sourdough." He called them a bunch of pansies.

Rachel and I pitched our domed tent on the outskirts of the camp, as far away from the action as we could get without appearing to be unsociable and thus drawing attention to ourselves. Rachel cooked dog food in a broth of crunchy snow. The dogs ate quickly, then slept. Rachel and I shared a tin of canned chili, but the aroma of seal meat had ruined my appetite.

"So tell me about Ralph the Obit Man," she said, punctuating her question with a mouthful of chili. She swallowed. "Aren't you hungry?"

"He's got a newspaper in Nome, the *Nome News*. The locals don't like some of his stories. Somebody tried to hang the family dog once."

Rachel looked worried, as if she knew the dog.

I told her how small-town newspapers work: how one man does five jobs; how the publisher stays on good terms with elected officials so that they will purchase lots of official advertisements with the taxpayer's money; how subscribers won't pay for their subscriptions and advertisers won't pay for their ads; how when somebody farts it's news, unless it's a friend, in which case it's slander. After my lecture, we ate some more chili and changed the subject.

It happened that night. The wind sang and our tent quivered and the cold pressed our warm bodies together. We fumbled with each other's clothes, in the inefficient way of anxious lovers. I tried to release her breasts from a brassiere while she leaned over to attend to the business end of things.

"Ouch! It's hard," she said as my trousers crumpled around my ankles.

She did not refer to my penis, which was indeed in an excited condition, but to my leg brace, which had banged against her forehead. By the time I unlatched her bra and she untied my brace, the cold air had wilted my magnificence. We smoked a cigarette and tried again. It was the best thing there ever was.

Afterward, we talked about childhood and childhood friends. I was my mother's only consolation. She was the youngest, with five older brothers, and had to milk the cow. I told her about the Puerto Rican street gang and other friends of mine. Rollie Beebop, Connie Yamani, and Miroslav Lipshitz were my friends. Lou Shue, Debby Putz, and Marilou Copjonovich were hers. Rachel wondered why children had such silly names, and where they disappeared to when they grew up. We slept. By the time we awoke and crawled out into the day, the Bohunk and the reporters had broken camp and were on their way to Skwentna, trailing Mad Dog and the rest of the leaders.

The contestants settled into three distinct groups—the leaders, the contenders, and the stragglers, who wasted time on the scenery and were just along for the ride. Mad Dog, Herbie, and five other veterans broke trail, followed closely by Susan Butcher, the Bohunk, and the Alaska press corps. Rachel and I traveled on the fringe of the second group. The air was clean and crisp, and we saw no killers hiding behind the trees along the way. After a while, I stopped trying to hide from the other mushers we met along the trail. As Rachel explained, mushers are notorious liars, and therefore the last thing people would think of rumors of a man in her basket was that these rumors might be true. We moved along, moved along through the City of God.

THE COLD FRONT

The City of God was full of rumors. My favorite had to do with unconfirmed reports that the lead dog of a Japanese musher was actually a battery-powered facsimile of Balto, the famous lead dog of history who'd been stuffed and enshrined in the Cleveland Museum.

Our sled was but a whisper in the wind. People born among cars and trucks don't know what silence is. Silence is riding a dog sled at night. Sometimes Rachel sang ballads to the team. But when she didn't, the only sound was the soft, steady crush of our sled over the frozen, crystal plain leading up into the Alaska Range. The dogs chugged along, billowing steam like thirteen little locomotives.

Then Skwentna was behind us and with it all semblance of civilization. The pack of mushers had thinned out into a line more than a hundred miles long. We kept dropping farther back in the pack, but Rachel still held the dogs to an easy pace with singsong commands to "gee" or "haw" and a rest stop every four hours.

I listened to the transistor radio for news of the race and other things. The girl on the radio said Mad Dog Dunnegan was already through Rainy Pass and well on his way to McGrath. He held a seven-hour lead over Robey and Herbie Ingnukluk, who were traveling together. Close behind them were Fred Tunny, Joe Harrington, Susan Butcher, and the Bohunk, who was still hanging back. These were the leaders, the first rank. Except for Dunnegan, each had won the race at one time or another.

Mad Dog's strategy was to push his dogs hard and fast and capture the bucket of silver coins awarded to the leader at the halfway mark. His dogs couldn't keep up that pace for 1,000 miles, but if he was lucky a storm would pin the others down on the wrong side of Rainy Pass and he could limp into Nome.

"Dunnegan's a criminal," Rachel announced at our first rest stop after Skwentna.

We settled around another can of stew. "How's that?" I asked, loosening a lump of something like meat from the rubbery stuff the label said was gravy.

Rachel pushed back her coat and fluffed up her hair, a wonderfully girlish gesture considering it was nine degrees below zero.

"He'll never win the first-place prize. Not the way he runs. No way. He'll maybe get the silver again, but then his dogs'll start to drop out until he's only got the regulation five left to carry him into Nome. I hear he does it for the attention—that and the halfway prize, just like a little kid. He likes to see his name in the papers, not that he can read. So he gets some early headlines and hurts some dogs and picks up twenty-five hundred in silver. Maybe he gets his ugly face on television and then everybody talks about how he's such a real wild man when all he really is is mean. He kills a dog or two every year and your reporter buddies just suck it all up. How come you guys let him get away with that? Where's the story about how he's always killing dogs, running them into the ground but he's never going to win? Ever. Where's that story?"

I nodded sagely and gave her the only reply that made any sense. "Could you pass some more stew over here?"

We took a short nap curled up against the dogs. When I woke up, Rachel was fussing with some dog booties—adjusting the bindings on some, replacing others, and setting aside torn booties that with a little mending still had some miles left.

I climbed into the sled, like a baby returning to the womb. We pressed onto the plain which narrowed into Rainy Pass. The world was all white and blue, the silence a most remarkable thing. Motion without noise lent a strange, dreamlike quality to our travels, as did the perfect blueness of the sky and the craggy arrogance of the mountains sprawled before us, where mistakes are punishable by death.

This is especially true of Rainy Pass. The only good thing about Rainy Pass is that the other way through the mountains is called Hell's Gate.

We passed a couple of idling teams, but many more passed us. The mountains played hide-and-seek—popping into view as we turned into a clearing, then disappearing behind a clutch of trees only to rise again like an angry wall every time we crested a bit of high ground. Distance had lent a perspective which proximity now shattered. No longer rises and bumps on the horizon, the mountains now became brutal worlds of their own hiding behind storm clouds of their own making.

Back on the other side of Skwentna, the mountains had looked like the heads of sleepy old men, with shocks of white hair on top and forests crawling up their chins like the stubble of a two-day beard. Now these old men became terrible gods. They weaved fierce storms from the winds which butted against their frozen certainty. The tallest peak had pushed the clouds down into a misty collar around the timberline, cloaking everything but the summit, which looked like a smaller mountain floating on a fog.

All the bad weather which the mountains wrought from the gentle clouds had to escape somehow. This is what Hell's Gate and Rainy Pass are for—safety valves so the storms won't explode as they build up one on the other in the space between the mountains. Rachel described mushing through Rainy Pass as like running through a bottle of milk. Hell's Gate was worse, and rarely used by even the most ambitious of men.

One storm was failing and another building up as we set up camp on the rise leading up into Rainy Pass. I built a fire while Rachel tended to the feet of her dogs, rubbing them warm when needed and making sure slivers of ice hadn't slipped through the booties to jam up and cut the soft skin between their toes. The dogs left her and crowded around me as I plunked frozen bricks of meat into a cookpot full of sizzling snow. Afterward, they fell instantly asleep, an ability which I was coming to admire as the lack of a good long rest was starting to make me woozy.

Rachel and I snuggled together around the fire and made moon eyes at one another over a reindeer steak. She'd purchased the meat at the Skwentna checkpoint while I hid behind a tree in an effort to elude race officials.

"I saw that reporter friend of yours in the general store," she said. "He was kind of creepy. He asked me how you were. I said you were in Anchorage, but he just smiled."

"Jamie Farrell, right. Tall guy with too much mustache?"

"I guess so. He didn't say his name, but he knew me all right."

After our meal, we listened to the radio for a bit and Rachel entertained me with some rumors she'd picked up along with the reindeer steak. Rumors and dog food are the chief currencies of the Iditarod. Jamie and the clerk at the Skwentna ACC had some good ones: Robey had the flu; one of Susan Butcher's leaders had been stomped by a moose; the Bohunk was already dipping into his beaver meat.

(Beaver meat is the high-octane fuel of dog sled racing. As such, it is best used in moderation and saved for the stretch run. Running an entire race on beaver meat is like trying to play football on coffee and candy bars—the frenetic bursts of energy which beaver meat gives the dogs can delay but not prevent a complete physical collapse.)

"I think it's a bunch of bull," Rachel added after repeating the rumor as if it was gospel. "The Bohunk's got it under control. He always does. He's just trying to turn some heads and get some people thinking that he's going to drop out soon. It doesn't mean a thing; just another one of his cheesy ploys."

"Confusing the opposition?"

"That's my guess. He's not using any beaver meat. Not yet, anyway. It's just a line of talk. He's probably got a sack that says 'beaver meat' filled with caribou. These guys are all liars. Never trust a word they say."

We nestled some more. It happened again while teams passed us in the night. "What's on the radio?" Rachel asked afterward, her round face like a pink moon in the light of the kerosene lamp.

The radio was mostly scratchy rock and roll from McGrath, the first town of any note on the other side of the Alaska Range. After a while, the radio guy said Mad Dog and Tunney were just a couple of hours out of town. Mad Dog looked like a sure bet to win the halfway silver, but now he and Tunney were being pressed by Herbie and a guy from Fairbanks who looked like the Rookie of the Year. Butcher and the Bohunk were slowly moving up, getting ready to make a move when they got to river country.

We tried to sleep, but two more teams passed by our tent, making some noise and reminding us that we were falling behind, dropping to the back of the pack. Pretty soon, we'd be stuck with the stragglers instead of up front where the action was; up front where Jamie should have been. The Anchorage Herald didn't get to be a great newspaper by covering the wrong end of a sled dog race.

"The crowd's thinning out," I whispered, not sure she was still awake.

She answered with an unfamiliar something in her voice—worry, maybe. "The clerk in Skwenta said there's still about twenty-five teams behind us. But most of those are just along for the ride, taking their time. They won't catch up to us for a couple of days. We'll be pretty much on our own until then.''

''I'm slowing you down. We'll never make it like this.''

I felt her smile through the closeness of the tent. ''You're not slowing me down. You're keeping me awake. Get some sleep. We hit Rainy Pass tomorrow and that makes for a long day.''

Chapter 22

THE STORM WINDS SLASHED INTO THE NARROW PASSAGE where two mountain hulks leaned against a sliver of sky. The snowflakes were as heavy as soggy sponges dropping from a thick sky which washed the mountains and the plain different shades of discouraging gray. The lady on the radio seemed to think the worst was yet to come.

"Ease up, my children of the trail. We've got a cold front coming in right now and another storm brewing in the Bering Sea. All aboard for the Siberian Express."

The dogs were in a tizzy. So was I. "My God," I said. "It's five below, we can't see shit, and the lady says the cold front hasn't got here yet."

As soon as we hit the trail, we started to hear a faint buzz that had nothing to do with stone or snow or wind or anything else that belonged in the City of God.

At first, I thought it was just some strangeness of the wind, or the first dull sign of a headache. But the buzz changed pitch, sometimes coming thin and steady like an electric shaver, and sometimes sounding more like a lawn mower. Rachel heard it, too. She leaned into the wind and told her dogs to hurry up. She sang to the dogs and tried to soothe them, but her voice betrayed an urgency which made them puff a little harder, despite the bad weather.

Somewhere along the trail, Coffee and Cream became tangled up. When we stopped to unscramble them, the buzz got louder and louder and then stopped altogether, as if the driver was stalking us, but not quite ready for the kill.

"Can you see him?" Rachel asked.

I said I couldn't. "That's good. It means he can't see us either." And he couldn't smell the trail, like Coffee and Cream, and he made a lot of noise.

The lady on the radio said the cold front hadn't slowed down much when it hit the coast of Shaktoolik. Now it was moving inland and messing up the trail. Weather forecasters predicted the storm would crash into the Alaska Range by sundown, clogging up Rainy Pass and severing the race in two—one race for the contenders who'd already traversed the mountains, another for the stragglers pinned down by the storm. We were on the fence.

The dogs didn't care. Rachel's voice was the only thing for them, and she said "On by! On by!" They bent low to their business, their tails starting to droop a bit. The buzz started up again as the slow rise into Rainy Pass twisted into a series of switchbacks headed straight up into hostile clouds.

As we climbed into the milk bottle, the wind picked up speed, urged on by the other storms behind it. The thin buzz sputtered and died as we negotiated switchback Z after switchback Z after switchback Z, traveling a thousand yards in half an hour just to crawl up a hundred vertical feet. Thin drools of icicle gathered on the panting chins of the dogs as they strained up against my useless weight. Rachel worked hard, too. The sky dumped trainloads of snow into the pass. The wind frothed it all up into a cornered tornado. Not like milk in a bottle. Like whipped cream in a blender.

Higher up, the storm had carved weird shapes into the walls of ice along the trail. Rachel ducked away from these sculpted arches and ledges, and from ridges of ice which swung out like bludgeons each time we turned into another upward-bound switchback Z. Everything was wind and cold, a bitter white. The dogs hauled us up by the skill of their noses, urged on by Rachel's command and the instinctual notion that to stop was to die.

We cut around another switchback Z into a wild howling and a crash. Something we couldn't see went wrong. Our own confusion was added to that of the trail. We hit a dip which made the sled fly forward with a sudden burst of speed into a large bump in the middle of the trail. Rachel screamed and tumbled off.

I looked back, straining against the fur bindings which tied me to the sled and saw Rachel disappear into the fluffy hell. The lightened sled lurched forward again, catching and crushing the heel of the rear-most wheel dog. The dog yelped in pain and spattered the snow with blood, but the others kept on pulling because in weather like this to stop is to die. Their wounded mate became twisted into a tangle of the line and they dragged the sled into the teeth of trouble. I held on for dear life, almost certain that Coffee and Cream were about to haul me into some crevasse. Desperately, I reached out for low branches and clawed the ground for some handhold that would slow our mad ascent. The cannonball charge continued until a low ridge of rock reached out and slapped us off the trail and into the welcome embrace of a snow drift.

We were stuck there for a moment, but then the panic of the dogs wrenched the sled out of the snow drift, tipping me and the other inert baggage out onto the trail. The panicked dogs chased each other in a frenzy until they became paralyzed by a tangling of the lines. Their wounded mate spilled his life out onto the snow.

I quickly untied two of the dogs which seemed about to strangle on the lines. I lashed the whole team to the trunk of a thin but sturdy tree so they wouldn't wander away. The rest of the team gathered around the fallen wheel dog. I hurried down the trail, backmarking through a confusion of tracks which were already being whitewashed by the storm. "Rachel! Rachel! Where are you?"

Only the wind answered. It said it was time for us to die.

I lunged forward, bumping trees and slipping on the ice, tumbling down into the same dip in the trail that had caused our troubles in the first place. I found her groaning at the side of the trail, her soft form already covered by a thin coat of the white death. Ten minutes more and we both would have been permanent features of Rainy Pass.

A thin line of blood slipped down her cheek and froze into a ruby drop. I washed away the blood with snow and pulled her to her feet. "Come on. Get up," I said, using the same tone of certainty she used with her dogs. "We've got to get moving."

She was groggy and a bit uncertain of the time and the place. It took us an hour to untangle the team and recover our provisions, and another hour to bury the wheel dog and mend the wounded. Rachel had a headache, but insisted on taking command. I might have argued the point had it not been obvious that I would eventually "gee" when I should "haw" and kill us all.

Up again into the white tornado—the dogs in front, Rachel in back, and me huddled in the basket with two simpering casualties. The wounded dogs were warm. One seemed more frightened than hurt. The bitch was in a bad way. She had a broken paw and might never race again. She could now look forward to a long and pleasant retirement in Rachel's dog lot. I envied the beast and caught myself imagining that a similar catastrophe had befallen me with similar reward.

Still, as Rachel and the dogs bent to the task of delivering me to Nome, I felt a little silly. If I was to be saved from death, it would be by the grudging respect which Rainy Pass granted Rachel and her indomitable team. I did nothing. I was just their burden. I concluded then that there is nothing more useless than a writer. I vowed for a moment never to write again, but then remembered I don't know how to do anything else.

Blinding snow, cutting wind. A pale yellow light blinking meekly through the storm. The dogs collapsed into exhausted lumps as soon as Rachel buried the anchor.

Woodley's Rainy Pass Lodge was a rough wood cabin that swelled out like a peeling blister from a nook in the stone. The house light flashed brighter and a hoarse, female greeting pierced the night. "Hurry up. Come on quick inside you two or you'll catch your death of cold."

Inside was warm and still and soft, a dark, quiet, female place. For a minute, the storm still echoed in my ears. When the sound died, I started to perspire for the first time in a week.

The walls of the lodge where generously hung with all sorts of animal skins, amateur photographs of relatives and friends and a dusty painting of two young people kissing by a lake. The cabin smelled of human beings and the walls had been cured a dark brown by the smoke of a hundred thousand meals.

The meals had presumably been cooked by the mountainous woman who welcomed us. Her name was Mabel Woodley. She was an official Iditarod Trail judge who could not officially condone the presence of an unofficial man. She dismissed me with a nod, hoping I'd go away.

"I thought you were just another rumor." Then, to Rachel: "Okay, dear. Let's see the goods."

The "goods" were the traditional articles which all mushers entered in the Iditarod were required to carry on the long journey from Anchorage to Nome. Rachel laid medicine and letters on the round wood table that filled Mabel's kitchen. The medicine is a reminder of Leonard Seppala's heroic diphtheria serum run, while the letters recall the original purpose of the trail and carry official Iditarod postage stamps, which are sold at inflated prices to people who have nothing better to do with their money.

Mabel sat down and checked these items off against a thick, spiral notebook. The old woman was as wide as she was tall, with deep, sad eyes and a gray, receding hairline. When she leaned over to examine the goods, her suckled-out breasts rolled over the table like downed hot air balloons.

The accounting done, she leaned back, curious. "Now you two are a surprise. I didn't figure to get any visitors tonight. The quick ones are already well on to Nome and the slow ones should have been socked in by the cold front comin' in. Travelin' together, huh? You two in love? Not much room for that kind of stuff on the trail anymore. My rule book over there says passengers'd be illegal, especially when they's men. That book over there says I need to mark you outta the race."

Rachel blushed. I sought to avoid the issue by slipping over to the old wood stove which filled one corner of the room. I stamped my feet to get the blood moving. I blew hot breath into the cup of my hands and then spread my fingers over the fire. A dribble of water leaked from the roof and sizzled into steam as it splashed against the rusty heat of the stove.

"How many have gone through so far?" Rachel asked.

Mable scratched the slalom on her ski slope nose. She

thought for a moment and then checked her book just to be sure. "Well now . . . let's see. Mad Dog was first in and first out on Wednesday morning—two days ago, that would be. That is an evil sonofabitch. He left two dogs here that're almost dead. They look ragged and start crying whenever I get close. I can't keep 'em with my own dogs because they always want to fight. So I stuck 'em in the tool shed. I bet he beats 'em for breakfast. I hope they don't freeze out there, but there's not any more I can do. Then we got the Bohemian and Herbie and this rookie from Fairbanks with a cute behind that all came that same afternoon. Them three is watchin' each other pretty close, I'd say. They all went to sleep with one eye open so as nobody might sneak out in the middle of the night. After that, it was just dribs and drabs mostly for a day or so—one at a time every hour maybe, except for these five Canadians who travel together like they some kinda sissy band. Man's gonna win this year after all. Susan Butcher scratched on accounta her dog Gravel really did get stomped by a moose after all. That's the thing about rumors. Every now and then a rumor gets to be true and you don't know what to think. Now let me see here . . ."

She paused over her notebook. "You two are twenty-seven and twenty-eight, except that I see the boyfriend here don't have no sled or any of the proper goods and could even maybe be a violation of the rules according to my book over there. I better just call it twenty-seven and probably forget about the rules."

Looking to Rachel: "You know, dearie, legal or not you can't finish in the money with the man along. Leave him with me. He can help tend to Dunnegan's dogs. I pay ten dollars for that kinda work. Yea, you can still win one of those hundred dollar prizes if you have some luck and the weather clears up for you and clouds up for everybody else. But I don't know. This storm's been slow in comin'

and I'm afraid it'll be slow in leavin', too. Anyone comin'
up behind you?''

No. Just a buzz with some death in it. You see lady, it's
a long story . . .

Rachel faltered before answering. ''I hope not. I mean,
it's hard to tell in this weather. You've got to be pretty
crazy to go out when it's storming like this.''

Mabel scowled. ''That's just what I been thinkin',
lookin' at you two.'' She let the matter drop. ''You got
yourself a fine bad-weather team, Miss Rachel. I'd say so,
runnin' up Rainy in a storm like this with a big old basket
full of man. What's wrong with your leg there, son? Bit
by the ice worm?''

I pretended not to hear the question. No one spoke for
a moment. We listened to the bad weather banging against
the windows. No buzz. Not yet, anyway.

''You there,'' Mabel said to me. ''Work up the fire a
bit as long as you're standin' there with nothin' to do while
me and your lady mess around the kitchen . . .'' Then,
back to Rachel. ''Your dogs ate yet?''

''No. I want to let them sleep first. They're too tired
for food right now. We had a pretty rough run up the trail.
We took a nasty spill about halfway up. We buried one
and two more are shook up pretty bad. One's got a broken
paw.''

I could sense Mabel's nurturing tendencies rise through
her body like a fast sweat. ''Well, you can leave them with
me when you go. Ten dollars a day for expenses. I'll even
fix the break if you want. I got splints and medicine and
such, too. And there's some canvass out back you can
string up between the trees so as to make them a little
sleep tent against the wind. Or maybe better yet, your
boyfriend can do it so we can talk like real ladies without
some man hangin' about. Then maybe we can put some
supper on the stove.''

THE COLD FRONT

I trudged outside without comment, listening for a buzz and watching for the telltale bobbing of lights. The wind whipped the snow into a fury as I wrestled with the dogs, who were already sleeping and really didn't care to be bothered. The dog with the broken paw snapped at me when I picked her up.

Mabel snapped at me when I dropped the bitch on her living room floor. "In the kitchen, boy. The kitchen. I don't keep no dogs in my living room. What do you think I am, a man?"

The dog cried while Mabel cleaned the wound and applied a splint. She charged ten dollars for the service.

Everything at Woodley's Rainy Pass Lodge cost ten dollars. She said it made bookkeeping easier. Ten dollars for a carton of cigarettes and ten dollars each for a full meal of potatoes, carrots, and ground moosemeat pie, which Rachel and I ate sitting at her feet, next to the old wood stove. I ate in silence while the women talked about the different times to use different brands of dog food. They also talked about rumors of war and the almost constant stupidity of men, my own stupidity not excluded. Mabel seemed to think the Democrats wanted to prove their manhood by getting into some kind of bloodbath.

"Weak men are much more worry than strong ones," Mabel suggested in a manner that seemed to brook no liberal backtalk.

Rachel said, "Yes. That's true." I didn't say anything.

Mabel: "I tell you, my George wouldn't notice a bulldozer in the outhouse if the motor weren't runnin'. Even back when we was younger he couldn't see the difference between my flirtin' and my fleein' to save a life. I almost had to wrestle him down before he would even speak to me, and then when we finally got to talkin', he told me about how all along he'd been lookin' at me lovin' like."

Again Rachel agreed that men were pretty stupid. Then

they talked about malamutes and huskies. Rachel used malamutes with a quarter wolf for wheel dogs because she wanted speed and stamina. Mabel preferred huskies because that breed, while slower, is stronger and more suited to hauling groceries home and furs to market. Both breeds, they agreed, were considerably wiser than men.

They danced off to other subjects, like fireflies in a mulberry bush. "Now I know you Anchorage folks think you started the Iditarod race, but that just ain't so." Mabel said this to me, since I was from Anchorage, then turned back to Rachel. "But if you want to know the truth, it was us folks who live along the trail. For us, it's like the circus come to town—our own little TV show. Only instead of havin' to buy cars and stuff, we get to sell stuff to all the celebrities. I got some beaver meat out back that'll make your dogs run like they tails're on fire. Ten bucks a pound and you'll be in Nome by Monday afternoon. The Bohunk says he only buys his beaver meat from me, because mine's got that extra get-up-and-go. Glacier-fed streams. That's the secret to good beaver meat."

Rachel laughed. Then I laughed. Then Mabel laughed and the circle was complete.

The old woman continued. "Yeah, it gets pretty slow around here in wintertime. I check the traps once a week and putter 'round the house and wait for spring and the race to come. If it's clear outside, I might take my dogs for a romp, but I'm getting old and most of the time I just sit around and watch the TV and wait for the race and talk on the shortwave radio to these two guys of mine that live over by Hell's Gate. Now sometimes, one or the other of the boys'll come over here if he be real randy and so maybe we'll trade ivory for furs, eat some supper, and then make love some. Nuthin' too excitin', mind you. We just do it so as not to forget altogether. But mostly I'm just waitin'. Waitin' for spring and waitin' for the boys from Hell's Gate and waitin' for the next musher to come on through Rainy Pass. Waitin' to die mostly, I suppose. It ain't the same now that George died. Maybe I'll go to Anchorage in the spring this year and do some shoppin' for my youngest daughter's baby. It's hell to be an old woman, but I'm damned if they gonna stick me in no old folks cage like one of Mad Dog's dogs."

She didn't cry at first. Her eyes were tough and clear. But when I asked her about George, she started to sniffle. She told us everything. Conception was about the only detail she omitted. It was a long story full of woe and inarticulate courage. He died of a heart attack while checking the trap lines.

"Not that I'm complainin', mind you. He lived a full life. Better than most no matter what the troubles, but just not long enough for me."

She got up from the table and started banging things in the kitchen so Rachel and I couldn't hear her cry. She came back to us and said to Rachel while looking at me: "A good man is just like a child. You make him. You love him. You build him into something and you set him all straight. You keep him out of trouble and you keep his belly full for days and months and years. And then one time, he's up and gone and you're more lonely than you ever were before he ever came around."

She blotted down a tear and took a deep breath. "So that's our story. Now I think you better tell me yours."

When we were done, Mabel said, "You got three days, maybe four if you really gotta get there for the finish of the race. Herbie and the 'Hunk are lookin' real good right now and there's clear weather up through the other side of the Pass. Mad Dog's gonna fade for certain, but Herbie and the 'Hunk are makin' good time and who ever knows about that rookie from Fairbanks. The weather's clear in the Burn right now and I sold them three enough beaver meat to launch a rocket ship. You need speed, kids, and your dogs don't have any left.''

''What we need is a snowmobile,'' I suggested, thinking of the buzz that stalked us on the trail.

Rachel scowled. ''I'd rather walk.''

''The man's right, Rache, but it don't matter. I'd give you my whole lodge if it'd help—for ten dollars, of course. But I'm kinda like you with my natural ways, so I don't got no snowmobile. I bet the nearest one's in McGrath. That's two days by most dogs, three days by yours. That's if there weren't no storm and there is. You'll never make it, as I can see, unless we figure something out. Whatta you say, Mr. Prester John?''

Mabel trundled off to bed. I stoked the stove and turned out the lights before pressing close to Rachel in a corner of the living room. It didn't happen that night and wouldn't happen again for quite some time. Still, our limbs tangled together and our bodies stretched out for maximum skin contact. Then we listened to the night, waiting for a buzz to pierce the storm. We slept for an hour or so, until there came a heavy knocking at the door.

Old Mabel tied up her flannel nightgown as she trudged to the door with a flashlight in her hand. ''Come on in, stranger. It's deadly cold outside.''

The stranger stomped the snow from his boots as he walked into the lodge. His shadow danced across the ceiling, his head as big as the refrigerator, his shoulders spread large and black between the rafters. I looked at Rachel and saw my own fear in her eyes.

Mabel said, ''It's awful thick out there, mister. You're lucky you found your way.''

His voice sounded like the grinding of ice on the Toyukuk River: "Thanks. You'll be saving me if I could stay here until the storm clears up."

Mabel said: "Well, you'll have to hush down a little bit. We got a sleeping man over in the corner there and a lady, too, if you believe that. They travel together, I'm told. In love, I bet. The lady was right up behind Mad Dog Dunnegan for a day at the start until her first leader got a busted foot. Now they just tagging along—sightseers, I suppose, like that Italian guy who won the TV game show. Takes all kinds. You see anybody out there? State troopers got a lookout for a couple of teams that be strayed in the storm."

There was a brief pause, a double sigh. "To tell you the truth, I couldn't see anything out there. I almost missed your light even. Maybe somebody else missed it, too."

"I expect you're right," Mabel said. "I hope them that's lost got firewood. If they don't they'll die out there for sure. But that's not us. Not tonight anyway. Warm yourself by the fire while I put some coffee on the stove and call in your time. I need your name, your bib number, and a peek at your goods before you go to sleep. A sleep here on the floor cost you ten dollars—a bed be another ten."

"What goods?"

"Your racing goods, sir. And your name and number for my log sheet. You're running a dog team, right?"

"No. Not exactly."

"Then what the hell you doing out here?"

"I'm a reporter. My name is Jamie Farrell. I'm covering the race for the *Anchorage Herald*."

"Well, shoot, boy. You're coverin' the wrong end of the dog. The leaders are all movin' up into Flat by now."

"So I've heard, but I'm working on a different angle. My story's all about the sightseers, the ones who just go along for the ride and the scenery."

* * *

Mabel went back to bed and soon stoked up a mighty snore that sounded like an old coal stove working too hard. Ed Hadley didn't get rich by paying reporters to look at the wrong end of a sled dog, and his name wasn't Jamie Farrell. The pretend journalist pretended to sleep. Rachel and I held each other tight and measured every breath. Morning's first light showed a sawed-off shotgun, an artificial hand, and a nose like a baked potato.

Mabel's snoring filled the lodge. "Mick the Pick," I said, in case Rachel had any doubt.

He said, "I want those papers. Right now. No bullshit."

Mabel stopped snoring and the lodge became quiet. A few moments later, she walked into the room. Mick the Pick was very polite. "Good morning, Mrs. Woodley. I want you to sit right there by your friends."

He laid the shotgun in the palm of his artificial hand. His knee started pumping up and down like a piston; nerves. Mabel tried to sit down slowly, but her knees failed at a critical moment and she collapsed on the floor like a dirigible making a crash landing. She huffed a bit, but otherwise acted like she hadn't stumbled at all. "You're a foolish boy. I don't know what you think you're doing, but it ain't gonna work."

"I'll keep that in mind. The papers, please."

"What papers?" Rachel asked.

"The ones you're sneaking into Nome on that dog sled."

I moved to get up. He turned the shotgun and leveled it at my head. I said, "If you want the papers, I've got to go get them. They're outside. In the sled."

He looked around the room. "Not you . . . You sit back down . . ." He pointed the shotgun at Mabel. "You. You go."

228

Rachel: "No. Not her. She's too old. She can't. I'll go."

Rachel moved to get up. The shotgun shifted a degree. "You sit." Then, to Mabel: "Let's go, grandma."

She huffed first, gathering air. It took her a great effort to stand up. First she rolled over on her knees. Then she straightened her legs and stood up with some help from Rachel and a nearby chair. The wind exploded into the room when she opened the door.

"Leave it open," Mick the Pick said. "I want to keep an eye on you. And don't be gone too long."

I tried to make small talk. "What happened to your stiletto?"

He told me to shut up. We waited. A bead of sweat inched down my temple. The wind reached in and slammed the door shut. This confused the man and caused his finger to quiver on the trigger of his gun. We waited some more. He was about to get up and peek out the window when the door cracked open and Mabel's massive body filled the frame like another door. She stepped in slowly, but then quickly moved aside.

"That one!" she screamed, pointing her finger at Mick the Pick.

A shot boomed out and the first dog exploded into bloody pulp. The second dog got a bit of leg. Then came the third, then the fourth, then the rest. Within seconds, Mick the Pick sank under a mass of angry fur. His second and last shot flashed out from the confusion, making a hole in the wall big enough for a thin man to crawl through. The dogs crowded in, fighting for a bit of throat. They poked a thousand holes into the fallen man. His cries of horror filled the room. Dog nails clacked on the hardwood floor. Clothes and skin ripped with equal ease.

"On by!" Mabel commanded. "On by!"

The dogs stopped before her second "On by!" was

done. They gathered around the old woman. One held a chrome and plastic hand in its jaws. He brought it to his mistress as if fetching a stick and dropped it at her feet. The stiletto popped out.

Mick the Pick kicked and punched the air, thinking the dogs were still on him. It was hard to tell where the clothes ended and the wounds began. He looked as if somebody had mixed red meat and cloth in a blender. I picked up the shotgun. Mabel rewarded her team with something called Doggie Bonettes. Rachel averted her eyes from the dead dog in the corner.

Chapter 23

"SO WHAT YOU GONNA DO, CHILD?" MABEL ASKED RA-
chel. The old woman had gotten into the habit of addressing all important questions to Rachel.

"We've got to get to Nome and we've got to get there
first. It's the only way even if Smalley knows we're coming," Rachel said.

I added, "Every big-time reporter within two thousand
miles is going to be in Nome for the finish of the race."
Mabel didn't seem to think this was important until Rachel
told her it was.

"Well then," Mabel said, "I guess you better get along.
I wish I had some gasoline, but like I said, I prefer to keep
to my natural ways."

She agreed to take care of our dogs for ten dollars a
day.

Rachel was so horrified by the very notion of the snowmobile we had confiscated from Mick the Pick that she
decided to let me drive. My ego swelled accordingly. The
lady on the radio said the Bohunk had stopped hanging

back. The rookie from Fairbanks had been disqualified for misplacing his official Iditarod postage stamps and Mad Dog was fading fast, stuck in Flat with three more lame dogs and the halfway silver.

No longer was our transit just a whisper in the wind, a dreamy sigh punctuated by the tireless chugging of the dogs. Now we were the simple baggage of a snarling machine that churned miles of unblemished wilderness into a thick spray of smoky exhaust. Our top speed on a flat straightaway was fifty miles an hour, just like the assemblyman's car. We were well rested and made good time.

By noon of the first day out of Rainy Pass, we'd passed a dozen irritated mushers, including the disconsolate rookie from Fairbanks. One of the mushers fired a gunshot over our heads as payment for frightening his dogs. Two others ate dinner out of a can and laughed while two of their dogs fucked each other amidst a wild tangling of the tow lines.

Fred Tunney of Homer, owner of the bitch, said in a tight-lipped deadpan: "I came here with ten dogs, and I'll leave with sixteen if we ever get your Barkem off of my Jelinda."

We pressed into the Burn. With the mountains now behind us, the world spread flat and wide like a frosted sea. The only life besides our own was the world-weary sound of Joyce the Voice, a deejay with radio station KROD:

"Put down your breakup blues, my friends. It's time to rock and roll. Tonight we got some of the Talking Heads, some Rolling Stones, and a brand new cut by Billy Joel. Angie says 'Hello' to Rick and wants him to come back home. She loves you, Rick. Go back home. Mabel says from Rainy Pass that we got two little chillens lost in the storm. That would be Miss Rachel Morgan and her unidentified squeeze. Rachel is a lady musher in the Last

Great Race and her squeeze is . . . well . . . unidentified. Joyce the Voice reminds them to cuddle close and light up a smoky fire so the state trooper rescue plane can find your camp. Iditarod Joe says two days more and it'll be time to lay down the red carpet and turn out the dogs. Mayor Bob says you got your NBC and your ABC and they all got fur coats and hairspray and are taking pretty pictures of themselves and the old hometown, too. Now here's one for Rachel Morgan and her unidentified squeeze. The Stones gonna give 'em shelter . . ."

And on into the Burn, death cooled over. In 1977, a wildfire did to the interior plain what man did to Belgium in the First World War. It had been a dry summer and there was a spark somewhere. Volunteers tried to slow the blaze, but the fire didn't stop until it had consumed all the available fuel. When it was over, there remained 360,000 acres of charcoal and swirling ash in what once were lush hunting and trapping fields.

Rachel and I zigzagged around the charred tree stumps, which poked up through the snow cover like the fingers of giants rising from their graves. We passed a few more mushers.

After the Burn came Nikolai, an old Russian trading town built by vassals of the tsar. Nikolai is a church, a store, and a couple of dozen homes surrounded by a herd of bison. The furry beasts had been shipped to Nikolai by Roosevelt in one of the stranger and more enduring of his New Deal recovery schemes. The bison cut our snowmobile a wide swath littered with turds the size and consistency of garbage can lids.

After Nikolai, McGrath. After McGrath, Flat, which rests where the Takotna River once dumped gold into a half-dozen tiny creeks. No one lives in the old ghost town of Flat these days. And no one visits either, except for the two weeks a year when the race comes through town.

THE COLD FRONT

The place is in those final days before the rusty nails hammered eighty years ago by dreamy clerks crumble into dust. In a few more years the last few joints will split and the last few wall boards will fall down, to be swept away by the wind and the drifting snow. But still the place clings to its shadow. Like an old photograph in someone else's attic, Flat has captured a frozen moment from the lives of strangers long ago forgotten.

We cruised past an old tavern full of empty bottles, toppled tables, and broken chairs. The general store was well stocked with putrefying canned goods and yellowing copies of the final edition of the *Iditarod Times*—August 25th, 1925. A player piano drifted forever on the foundation of a lost building, the walls of which have been stripped away by scavengers and the elements. The bank vault was rusted open and a church bell clapped in the wind, calling the congregation to come back and clean up the mess they'd left behind.

Mad Dog was just leaving Flat when we arrived in a blizzard of smoke and haste. He was a scrawny man with ferret eyes, an uneven beard, and a large, broken nose that hadn't mended too well.

We parked on a clearing of frozen mud next to the church and watched out of the corners of our eyes as the musher jabbered with a handful of race officials who had set up their judging table in front of the general store. A faded sign on the door behind them said: "Chopped Meet Clearance Sail: 15¢ a pound." I wondered what kind of meat it had been and where the butcher had gone.

Rachel cursed Mad Dog under her breath as the judges marked off his goods against the same sort of notebook Mabel had used. When the accounting was done, Mad Dog hopped on the runners of his sled and barked a command to his weary dogs. As he pulled away, he turned back and gave us a long, slow look. I felt a chill. It wasn't the wind.

"He'll have some more trouble down the road," Rachel said. "He's got his wheel dogs up front now. That means his fast dogs are tired out."

"Trouble down the road," I repeated, just to hear how it sounded.

Rachel went on, "The wheel dogs are the strongest ones. You put them in the back so they can turn the sled around curves and such. But he's got them up front right behind the leader so they can pull the other dogs along. He's pushing them too hard. When his wheel dogs wear out, he's finished. We'll see him again real soon."

The race officials talked about us and gawked at us for fifteen minutes before one of their number walked our way. Round, rosy cheeks bobbed atop a mountainous bulk of fur and imitation leather. "Why, hello there, folks," he said, as if he'd just noticed our presence at a crowded party. "That's a nice little machine you got there."

Rachel let me do the talking. "Thanks," I said.

"So, what brings you to Flat?" he asked, as if the town had many attractions to choose from.

I improvised. "We're from the International Snowmobile Association. Our board of directors wants to run their own machine race alone the Iditarod Trail. We figure if dogs can do it, so can a machine. We're hoping for next year, if we get the permit."

"Snowmobile, huh?"

"That's right. We want to call it the Iron Dog Iditarod and we're scouting the trail and talking to people. What do you think? The race would be real good for business. We need judges, too, and people who live along the trail could sell us food and gasoline. So what do you think?"

"I don't care. I don't live here. I'm from Shagaluk. Nobody lives here, you know. Flat's a ghost town."

The man grunted as he walked away. Five minutes later, another man bopped over to us on incredibly thin toothpick legs. With the thin limbs and a furry trunk he looked like a candy apple gone to mold. His name was Ralph Tok and he was sure that Rachel was the prettiest thing on the trail.

"I agree," I said.

"I'm not a thing," Rachel replied.

Ralph Tok paused a moment. He thought about it, then nodded slowly, as if, upon further consideration, he too believed that Rachel was not a thing.

"I agree," I said again.

Ralph Tok continued. "Yes, sir. We don't get many pretty women coming into Flat. Most look like they should be on the other end of the sled. They pay you a lot for this kind of work?"

"It's not work. We're volunteers," I said, giving the lie a life of its own. Rachel turned away.

"Yeah, sure. I bet," Ralph Tok said. "Well, you two listen up. I'm pretty sure you must know the rules by now, but as the chief judge of Checkpoint Flat, I gotta say them anyway. You shouldn't pass a movin' team and you got to turn the engine off when you're near a hundred feet of any running dogs. We'll have no littering and no hunting except for a male moose if you got a proper permit and as long as you bury the part you don't eat. And no making a lot of noise at three in the morning. Don't want to wake the dead. We don't want to hear no complaints about you snowmobile folks bothering the dogs. If all that's okay, we'll get along real good."

"Who was that who just left here?" I asked for no reason other than to change the subject.

Ralph Tok's big cheeks dipped down into the collar of

his lumberjack shirt. I didn't notice he'd been smiling all the while until he stopped. "That was Mr. Brian Dunnegan—the Mad Dog, they call him. He's a real asshole. If you run him over on the way out of town, we'll all pretend it didn't happen."

"Why's that? What about the rules?"

"That man don't play by the rules. He's a real mean one. His dogs look like they been hauling gravel—worn-out and mean, just like their master."

"We'll keep that in mind," Rachel said, rejoining the conversation.

At the sound of her voice, Ralph Tok's cheeks smiled back up to their normal elevation. "Well, that's just fine, you bet. Now how about if you folks come over our way for a bite to eat? We got steaks and rice just shipped up from the lodge in McGrath."

My own cheeks swelled from a rush of saliva saved up during a week and a half of mostly stew. Rachel tucked her elbow between two of my ribs and started drilling. It was as if we'd been married for thirty-five years. "No thanks," I said. The drilling stopped. "I think we're going to bed now. We've got a big day tomorrow. We want to catch up with the Bohunk and ask him about the trail before he gets too busy with the TV cameras. He looks like the winner. That's the word, anyway."

Ralph Tok shrugged. "Suit yourself. But don't you be running Mad Dog down while his dogs are moving. I was just kidding when I said you should run him down. He's an asshole for certain, but the rules are for assholes, too, and his dogs are still dogs even if they are mean. We got to take care of them. You don't get to pass him up until he takes a rest stop. Got that? You gotta wait until he takes a rest, you hear?"

"We hear. Thanks."

Ralph Tok toothpicked his way back to his mates and,

sure enough, we were soon tormented by the aroma of steaks cooking on an open fire. My stomach growled, but Rachel would have none of that. She opened yet another can of stew.

We crawled into our tent, listening to the wind and talking about life as a kid. She was a farm girl, I was from the city. My parents met in school, got married, conceived me. My father left me, my mother birthed me and named me Prester John to remind me of a man I'd never met. Rachel's parents grew up in the same Kansas county and met in the 4-H booth of the state fair. They married and were lured to Idaho by talk of big potatoes. This reminded me of food, but Rachel wanted to talk some more.

She wore braids and hand-me-downs and had five older brothers to feed and dozens of crusty socks to mend. At the age of eleven, she vowed never to marry unless she could be guaranteed that the union would produce no males. She renewed the vow three years later when her father died of a heart attack while weeding the turnip patch. Mama took over and raised six children on hash browns for breakfast, a cold baked potato for lunch, and potato soup for dinner. Rachel still hates potatoes, even though she hasn't eaten one in fifteen years. She blames them for the amplitude of her thighs.

"I love your thighs. They're beautiful," I said, but she would not be consoled. After a while, we drifted off to sleep. She breathed easily while I dreamed of cheeseburgers in Flat, Alaska.

But the burgers went bad and so did the dream. In my dream, a statue of Smalley spoke to dead people congregated in the church in Flat. With stone-cold lips, he said: "Bring now to me the unfed children of the world. I will make of them a nation of satisfied customers with full bellies and empty hearts. They will chant my praises and vote for True Believers in the November general election. Those who doubt me should consider the lesson of the Irish, who once tried to make potato soup without potatoes.''

I woke up with a start, my body drenched with a sticky sweat that glued me to the plastic lining of our sleeping bag. Rachel stirred in her sleep but didn't wake up. I unzipped the sleeping bag and cracked open a flap of the tent. I was snapped to my senses by a draft of cold air streaming over my fear-drenched skin. I got up on my one good knee and peeked outside the tent. Flat was still and dead, except for a low laughter from the judges and the slow chime of the church bell summoning the dead to prayer.

I don't know when we decided that Mad Dog meant to kill us, or even if we talked about it at all. But some time after leaving Flat, we saw the same danger and thought the same thought without the need for uncertain words. We looked at each other, and that was enough.

Mad Dog and his team were a gray knot in the trail. The sun spanked the snow so hard the temperature had crawled above zero for the first time in a week. But our breath still smoked and a layer of frosted exhaust had attached itself to the patchy beard I'd produced.

The geography of our predicament was this: off to the west, a desolate plain slid into the Bering Sea; to the east, more plain without rise or horizon. The trail itself was a rutted thread buttressed on either side by chunky ridges of snow which had been cleared away to make room for the thin groove over which the mushers prodded their weary dogs.

We veered off the trail, heading west toward the sea, so as to avoid Mad Dog and the trouble written all over his cruel and stupid face. At first, we went at a right angle from the trail, then cut back north into a wide turn over rough terrain that would take us past Mad Dog and then back to the trail.

As soon as he spotted us, the musher scrambled into his sled and whipped his dogs in an effort to cut us off. The sky spat out a twin-prop Cessna with skis for landing gear. As we bounced over the rutted ground, the plane dipped low to take a good look at us, then climbed back and turned into a long, slow curve.

I pushed the snowmobile to sixty miles an hour, leaving a blizzard in our wake and passing a couple of hundred yards to the west of Mad Dog. But there was no place to run, no hiding place, and the Cessna mocked our flight with long, easy turns, like a buzzard with plenty of time on its hands.

I stopped the machine, just to see what the buzzard would do. The Cessna circled once again before climbing back into the sun and turning around. With the blinding sun at its back, the only clue to the plane's approach was the ever-louder cry of its engine and the twin staccato of rapid-fire shots. Two sounds filled our ears—the sharp explosions of the machine gun and the soft, more disturbing thumping of the bullets as they kicked up a dotted line some ten feet to our left. I slipped the machine into gear but forgot to step back on the stand. The nose of the snowmobile kicked up and I lost my footing like a drunk on the dance floor. My hands sweated up a film of oil and I almost slipped off, but I was somehow able to cut the engine back and regain my footing.

The Cessna climbed back into the sun. Rachel looked back at me. Her hands flashed a wild gesture and her eyes were wide and quick. "Pres, quick . . . get back on the trail . . ."

I did as I was told. As we cut against the grain of the drifting snow, the machine lifted and flopped over the spongy ridges, lifted and flopped like a late-model Chevrolet attempting flight. Rachel sat up straight and proud, facing into the wind. My own heart raced like a BMW with valve trouble as the Cessna dipped back down and laid across our path another round of shot which came thick and heavy like a thousand baseball bats hitting a thousand pillows in ten seconds' time. I remember that sound and I remember thinking that I should have worked harder in high school and been nicer to my mother. The brain does strange things when it's about to explode into bone and gray and blood.

The Cessna climbed again. I looked back and saw the most remarkable thing. Mad Dog had stopped dead in his tracks. He was laying on the whip as hard as he could, to which the dogs responded with a howling frenzy. But they weren't going anywhere. They had had enough. When a dog won't move, a dog won't move.

I pushed a little harder on the accelerator as we neared the side of the trail, which was protected by a thick berm where the deep snow had been pushed away to make a path for the mushers. I slowed down as we prepared to climb the ridge, but the snowmobile found a soft spot and its skis dug into the lumpy crest of the snowbank. The back end kicked up and for a terrible second we stopped dead still, the nose of the machine buried in the punchy snow and the caterpillar wheels spinning foolishly six inches above the traction of the ground.

The Cessna laughed. Rachel bowed her head in prayer. I jumped off and hunched my shoulder into the back of the machine, shifting it a little. I climbed back aboard and hit the accelerator, but the tracks still spun without effect, except maybe to push us deeper into the snowbank.

Rachel and I turned back and saw Mad Dog throw down his whip and pick up his rifle. He fired two measured shots. The first slammed into my arm, knocking me over the steering wheel and into Rachel's lap. The second shot creased the nose of the snowmobile. Somehow the combination of the two impacts dislodged us from the trap. We slid into the trail and the machine pushed ahead of its own accord, blindly following the rutted path laid down days before by Herbie and the Bohunk. Rachel crawled out from under me and grabbed hold of the controls.

The night was as dark as my fevered brain. My arm felt dull and heavy, like an oak two-by-four being pounded with a six-inch nail. When I came to my senses, I was back in the womb. I said something that made no sense and Rachel stopped to give me some water. She adjusted my bandages and asked me if I was going to be okay. I said I was. The ringing in my ears changed to a slow buzz, a bit like that which had chased us into Rainy Pass. I looked up and saw a cluster of blinking, circling lights. "Him again?"

She let out a muffled sigh. "No. That's the second one. When the first plane got low on fuel, this one came up and took its place. No shooting though. He's just watching us."

We moved on for a while. My arm throbbed with a swelling pain no longer confined to the immediate area of the wound. The bullet had passed right through the fleshy part of my upper arm, but there was little bleeding and the hole was awash in antiseptics, lovingly applied. Fever came and went.

The two planes monitored our progress. They displayed no further desire to kill us and seemed content just to watch us so long as we stayed on the trail and kept moving in the direction of Nome.

The Cessna that shot at us was white and blue and circled high in an uncoiling spiral reminiscent of Slinky, the children's toy that walks down stairs. The other plane, red with yellow trim, was more adventurous and amused itself with playful spins and dives—climbing high to hide behind a cloud, then roaring down with the sun at its back to see how close it could come to our heads without actually chopping them off. After the first few scares, Rachel and I refused to duck, clinging to the last shards of dignity.

More travelogue. A light snow dusted the trail and was blown into a swirling haze by a brisk, wet wind headed inland off the Bering Sea. The temperature had risen to near zero. The land was as flat as the sea itself. We passed some more mushers and quickly narrowed the gap between ourselves and the two leaders. We traveled eight or nine miles to their every one and didn't have to stop to feed and rest dogs or change their booties. Rachel was getting used to the snowmobile and even confessed at one point that its ungodly speed might save the day. Still, she could not resist a worried laugh when there was no fuel to be had in either Shageluk or Anvik.

At Anvik, we turned west again as the ancient trail cut straight down the middle of the frozen Yukon river. Twenty-five miles later, we took a short cut off the big river across the Big and Little Yentna rivers before turning back to the Yukon near the town of Grayling. We were met at the Grayling city limits by a scruffy gang of Native kids riding big three-wheelers imported from Japan.

The three-wheelers bounced around on oversize tires, a parody of tricycles. The children who drove these noisy vehicles were of all shapes and sizes and colored a milky brown mixture of Native and caucasian, with straight black hair and eyes from someplace else. Their apparent leader was a sniffling pre-teen of indeterminate gender. I asked him/her where they got their gasoline and he/she pointed down past a side street lined with corrugated buildings and enormous banks of snow littered with planks of wood, broken furniture, and metal scraps of forgotten purpose.

"Nice ride," the leader said. The words reminded me of the schoolyard, while the tone was that of a younger boy or growing girl.

Before we could respond, the leader said "Race ya!" and scooted down the frozen clay boulevard with the others in his/her wake. Rachel put the snowmobile in gear and followed them at an easy pace to an old tin hut advertising "Food, Gas and Other Things."

The leader got off his/her machine and walked inside. The rest of the gang charged off to other mischief. We went into the store.

"Grandpa! Grandpa!" the child yelled. "Customers here."

He/she employed the rapid-fire delivery of a seasoned huckster to list the available products while taking off his/her coat: ". . . and we got cigarettes, canned peaches, and magazines all the way from New York City, which is pretty far away on a whole 'nother ocean. Out back we got some car oil, spark plugs, and ninety percent gas if you want some, lady. Papa shot a moose the other day, so we got some real nice steaks for twelve bucks a pound if you don't tell the state trooper and you don't mind the gamey taste. And there's some hamburger just in from Fairbanks if you don't like moose meat that much anymore or feel like you can't eat when it's not legal. I'm getting pretty tired of moose meat myself. This is the third moose Papa's shot so far this year. Stay here a bit and I'll go get my grandpa to open up the cash register."

The unraveling of a half-dozen winter wraps revealed her gender at last. She was thin and pretty and nearing the age when Papa would start worrying that there might be guys like him around. She came back into the room with a leathery old man leaning on her shoulder. The old man had big hands. He shuffled when he moved, his knees locked in place, his feet never leaving the ground.

The child and Rachel started talking right away, as women tend to do. "What's your name, dear?" Rachel asked.

"I'm Carmen."

"Well, I'm Rachel and this here is Prester. Say 'hello' to Carmen, Pres."

"Hello," I said. That was all I had to say and all they cared to hear. The old man and I traded smiles but held our tongues so that we could eavesdrop on their conversation.

"I'm in the eighth grade and Papa says I can go to school in Fairbanks next year if I get good grades. But that's so far away."

"Well, Fairbanks has a very good school for young ladies," Rachel said with the voice of an indulgent aunt. Then as the jealous sister: "Where *did* you get those boots?"

"Mama made them from a seal skin Uncle Bobby sent us down from Nome. Do you like them?"

And on and on. I picked up a two-week old copy of *Time* magazine. The editors were all in a tizzy about Iran (bad), a neoconservative revolution in women's fashions (good), and the decline of trade unions (depends on your point of view). I was about to exchange the magazine for a three-week old copy of *Newsweek* when the old man cleared his throat and fastened his eyes on mine. His skin was brown and folded into deep wrinkles around the eyes, as if he'd been squinting for a decade or two.

"We used to be called Hoolikachuk when I was born. Hoolikachuk was a village ten thousand years back, when your Rome and New York City were a couple of rock piles waiting to get built . . ."

He paused, estimating my interest. I said, "Hoolika-chuk?"

"That was the old town before Grayling became the new town. We used to sing in the winter and tell stories and then, you know, in the summer we'd hunt and fish so's we could eat and have something to tell stories about. Every now and then, the glaciers way up in the mountains way up river would turn to water too fast and then there would come the river with chunks of ice as big as that church over there. We'd just fold up our houses and pack up all our stuff and move on up to the high ground so we could get a view and watch the floods come through. Then when it was done, we'd go back down and put all the houses back up and it was no big deal so nobody cared anyway. Then about '56 we got electricity, so here comes toasters and TV and rock radios and blenders and all that kinda stuff so as when '62 comes and also too another flood, all the wires got soaked and the TVs all got shorted out and even some people had wood houses by then and the wood houses all got flooded too and it was a big mess. Think of that. We had a thousand floods in six thousand years, I guess, and nobody cares too much. But we get the electric power and TV sets and even the flood gets to be a big deal. So we all packed up and moved the whole village up here to the high ground where the water never goes. Now we got to walk two miles to go fishing and the creek out back where the sewer pipe goes smells like old pee every spring when the ice melts. All that just 'cause of the TV. And what do you get from the TV but a lotta junk we don't need? We called the new village Grayling which is a white man's name even though we're all Indians and we all come from Hoolikachuk. Say, mister, you okay? You don't look so good."

I didn't feel well either. The old man grabbed my elbow

and we shuffled to a folding chair tucked behind the magazine rack.

"Say, women," he said, interrupting an animated conversation. "You got a sick man sitting here and all you do is talk about clothes and how to spend his money. Carmen, you go in your papa's house and get your mama's medicine box. And you, lady . . . you better fix your man back up or he ain't gonna make it to Nome."

I had trouble breathing. My arm throbbed a warning. I should have laughed, but I couldn't. Rachel asked me if I was okay, then said to the girl, "Carmen, get aspirin, a towel, and some cool water—not cold, cool. Warmer than you'd drink."

Carmen returned with a pitcher of water and a shopping bag bulging with a variety of seemingly modern medical utensils. The child patted my head with a damp towel while Rachel unbuttoned my shirt. The grandfather seemed disappointed that I had no hair on my chest. He wrinkled his nose and clucked his teeth when my sleeve was peeled back to show a mess of purple skin and a bloodstained bandage with a new wet spot. The child, coolly efficient as a veteran nurse, helped Rachel dress the wound. In Grayling, it seems, doctoring is women's work and home surgery is a commonplace occurrence. The child told her grandfather to open the door. He did so. The fresh air revived me.

"We'll never make it," I said.

"We will. We must," Rachel insisted.

"What's wrong, Mr. Prester?" the child asked.

"Too much TV," the old man replied.

I slept with the old man, who's snoring sounded like the flatulation of a large animal. Rachel slept with Carmen. They giggled and talked for several hours before falling asleep. Despite all the noise, I slept deeply and felt much better in the morning.

We ate breakfast, filled up the tank, and hit the trail. The Cessna picked us up as soon as we passed the city limits, wherever they were.

Dawn and more travelogue, through the vast sameness of the solid sea, a sparkling flatness beyond compare. Rachel astonished me with her obscure talent for distinguishing one sparkling flatness from another, for knowing the difference between two seemingly identical knobs of stone. She chattered about Eagle Slide and Eagle Island and actually knew which was which. Past Kaltag and Kaltag Portage, the Nulatto Hills, North River, Egavik Creek, Junction Creek, Beeson Slough, Reindeer Hills, and on past Shaktoolik and into Norton Bay, a frozen slab of the Bering Sea.

And all the while, the Cessna circled above us. The ice pack of Norton Bay creaked and groaned and the girl on radio station KROD said Herbie and the Bohunk were neck and neck less than a day's run from the finish line in Nome. The TV cameras were waiting for them, and Smalley was waiting for us.

Chapter 24

THE FAHRENHEIT AND THE CENTIGRADE DROPPED A DE-
gree every ten miles or so. Rachel wasn't bothered by the
cold. She guided us north.

The pilot who liked to fly high tracked us through Koyuk, Moses Point, and Elim. His partner took over at Golovin and buzzed us as we passed over frozen Golovin
Lagoon. After that, the plane was kept at a more comfortable altitude by the low ridges of the Kwiktalik Mountains and again by the sloping walls of Topuk Funnel, a
slippery canyon that worked like the nozzle of a garden
hose: as the passage narrowed, the velocity of the wind
accelerated. The pilot resumed his teasing, diving tricks
after we passed through the funnel and bothered us again
as we traveled the flat shoreline leading to Nome. He
stayed close until we caught up with Herbie and the Bohunk just outside of Port Safety, twenty-two miles from
the finish line. Twenty-two miles. That's four hours by
dog, a half hour by snowmobile. Ours needed a tune-up.

We slowed to a halt just outside the amber glow of their
campfire. "Son of a gun gonna spook my dogs," Herbie

said, shaking his fist at the diving plane. He leaned down and whispered something to the Bohunk, who nodded once, not wasting any motion on his chief rival's problem.

The low buzz of the plane drowned the soft whispers of the men. When the plane dipped low for another pass, the Bohunk handed his shotgun to Herbie. The Eskimo blasted a round of shot at the plunging Cessna, which thereafter adopted the more conservative flight pattern of its mate.

Rachel sighed. I smiled buffoonishly. We looked at the gun, admiring its easy authority.

"Nice night," Herbie said, The Bohunk groaned his own harsh greeting and then lost his thoughts in the campfire. He didn't want to be bothered.

"What a beautiful night," Rachel gushed. "This is how it was meant to be: the night quiet and full of stars."

"Yeah, right," the Bohunk barked, although his voice betrayed just a hint of excitement. Rachel reminded him of that which he had not had. "Right," the Bohunk repeated, although this time it seemed like he meant it. "God's own light. What're you doin' out here? You two one of those reporters from New York come to ask the 'Hunk how he do it?"

"No," I said. "We're just passing through." But they both ignored me and focused on Rachel, who added, "Mind if we join you?"

They didn't mind at all. In fact, they stumbled over each other clearing her a nice, warm spot by the fire. I was left to hang out on the fringe of the circle, making the best of the few currents of warmth drifting my way. The pain in my arm had subsided to a dull throb.

"Wouldn't you be Rachel Morgan?" the Bohunk asked.

"Yes. That's right. And this is my friend, Pres Riordan."

The two men looked at me and nodded, wondering, no doubt, how a guy like me got a girl like her.

Herbie: "Yea, we heard about you two on the radio. They said you got stuck in the Burn, just this side of Rainy."

The Bohunk, to Rachel: "That's what you get for carryin' a trail mate in your basket. I won't have a woman on the trail unless she's got her own transportation or she's ugly enough to leave behind, although I guess he's ugly enough. Where's your team?"

Rachel: "He's not ugly. We left them back at Mabel's place. They were too tired to finish, so we thought we'd come on ahead and see which one of you guys get the gold this year."

The Bohunk laughed: "Hell, lady. You don't have to go to Nome to figure that one out. You coulda knowed that before the race begun. I'm gonna win. I always do, unless I get a kind heart on or don't feel like it."

Herbie coughed into the fire, paused for thought. He used bare fingers to rake something from his beard. He threw the catch into the fire. Whatever it was made a sharp, crackling sound as it burst into flames. He mumbled, "Wouldn't talk like that if Susan Butcher was still in the race."

I nudged closer to the fire. Its flames illuminated the men and gave me my first good look at our hosts. They had the featureless profiles men display in the northern precincts of Alaska. Both wore thick, furry coats and stained racing bibs. They blew large clouds of smoky breath into the fire and up into the night. Voices and beards and the Bohunk's boasting ways were the main distinctions between the two. The Bohunk had a low, rough voice while Herbie talked in a light, twangy tenor. Herbie had a black, stringy beard while the Bohunk's was red and fluffy. Herbie was quiet; the Bohunk couldn't stop talking about himself.

"Yep, I think I might just have to take the lead here

pretty soon. Only twenty miles left, so I suppose I got to stop hanging back sometime. How's Cupcake doing, Herb? She looks a little lame to me.''

"She's doin' fine and you ain't goin' nowhere. You followed me this far and you'll follow me down Front Street.'' He turned to Rachel. ''The 'Hunk here runs a coward's race. He been trailin' me by a thousand yards ever since we left Flat, a day or so before the storm that socked you in. I could wait for three days and he still won't blaze the trail. But as soon as I start out, he follows right up close behind like pups after mama.''

"You hurt me, Herb,'' the Bohunk pretended. ''I let you win one back in '79 and that's how you got to talk about your old buddy the 'Hunk.'' Then he, too, turned to Rachel, as if she were the referee. ''Yeah, I let him win one so his 'Skimo buddies would have something to talk about and this is what I get. That's gratefulness for you.'' Then, whispering to her, as if Herbie and I couldn't hear: ''Can't say as I blame him, though. You cut the trail from Anchorage to Safety and just when you're about to catch some gold, the old Bohunk moves up and grabs the fifty thou.''

Louder now, and back to Herbie: ''Must be kinda frustrating, hey, Herb?''

"Kiss it, 'Hunk,'' Herbie said, angry. ''Now I change my mind. I ain't movin' away 'til you do. I'm gonna sit right on your tail for a couple of miles. I bet you don't know what to do without my asshole to look at. I'll let you flatten out the trail for a bit, and then I'll pass you real quick when your dogs get worn out in the deep snow. You goin' first. I'll wait here for a week if I got it. Wait here 'til Mad Dog comes up behind us if that's the way it's gonna be.''

The Bohunk clapped his hands and rubbed them over the fire, his eyes glowing with mischief. ''Maybe so,'' he said, looking over the fire and into Herbie's eyes, like a card player trying to tell the difference between a bluff and a flush. "Yea, maybe so. But I'm looking at your little Cupcake over there and I'm thinking that she ain't lame at all and that it's just a play and that the real thing is she's starting to act a little antsy in her sleep and wouldn't mind at all if her 'Skimo daddy tried to make a break for it."

Herbie got mad: "I'm no 'Skimo. I am an Inupiat Eskimo. Got it? Inupiat Eskimo. There ain't no 'Skimos on God's good earth."

Then he blushed and turned away, as if embarrassed by his own anger. He stood up and picked his way through a patch of snoring dogs. He retrieved a handful of dog booties from the carriage of his sled and brought them back to the campfire. The Bohunk prodded him again about sneaking out when he wasn't looking, but Herbie ignored the comment and concentrated on the booties—sorting them into groups of four—two red and two blue in each set.

Then it was the Bohunk's turn to tend to his dogs. He fetched a large plastic bag from his carriage and poured thick brown goop into a black metal pot.

"What's that?" I asked. He ignored the question until Rachel asked it again thirty seconds later. "It's my own special recipe. We got a quarter part of Mabel Woodley beaver, a half part caribou, and a quarter part of something I wouldn't tell you what even if you promised to sleep with me when I get to Nome."

Rachel smiled coolly. Herbie protested. "Hey now, 'Hunk. You just cut out that kinda talk or we're gonna have it out right here and now."

"Yea, cut it out," I added weakly.

The Bohunk changed the subject. "Good news, Herbie. My pups are eating just fine. How come your dogs ain't et yet?" He looked at me, desperate for an audience. "A lotta dogs be too tired to eat this far along. Dogs is smart that way. They know if you can't make 'em eat, you can't make 'em run. Won't eat if they don't wanna run. I remember one time—I think it was '80 or '81—I come outta Shaktoolik taking it easy like I like to do sometimes, and there was old Jeffrey Marquardt by the side of the trail trying to force his played-out dogs to eat. 'Come on, Ramjet,' Marquardt says, and Ramjet—that's his second leader—he just lies down and rolls over like a house dog trying to rub out some fleas. So Marquardt takes a big old fistful of beaver meat and starts to shove it down old Ramjet's throat. Clamps his mouth shut so as he doesn't spit it back out and then moves along to the next dog and so on. None of 'em wanted to eat, 'cause a sled dog might be dumb but he ain't no fool. Of course, by the time he got done, Ramjet had throwed up and the others all followed suit, Ramjet being the leader and all. Musta taken Marq all day to feed seven dogs. I won that race, too.''

Herbie said, ''You win 'em all 'Hunk. You win 'em all. Leastwise you win 'em so long as Susan Butcher don't be runnin'. Too bad her leader got stomped by the moose or maybe we'd have some quiet out here. Now how 'bout shuttin' up so's my team can get some rest before we show you the way to Front Street.''

''Now come on, Herb. Don't say all that. I don't win 'em all. Don't forget I let you win one in '79 just so you and your Innn-ooo-peeee-at Eeeskimo buddies wouldn't feel so left out.'' Then to Rachel: ''And maybe if you're nice, I'll let you win one, too. Maybe next year. You wanna be nice to the Bohemian? You wanna win one sometime?''

''You wanna go fuck yourself?'' I said.

The faces around the fire—mine included—registered something between amusement and shock. The Bohunk could have broken my back with his bare hands, but instead he laughed and leaned over the fire, slamming me on the back with his meaty paw.

"All right! All right! Your boy's got a little life in there, Rachel. I worried there for a bit. I like to see a little life in a man. It helps keep his eyes open. Okay . . . now that everybody's awake, why don't you tell us what you're doing out here. Herbie wants to know how come that asshole pilot up there is chasing you around and agitating his dogs."

The wind held still and easy, now and then rolling over our camp to be licked by the flames of the open fire. The stars burned brighter than they ever had before and the firewood snapped sometimes. The embers subsided into a pulsing glow.

Rachel talked first and when she was done, they asked me to read my story out loud. I had to invent the first few paragraphs because they weren't written yet. The words seemed lifeless and very much out of place under the sort of stars that had come out that night. There was a lot they didn't understand, so they made me read it back and they pestered us with questions and made us explain some more. Herbie didn't understand farming too well. Rachel explained it. The Bohunk wanted proof, so we uncurled the bundled tube of Jeffrey Williams's last will and testament. The Eskimo held the tube in his hand, measuring its weight as if pounds were truth.

The Bohunk wanted more proof; I showed him the scabs where my toes had been and the gunshot wound in the flab of my arm. Rachel talked about the airplane circling above our heads. I added, "Why else would a girl like her run down the trail with a guy like me?" This the Bohunk was able to understand, although Rachel insisted it was more than that.

Herbie leaned over the fire. "I got a cousin Jean who

married a guy from Toyukuk City. Tell the part again about how the babies got born dead already.''

Rachel told him again and when she was done he suggested they flip a coin for the honor of it all. The Bohunk said he didn't have any honor and he didn't have any relatives from Toyukuk City.

''I got to say it's not my problem. Now I'll help you, of course, if I can. But my main thing is the fifty thou.''

We shared the moose meat steak Rachel had purchased in Grayling and Herbie finally fed his dogs. Cupcake wasn't lame after all. Her tail was high and she was downright pleased that I had agreed to cut the trail with a stolen snowmobile.

I jumped aboard and headed for Nome. The cold front banged against the shore and hell was made of ice instead of fire and the wind was so cold it seemed to burn the thin wedge of flesh exposed around my eyes. After a while, I didn't feel the wind anymore and I kept myself company with a speech I'd rehearsed but never given: ''I'm going to Nome and I'll tell you why. It's not for the starving children of Africa and it's not for the unborn children of Toyukuk City. It is for you, Rachel Morgan. I'm going to Nome because you want me to. You make me alive and I'd rather die as a live man than live as a dead one.''

Chapter 25

NOME WAS MANY THINGS THAT NIGHT. FIRST IT WAS A memory from a book I'd read one time which described the gold rush of 1898, and a beach crowded with 20,000 prospectors and the tyranny of Judge Arthur Noyes, who resolved all disputed claims by taking personal custody of the gold. When I reached Cape Nome, a rocky suburb to the southeast, Nome became a low but full murmur like a sea change in the making. When I turned onto Front Street, the murmur became singing and laughter and loud conversation and Nome became a throbbing glow of festivity.

I reached town shortly after midnight, but no one would sleep that night. Front Street was decorated with banners and flags and the unearthly white light of a dozen television cameras illuminating hundreds of besotten faces. NBC held court from a large pipe scaffolding bigger than any building in town. An ABC crew sucked local color into a cathode tube. The townspeople and their guests celebrated the biggest day of Nome's long, cold year. A band played a tune from the gold rush days.

The finish line of the race was marked by something

called the Great Burl Arch across which was strewn a banner which read: "The Iditarod Trail Champion Sled Dog Race—1,049 miles from Anchorage to Nome." The burls were the tumors of a tree cancer which caused the trunks to balloon into a bulbous, pregnant swell. Four such afflicted trees had been lashed together into a square, polished down, and varnished to mark the end of the most grueling task man has devised for dog. A handful of children clung to the top crosspiece of the arch and fought for custody of a seat on the burl.

My appearance was the cause of a brief pulse in the general excitement when someone mistook my snowmobile for the winning dog sled. Disappointed fans hooted and hollered at me as I passed through the finish gate. A Nome policeman growled at me to get out of the way. A man wearing a fox fur hat with the poor beast's face still attached shouted to ask me if I'd seen Herbie or the Bohunk.

"Neck and neck," I shouted back.

The crowd pitched for a second in reply, then quickly subsided to its normal roar.

The town was mostly dark on the other side of the Great Burl Arch, with only a house light or two poking through the big arctic night. I scanned the shadows for trouble, but the only sign of life at this end of Front Street was the merry din leaking through the Great Burl Arch. The band played ragtime. A woman's scream shattered into hysterical laughter.

One of the house lights came from the office of the *Nome News,* which was tucked on a side street between a general store and a low-slung building with lace curtains that looked like a Currier and Ives portrait of a whorehouse. The front office was dark, but a bright light spilled out from a room in back. I tapped on the storm window and the light was blocked by a large shadow belonging to a small child. I bent close to the glass so the little boy could get a good look at me. This sent him hurrying back into the light from which next emerged the figure of Mary, wife of Ralph the Obit Man. She recognized me and opened the door.

"Prester John," she said. "How you been? You look like you been on a bender."

This put me off a bit, since I hadn't had a drink in quite some time. But then I remembered that I hadn't seen a mirror either. "I've been on the trail, Mary. All the way from Anchorage just to see Ralph."

Mary drifted back into the light, which came from the composing room of the *News*. Her three youngest children had made an assembly line for the cutting and pasting of advertisements for a special Iditarod edition of Alaska's Widest Newspaper. My intrusion brought their work to a halt.

"Back to it, kids," she said. But before they could bend to their tasks, she grabbed the youngest and set him down on the swell of her wide and comfortable hip. The other two dropped their Exacto knives and gathered around their mother. It was a picture of a worried family. Mary said, "You got a face full of trouble, Pres. Don't you bring your trouble into our home. We've got plenty of our own already."

I gave an awkward and not very effective account of the situation. Mary was not impressed. "So? We're a local newspaper. Nobody reads us in Toyukuk City or any of the places you're talking about."

"But Mary . . ." I said, then changing course in mid-sentence: "I should really talk to Ralph. Where is he?"

She pointed her nose out there somewhere and showed me the door. I walked close to the buildings on the dark side of the Great Burl Arch, hiding in the shadows for protection.

* * *

THE COLD FRONT

There must have been about ten thousand racing fans gathered for the finish of that Iditarod. Most of them were residents of Nome or nearby villages, but there were plenty of visitors from Anchorage and points south.

About half of the revelers warmed themselves in the taverns, milling about on floors sprinkled with sawdust, which in its turn was sprinkled with beer, spittle, cigarette ash, and sweat until it achieved the consistency of a lumpy brown pudding. The rest of the spectators lined either side of Front Street. They were just as drunk as their warmer mates and a few had tucked their bodies into door frames, window sills, cardboard boxes, and an old rain barrel for protection against the bitter cold wind blowing in off the Bering Sea. This jubilant throng made a great noise and a great cloud of steam which the lights of the television cameras painted an eerie blue.

I searched for Ralph among this confusion, starting with the crowd outside. Time was short and I wanted to be in place when the first musher arrived.

I've never searched a more congenial crowd. I poked my nose into other people's faces and I was offered free drink, free food, and a warm place to stay. Usually, people in a crowd wear psychic armor and hunch their shoulders to avoid contact with the next person. But this crowd enjoyed one another and crushed together for warmth, especially in the vicinity of the Italian television crew, who still had a long wait for Gino DeVino, the game show winner. Various women responded to my earnest search with a kiss, hugs, two unambiguous invitations, and a grope. Despite this encouragement, my search was futile, although I did see on a small grandstand set up for the press near the Great Burl Arch, Jamie Farrell scribbling furiously in his reporter's notebook.

My search for Ralph the Obit Man moved indoors. I started at the Board of Trade, a honky-tonk as old as ragtime itself. The swinging doors were plastered against the outside wall, as if the place had burst from the dense concentration of festivity within.

This was not a job for someone as short as I. I used my left shoulder as a wedge and slowly inched my way sideways through the crowd, using tiny slide-steps and taking advantage of every opening, no matter how small. I saw a lot of male shoulders and a lot of female breasts, but only a few faces and none resembling Ralph's. It seemed to be a hopeless task, but I inched into the Board of Trade toward a red light stage where dancers with heavy lipstick and garter belts did the cancan. I hopped on the stage and for a few seconds had a good view of the crowd. Then a large man with a beard and a flashlight told me that if I didn't get off the stage right now he would put me on the floor himself. I worked my way back outside again with no result other than the acquisition of a thick coat of sawdust on my shoes and the cuffs of my blue jeans.

Next I entered the Gold Nugget Tap, which was smaller and even more crowded. This place featured a banjo player who could not be heard by anyone other than himself. Then I tried Dirty Dan's Pub and Carlotta's CanCan Café, still to no avail.

At Bob's Bar I spotted Phil Norwood, city editor of the *Anchorage Herald,* in an intense and animated conversation with a pretty native girl half his age.

"How you doing, Phil?" I shouted into his ear.

His jaw dropped. His eyes widened. He tried to speak but couldn't. His girlfriend gave me a peck on the cheek. "You from Anchorage, too?" she asked. I nodded. She said, "There's a big party over at the Nome Air hangar after the winner comes in. You come too and we'll have a lot of fun. I'm pulling for Herbie now that Susan got scratched."

I nodded and shouted at Phil, "Stick around and that

story's going to pop. I got to find Ralph. Have you seen him around?''

Phil said something I couldn't hear. It looked like ''No.''

I lost count of the bars and have forgotten their names. Each place was packed to the rafters with drunks and smelled like beer and day-old sweat. Each time I entered a place I felt like the fifth pound of potatoes in a four-pound bag. Each time I left a place, I felt like a champagne cork that had just been popped. My search continued until I popped out of one tavern and happened to look up at the Great Burl Arch, atop which sat Ralph the Obit Man fiddling with a camera.

''Hey, Ralph!'' I screamed, with all the effect of a whisper at the Super Bowl.

The Great Burl Arch was slippery with varnish and ice, but I managed to climb aboard thanks to a good handhold on one of the burls and a boost from a young man anxious to show his girl how strong he was. The commotion caught the attention of Ralph, who helped haul me up the last foot or so. He directed me to a flat spot. I leaned against a burl and straddled the arch to steady myself.

It was the best seat in town. Behind us was the darkened part of Nome here the *News* was located. The crowd milled below us while the trail spilled out from the Great Burl Arch into a channel of glittering light and snow which turned gray and then black again after five hundred yards.

''Nice setup Ralph,'' I screamed.

He smiled, nodded, and took my picture. A flash wasn't necessary thanks to the television lights. He screamed back, ''They always save this spot for the *News*. It's one of the perks I get for living here all year round.'' He paused a second to advance the film and fuss with the light meter. He pointed the camera this way and that and set it on his lap. "What're you doing here, Pres? I thought you got canned."

The Great Burl Arch was very cold. I shifted around and sat on my hands. "I'm working freelance. I've got a story for you."

He lifted his camera and pointed it at me again, but didn't take a picture this time. "What kind of story?"

I eased my hands from under my seat and pulled a thin fold of paper from an inside pocket. The excitement of the crowd pitched again while Ralph hunched over the story. He didn't bother to look up; he knew a false alarm. I figured the first musher was still a good hour away. Ralph folded the papers and handed them back to me. "This is a national story. Where's the local angle?"

I put the story back in my pocket and my hands back under my seat. "The local angle's coming. If it's a good one, will you print it?"

Ralph turned away from me and took a picture of the crowd. "Will it get me sued?"

I shouted back, "Hell no. It'll get you a goddamn Pulitzer Prize."

Ralph seemed to think that would be okay. "We'll talk about it later."

"We've got to talk about it now. I want you to run it in the special edition tomorrow."

"No way. That's just for the Iditarod and nothing else."

Now it was my turn to smile and nod. "But that's the local angle."

It wasn't until I was back on the ground and heading toward the *News* that I realized our entire conversation had been observed by Jamie Farrell from the press box and by Monique Peterson from the doorway of the Gold Nugget Tap. I saw Jamie pick up the telephone and I saw Monique and two of her companions advance toward me. I saw Ralph taking pictures, oblivious to it all.

It was the sort of slow-motion chase for which I am well equipped. I might have escaped if I'd had someplace to go. I turned around and crossed the street, stumbling a bit as if I'd had too much to drink. This gave me a pretty good sideways glance at my pursuers, who were as anxious as I to avoid a scene, although it's hard to imagine that anything would constitute a scene in Nome at the finish of the Iditarod. They slowly narrowed the gap between us until I reached the swinging doors of the Board of Trade and performed what I consider to be an inspired and acrobatic maneuver: I dropped to all fours and plunged into the jam-packed tavern at knee level.

People are thinner at their ankles than at their shoulders, so I made much better time than on my previous expedition through the Board of Trade. With two exceptions, nobody paid much attention to me. One woman thought I was trying to look up her dress, but by the time she notified her boyfriend I was long gone, like an insect scooting through tall grass. Another woman thought I had invented a new dance and wanted to join me. She followed me all the way to the alley, where I gently explained that I was some sort of lunatic and no, I didn't want to go to a party either.

The alley was full of drunks and howling dogs. The drunks where asleep and the dogs were locked up and howling mad because they sensed there was some sort of dog excitement in the air from which they had been excluded. It was pitch dark and the ground was made of a slick mud covered with a slicker glaze of ice. I tried to brush away some of the wet sawdust which had attached itself to the front of the clothes during my crawl through the Board of Trade, but the sub-zero air had frozen the goop in place.

THE COLD FRONT

I must have looked pretty disgusting when I knocked on the front door of the *News*. Mary answered the door with the assistance of Mick the Pick, whose face looked like it was inside out thanks to Mabel's dogs.

As they ushered me inside, Mary hissed, "You bastard! How dare you bring trouble into my home. We have young children here, you bastard."

Chapter 26

HUGH SMALLEY HELD COURT BEFORE A TELEVISION SET IN a corner of the pressroom crammed with yellowing copies of the *Nome News*. He wore camouflage green of the sort affected by hunters who approach the killing of animals as a military exercise and sat on one of the oversize rolls of paper used in the manufacture of Alaska's Widest Newspaper. At his feet was Monique Peterson. Her hair was blond again. Smalley caressed it.

"The man of the hour," he said to me. Then to Mary, "Go about your business, madame. We'll stay out of your way. Joseph will assist you."

A guy named Joseph grabbed Mary by the elbow and led her into the composing room. She glared at me. Monique smiled. "Hello, Pres," she said. "How've you been?"

While I tried to think of something clever to say, Smalley answered on my behalf. "Mr. Riordan has been a very busy boy, Neekie. You can tell by the sawdust on his pants."

"Who won?" I asked, nodding at the television.

The black-and-white flickered in silence, lending a pasty aspect to Smalley's already somber countenance. His face was a question. He did not understand.

"The race," I said, in explanation. "The Iditarod. Who won?"

"Nice clothes," said Monique. The sawdust had started to melt. A clump plopped to the floor.

Smalley made a motion at the television set and a dutiful assistant turned up the volume. The blondly confident local newsman chanted clichés to fill the time between advertisements:

"Well, folks, we've got a photo finish here. At last report, Herbie Ingnukluk and the Bohemian were within seconds of each other just outside of Cape Nome. The winner should be here within the next twenty minutes, but we still don't know who the winner is. Herbie's got his malamute Cupcake in the lead this year. Cupcake was just a wheel dog when Herbie won in '79, but he's lost some weight and gained some speed. Wouldn't you say so, John?"

"That's right, Bob. Cupcake used to be a wheel dog."

Smalley flashed another signal and an eager assistant turned the sound down, leaving one of those uncertain quiets waiting for someone to speak. We all looked at Smalley. Smalley looked around. We all followed his eyes.

The room was built around the printing press. At one end were heavy rolls of paper and dirty barrels with ink inside. At the other end were neat mountains of newspapers lashed together with plastic straps. In between were crazy piles of newspaper mistakes: smeared papers with too much ink, or too little. Alaska's widest page negatives spilled from a plastic garbage can.

Page one wasn't ready yet. It was pinned to a corkboard

and had a big blank spot waiting for a story about the race and a picture of the winner. Smalley peeled the page off of the corkboard and waved it over his head.

"I sometimes wonder why people read newspapers anymore. Television is so much faster and much more real. And it does all your thinking for you and saves a lot of trouble. I prefer TV myself. It has a great reach but little grasp and allows the viewer no time for reflection. Television is perfect for a scoundrel like me. Wouldn't you say so, Mr. Riordan?"

Someone turned the sound up and the television said, "The Bohunk . . . excuse me . . . I mean the Bohemian is probably the best musher in the field now that Susan Butcher has scratched. He's got a strong team and he is a master at confusing the opposition. Isn't that right, John?"

"That's right, Bob. The Bo . . . Bohemian . . . certainly has the psychological edge, but at this stage of the race speed and strength are what really matter and that brings us back to Cupcake."

Smalley shifted gears. Monique was transfixed by his ravings, which came out of nowhere. "Think about the Bomb, Mr. Riordan. Let the words roll around on your tongue like a piece of hard candy. The Bomb. Nine million soldiers died in World War One, but that wasn't enough, so the same fools waged World War Two and twenty million more died. Then came the Bomb, and we hate it but if we think about it at all we don't know what to think. We haven't had World War Three yet because of its evil genius. How can something as ghastly as the Bomb save the world? The Reverend Malthus would have understood. He wasn't afraid of the truth."

The television set flickered and then went black as Channel Five had some more technical difficulties. Mick the Pick started fussing with his artificial hand and used it to scratch one of the scabs on his face. I wondered how he'd escaped from Mabel, but I feared the answer so I didn't ask the question. Channel Five solved its problem and the television set crackled back to life.

"One thing is certain. The recent dominance of women in the Iditarod is about to end. Isn't that right, John?"

"That's right, Bob. The ladies have won this race every year since 1985, when Libby Riddles broke the ice. Since then, it's been all Susan Butcher and it could've been Susan again if her leader hadn't been stomped by that moose. You can't run too far without a good leader, Bob. That's one of the unwritten rules of the Iditarod."

The television camera scanned the crowd. Ralph the Obit Man was still perched atop the Great Burl Arch. There was no sign of Herbie or the Bohunk.

Smalley looked away from the screen. He was staring at something, but he wasn't staring at anything in the pressroom of the *Nome News* or anything in this world as we know it. He was possessed by a vision all his own. Monique stroked his camouflaged knee. Smalley said, "They will sell their freedom for a penny, I'm sure. Most people will choose prosperous bondage over impoverished freedom any day."

He blinked twice and came back to Earth. "But enough of that, Mr. Riordan. History calls. I'd like the papers, please."

"Papers?" I said. I tried to sound casual, but I'm sure I sounded frightened.

Mick the Pick shifted in his seat and stood up. Smalley said, in a tone of strained patience, "Yes, the papers. The last will and testament of that thief Jeffrey Williams."

"I don't have them."

Smalley looked down at Monique. She touched her left breast and pointed her eyes at me. Smalley flashed a hand

269

signal and Mick the Pick advanced. The cheerful babble of the television was the only sound in the place:

"This is it, folks. Our spotter says we've got a team on Front Street. Get me a bib number, John. Is it Herbie or is it the Bohunk?"

It happened very slowly. His artificial hand closed into a fist and dropped to his side. I could hear the sputtering piston of my heart, and his breath, quick and uneven. One of Mabel's dogs had taken a big bite out of the baked potato that was his nose.

One of the TV guys said, "What do you mean neither? It can't be neither. Who is it?"

Mick the Pick pressed a button on his cuff and the stiletto popped out of a plastic knuckle. He charged. I ducked. The stiletto poked an X-shaped hole in the tin wall of the *News* pressroom. Mick grabbed me with his other hand.

One of the TV guys said, "No! It can't be. What's her name?"

The punches and kicks fell like a rain of bowling balls. I soon lost the trick of telling one pain from another, of knowing where the shattered elbow stopped and the hemorrhaging gut began. Blackened eyes melted into ringing ears. My senses became a dull mush. But for some reason, I was able to focus my eyes on a naked lightbulb swinging from the ceiling. The lightbulb was real to me— the lightbulb and the concrete floor, which felt cool against my cheek and seemed to tremor ever so slightly, as if from an earthquake thousands of miles away. Mick the Pick leaned over me, his breath heavy and fetid. He dug the strong fingers of his real hand into my throat, feeling around for that special soft spot that only guys like him know about. He found that spot and started to squeeze. My ears were filled with a different hum. The lightbulb on the ceiling exploded into a thousand dancing stars. The last thing I heard was Rachel's voice, crackling over the television set.

"I know you've got a lot of questions, and I'll answer them. But first there's something I've got to say. Jeffrey Williams was a friend of mine . . ."

Chapter 27

THE SPRING THAT HAD ONCE PROMISED SO MUCH TROUBLE waited until the last possible moment, then broke free with frantic energy. The late thaw gave the Alaska Department of Environmental Protection just enough time to drain the sludge pit and put the Toyukuk River on the comeback trail. They're still fighting over where to put the stuff.

Smalley made the cover of *Time* again that year, but so did fifty-one other men, women, trends, and events. The story flared white hot for a while before subsiding into the fuzzy fringe of our national memory. Ralph didn't win the Pulitzer Prize, but he did win the Horace Newberry Award for Business Journalism, which included a check for $10,000. He sent me a thank-you note.

Like a true local journalist, Ralph had changed my lead to beef up the local angle and pushed the important stuff back to an inside page. But he left most of the story alone, swearing he'd strangle me if he got sued. He didn't get sued. If, by chance, you missed the March 24th special Iditarod edition of the *Nome News*, my story started out like this, minus some typographical errors which Ralph tried to blame on me:

NOME STUNNED BY CHAOTIC
IDITAROD FINISH

By Prester John Riordan
News correspondent

Nome residents received a big surprise Tuesday night when the first Iditarod musher came through the Great Burl Arch. They were expecting Herbie Ingnukluk of St. Mary's or Beau "The Bohemian" Dremysl of Palmer to end the recent dominance of women in the Last Great Race.

But again this year, the first musher to the finish line was a woman, bearing incredible allegations of murder, fraud, and crimes against the Earth on the part of one of Alaska's most prominent citizens. Rachel Morgan of Talkeetna was later disqualified when it was learned that the dog team which carried her into Nome was registered to Ingnukluk.

The St. Mary's musher apparently gave up an excellent chance at the first place money so that Morgan could use the Iditarod spotlight to state her charges against Hugh Smalley, chief executive officer of Entco Investments Corporation.

Dremysl claimed the first place prize when the judges made their ruling several hours later. But by then, the television cameras were packed up and Nome residents had already finished celebrating the most incredible dash up the Iditarod Trail since Leonard Seppala and associates delivered life-saving diphtheria serum to Nome more than sixty years ago.

"I had reporters on my butt for a thousand miles and now that I won it nobody wants to talk to me,"

273

Dremysl said after being informed that he had won his third Iditarod Trail championship.

"I'm just a Native man helping his Native brothers way over there about a thousand miles away in Toyukuk City," said Ingnukluk when asked to explain his selfless decision to let Morgan mush his dogs into Nome.

Reporters from the state, the nation, and even Italy were befuddled by the false finish and by the serious allegations Morgan made in front of live television cameras.

Morgan accused Smalley of . . .

Ralph put Alaska's Widest Press into overdrive for the occasion. Mary didn't like it, but she and the kids pitched in. The press broke down twice and some of the pages were smeared. But the photograph of Rachel amidst a sea of astonished faces, with dogs at her feet and a thick tube of paper in her hand, was crisp and beguiling. The paper got out before the people of Nome and the visiting newsmen had recovered from their post-race hangovers. We made sure each of the bewildered sports reporters had a copy of the *Nome News* to help them explain to their editors the bizarre dispatches they had filed the night before. The Italian TV crew was most excited, because they still had several days to kill before Gino DeVino would cross the finish line. They turned on their camera and peppered Rachel with questions she didn't understand.

Smalley was last seen fleeing from a reporter for the *New York Times* who usually wrote about sports but had a couple of questions he thought he should ask.

Even so, it took several days for the story to make the top of the news in the Outside media. The day after the race, NBC made a short comedy of the whole affair by turning Rachel's speech at the finish line into an "aren't people funny?'' story. That same day, United Press International put out a wire service account describing some paranoid fantasy Herbie and Rachel had hatched in the arctic wilderness. An all-purpose psychologist attributed the whole thing to cabin fever. Another blamed Rachel's rantings on the rigors of the trail. The *Anchorage Herald* ran this story next to a local feature about the hazards of constant darkness.

But the Associated Press took a careful second look at the documents, which had been copied by Ralph on the Xerox machine in the Nome City Hall. The *New York Times* assembled a panel of experts and locked them away with the same documents in a conference room on the fourteenth floor. On the Friday after the race, the Associated Press ran a tentative story with a lot of questions and a couple of answers which prompted the *Seattle Journal* to reprint my story after carefully deleting any reference to homicide. UPI published a prepared statement in which Smalley said he knew nothing of the sort.

And on Sunday the *New York Times* finally spoke with all its ponderous authority. They started on the top of page one and plodded on for page after page, through fourteen dense columns relieved only by a single, muddy photograph and a sidebar profiling Smalley's roller-coaster career. The rest of the news outlets followed in typical order, starting with the apologetic networks on Monday, the Italian television network on Tuesday, and the *Wall Street Journal* all week long. The next week, Smalley made the cover of *Time,* Herbie the cover of *Newsweek.*

This was just the beginning. *People* magazine and the *Atlantic Monthly* had yet to be heard from. The orgy lasted all through the spring and well into summer as reporters crawled all over one another in search of the inevitable back-tracks and follow-ups.

The market for ReapRight collapsed and African farmers started using the cleaner, cheaper product Dr. Williams had bequeathed them. Brazil followed suit. Herbie became a national hero and he and his buddy the Bohunk were folk legends for a month or so. Smalley's shattered empire and efforts to confirm some of the more obscure elements of the story became the subject of bilesome editorials and constipated think pieces. PBS did a half-hour special.

Then came the Jeffrey Williams story, as told to the *Chicago Tribune* by his mother and Evey. Several attempts at the definitive Smalley story were frustrated by the uncooperative attitude of the subject. *Sports Illustrated* focused on how fame had ruined Cupcake by making her fat and slow. Then came the story of the story. Moments after all this information was disseminated, it was forgotten by a public all too familiar with and wisely suspicious of such overcooked extravaganzas.

We only talked about it once. We both had our reasons for wanting to forget about Jeffrey Williams, a man I've never met.

It was winter of the next year. Rachel and I had moved to the town of Baranov on the Kenai Peninsula, home of the world's largest salmon. I'd gotten into the habit of taking Chena on long walks along Kalifornsky Beach, which has the most beautiful winter sunsets in the world if you don't mind the cold and have no pressing obligations at two in the afternoon.

Chena tried to eat a frozen piece of what used to be one of the world's largest salmon. The sun made a red halo around the blue barricade of Redoubt Volcano. I danced with the high tide and sang a song that used to make me cry. It was written by John Prine, who comes from Maywood, Illinois, the place where Jeffrey Williams was born. The part that used to make my cry goes like this:

And he loved every girl,
In this curly-headed world,
But no one will know his pain,
'cause two twisted legs
And a childhood disease,
Left Billy just a Bum in his dreams.

It used to make me cry. Now it only makes me sad—
not a bad sad, but a good sad: like remembering the last
time you and a close friend went bowling and then he
died.

So I was already feeling sad when Rachel ran down
from our house with a newspaper that said Mabel Woodley
had died in her sleep and was survived by five daughters,
three sons, countless grandchildren, and two old codgers
from Hell's Gate who used to "make a little love sometimes, but nothin' too excitin', mind you."

So that night we talked about it and then never talked
about it again. I told Rachel that when I wasn't too busy
being editor of the *Baranov Beacon*, I'd called around to
see how everyone was doing. Here's how everyone did:

Ralph the Obit Man sold the *Nome News* and moved
back to New York City. Mary couldn't stand it. She and
the kids returned to Nome.

Evey Williams and her mother sued Entco Investments
Corporation for $30 million and settled for $4 million.
Soon thereafter, Evey was impregnated by a man who
didn't love her. He married her and tried to get his hands
on her money. She dumped him and took Grandma and
baby Jeff on an extended tour of Europe.

Mick the Pick is under the protective custody of the
State of Alaska. Although he has not been convicted of
any crime, he tries to strangle anyone who comes within
his reach. His mental condition has deteriorated to a state
far beyond what even the most optimistic psychiatrist might

call the point of no return. His room is well lit but the windows are made of heavy plastic and fortified with iron bars.

Dr. Bob Brown and his family moved to the Sahel region of central Africa, where they supervise the production of the miracle fertilizer which Dr. Jeffrey Williams bequeathed to that part of the world.

Phil Norwood took a job as editor of a small weekly in Port Washington, Wisconsin. Upon learning of my appointment as editor of the *Beacon*, he sent me a package of Rolaids.

Ed Hadley is still plugging away. He didn't get to be a great newspaperman by knowing when to quit.

Monique Peterson hasn't been heard from since.

Nor has Jamie Farrell.

Naknek disappeared, too.

Andrew Finkelstein elected two state senators and one state representative. The Libertarian was humiliated at the polls but still paid the outrageous bills for the services with which Andrew provided him. On the day I came to pick up Chena, he offered me $50,000 a year to write press releases praising people I wouldn't even invite into my home. I declined the invitation.

Hugh Smalley dwells among the faceless poor. He made it through the Williams litigation with a good part of his fortune intact. But then a bank called in one of his notes and he couldn't find another bank to bail him out. The house of cards collapsed, leaving a debt of $3.5 billion secured with worthless Entco paper and molybdenum mines worth only $1.2 billion. The Mercedes fetched $230,000, the Lear jet several times that. Condos in the Barbados sold for a couple of million. The banks ate the rest—more than $2 billion. Some banks failed and some executives lost their jobs.

Although no one was ever charged with the murder of

THE COLD FRONT

Dr. Jeffrey Williams, the poverty to which Smalley was sentenced by the U.S. bankruptcy court held horrors far greater than anything to be found in the Alaska prison system. IRS agents and lawyers for various creditors hounded Smalley wherever he went, checking out various rumors that he had salted away some of his money. He retreated to his late grandfather's farm and started picking rocks. I believe this is some sort of self-assigned penance, not for what he did to Jeffrey Williams or to the Toyukuk River or to the unborn children conceived along its banks, but for acquiring so much money and then losing it in such a spectacular fashion.

Herbie suffered the strange degradation to which our society treats its heros. First came the talk shows. Then the commercials in which, for a handsome fee, he endorsed products for dogs (food) and men (beer). Now he and Cupcake are both too fat to run the Iditarod, but they may be the subject of a three-part miniseries.

Rachel moved to Baranov with me. She took a teaching job in the Baranov public schools and spends her summers cooking for commercial fishing crews that harvest the world's largest salmon and other fish. Either the students or the fish or the walks along Kalifornsky Beach have aroused in her some primeval need to talk about children, a topic of conversation I'd just as soon avoid. But that's another story, of which more later.